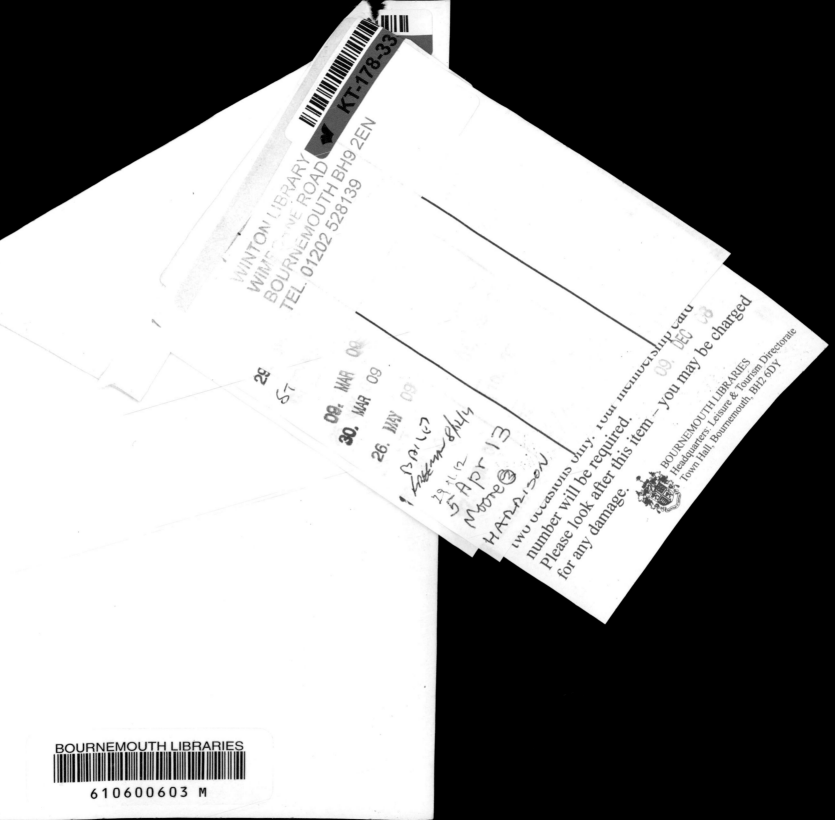

29

ST

09. MAR 09

09. MAR 09

30. MAR 09

26. MAY 09

09. DEC 08

5 Apr 13

Moore

HARRISON

HEAR ME TALKING TO YOU

HEAR ME TALKING TO YOU

David Craig

This first world edition published in Great Britain 2005 by
SEVERN HOUSE PUBLISHERS LTD of
9–15 High Street, Sutton, Surrey SM1 1DF.
This first world edition published in the USA 2005 by
SEVERN HOUSE PUBLISHERS INC of
595 Madison Avenue, New York, N.Y. 10022.

British Library Cataloguing in Publication Data

Craig, David, 1929-
    Hear me talking to you
    1.   Women detectives - Wales - Cardiff - Fiction
    2.   Detective and mystery stories
    I.   Title II. James, Bill, 1929-
    823.9'14 [F]

    ISBN 0-7278-6202-2

Typeset by Palimpsest Book Production Ltd.,
Polmont, Stirlingshire, Scotland.
Printed and bound in Great Britain by
MPG Books Ltd., Bodmin, Cornwall.

One

Bad, of course. Wrong, of course – wrong to be here alone. If what she'd been told was going to happen did happen, could she stop it, on her own and unarmed? Crazy. So, why was she here on her own and unarmed? She never did work armed, anyway. She had answers, but not good answers, not good enough to satisfy herself, and definitely not good enough to satisfy others if eventually it came to a formal inquiry. And a formal inquiry is what it *would* come to should things turn out bad and wrong. By others she meant her superiors. There were plenty of those at plenty of levels and they could pile up plenty of dissatisfaction. In fact, Sally considered it was the distinguished quality of her superiors' dissatisfaction with failure that actually qualified them as superiors – Raging Bullfinch, for instance, an assistant chief.

At least she was at pavement level, which should help if she had to act fast. Act fast? Doing what? Probably even now she could still put this situation more or less right – call up help in quantity, some of it armed help. But Sally delayed. And so, here she was, watching solo from a car. That might be less obvious than foot-patrolling the pavement, but not much less obvious. In theory, and in TV cop films, a car gave secret observers fair cover. However, an immobile saloon with someone inside also grew conspicuous after a while, even if it stood among other vehicles, and even if parked facing away from the target on the opposite side of the road, all observation done via the mirrors or back window, in absolute line with snoop training. Parked

1

cars had lost their innocence a long time ago, and not just because some of them in Jerusalem and Iraq were bombs. According to her information, people in that chic, marina-style house framed by her inside mirror would be alert. Her information. *Her* information. Only hers. It had come the way such information usually came.

'I want to speak to detective constable Sally Bithron.'
    'Speaking.'
    'That's Detective Constable Sally Bithron?'
    'Speaking.'
    'Look . . . well, it doesn't sound like you.'
    'There's a lot of noise around. Hold on. I'll switch it to a cubicle.'
    And then, when she'd done that: *'O.K. now.'*
    'This is Godzilla.'
    'Yes.'
    'We must meet.'
    'Right. Same place?'
    'When you switched – you know, just now, that's not so you could record, is it?'
    'For quietness.'
    'I haven't said a thing, anyway.'
    'Of course not.'
    'I wouldn't like to be on tape.'
    'You're not.'
    'I feel stupid saying Godzilla.'
    'But, Godzilla, it was you who chose Godzilla as your code name.'
    'Just now, it didn't sound like you.'
    'Yes, me. Don't be nervous.'
    'Yes, nervous. Yes, same place. You won't bring anyone?'
    'Do I ever? Would I ever?'
    'Only, it didn't sound like you.'
    'Absolutely me, Godzilla.'

*   *   *

This was the kind of conversation that put you among expensive properties in Schooner Way, one of Cardiff Bay's most modish streets, trying to watch things through mirrors or with your head twisted around. Yes, on the phone, talking to Sally at the nick, Godzilla could be nervous. That was understandable. Anyone talking to big organizations by phone or otherwise should be damn wary. Think Kafka. Under the influence of a boyfriend, she'd read some once, but not much – it scared her. Anyone talking to a police organization by phone or otherwise should be extra damn wary.

But when she and Godzilla met in the established spot, he would sometimes be quite playful and liked to tease. You could see how he might come up with the jokey cover name for himself. In fact, meeting spots should not become too established. Habit was carelessness. But she'd thought it would be OK this time. They could agree a change.

'Tell me, now, Detective Constable Sally Bithron, where, these days, do you think robbers might find cash – reachable, big cash?'

'What do you mean – "these days?" Are these days different from—?'

'From twenty, fifty years ago? You know they are. Who tries a bank snatch in 2003? Bulletproof glass up to the ceiling. Cameras. Super alarms. Banks are little forts. Not even Jesse James would try.'

'Post offices,' Sally said.

'Post offices are takeable. But do they have enough on the premises to make it worth taking – especially now pensions all go into bank accounts?'

'Cash in transit,' Sally said.

'Vans like tanks. You need another tank. Possible but tough. Likewise money deliveries at airports. You can't do it without someone inside for the signal. Possible but not

3

easy, and it would take a while to set up. People haven't got the patience. And, in any case, so many armed police at airports these days for other reasons –not conducive.'

'So, what are we—?'

'And yet, cash does exist – exists to be grabbed.' ˙

'That's so, is it?' Sally replied.

The established spot was in a garden centre, among good potted fuchsias, a mild artificial waterfall backed with green plastic nearby.

'Buying and selling.'

'Right.'

'Buying and selling, where cheques and credit cards can't be used because of the danger of it being traced.'

'Crooked buying and selling?'

'That's why I say the house in dockland's Schooner Way, with its sweet little scarlet, wrought-iron gate.'

'Crooked buying and selling of what, Godzilla?'

'I want you to think of a bulk sale for bulk cash. All right, prices have nosedived a bit, but a lot of stuff still draws a noble quantity of cash.'

'We're talking heroin?' Sally said.

'Mostly. H still holds its price. Some other Class A with it. Yes, mostly H, obviously.'

'A wholesaler supplying one of the networks?'

'Now you know more than even the brass,' Godzilla replied.

'What wholesaler? What network?'

'That's not what it's about.'

'What?'

'My information. What I hear concerns the cash.'

'Someone will try for it – grab it while the deal's being done?' Sally asked.

'Along those lines.'

'Who?'

'That's what I mean.'

'What?' she said.

4

'*This is one of those few times and places these days where big money is there to be snatched. Like mugging, but multiplied.*'

'*Someone – someone outside – someone knows about it?*'

'*What?*' he said.

'*The meeting. The deal.*'

'*That's my understanding.*'

'*Hijack?*'

'*In the proper sense. Villains robbing villains.*'

'*When?*'

'*When what?*'

'*When is the meeting, of course.*'

'*Some spells of watching for you in Schooner Way. Lovely waterside setting. I want you to do this by yourself, Detective Constable. No big team from the nick. No Brade. No Jenkins. You tell a big team and the word gets out that there's a big team. People wonder –why a big team? Inquiries. If there's a big team, the word nearly always gets out, doesn't it? And if the word gets out, there's no meeting, no deal, obviously. Or, yes, there will be a deal, because the holy main-line traffic has to keep moving, hasn't it, as we all know, including me –but they'll shift it to somewhere else at some other time, not Schooner Way. And, secondly, if the word gets out, people also start wondering how Schooner Way became known, and then there could be awkward· deductions.*'

'*About what?*'

'*Me.*'

'*As informant?*' Sally replied.

'*So you see why I say you have to do this on your own – sort of stumble on the incident by gorgeous fluke.*'

'*Which incident?*'

'*The money raid. Then you bag them all – the raiders, the buyers, the sellers.*'

'*I get them all – me, solo?*'

'*You see everything. You can describe, identify maybe. And you can bring in the big team once things are under way. You*

5

*make an emergency call for aid, based on what you've acci-
dentally witnessed, as it were. Perhaps they'll arrive while
a battle is still on. Or perhaps they'll pick them all up later
from your descriptions. It would still be your collar. Trained
in descriptions, aren't you? Height, weight, race, hair, clothes,
age, shoes. You'll do all that damn well. You're a clever kid.
You must be, or you wouldn't have a gifted grass like me for
your own personal use, would you? Yes, clever.'*

Perhaps so, or then again, perhaps not. The difficulties of
running an informant scared Sally now and then. Looking
for comfort, she had discussed this with friends and, some
while ago, one of them, backpacking in Australia, sent her
a cutting from the *Sydney Morning Herald*. It reported the
retirement speech of a New South Wales police chief superintendent. He bemoaned the reluctance of young officers to
train as detectives any longer, dreading corruption accusations if they did what effective detectives had to do and
cosied up to crooks for tip-offs. New South Wales was four
hundred detectives short. British police forces, including
hers in *Old* South Wales, recognized this problem and had
devised an approved system for handling informants. It
rested on the rule that a nark belonged not to an individual
officer but to the police force as a whole. Informants should
be officially registered, their names set down in a list and
known to a very senior officer.

Fine. The trouble, though, was that some voices, like
Godzilla, rejected these guidelines. They would do one-to-
one talking but feared leaks once things moved beyond.
Godzilla and many other message-men, and women, were
obsessed about leaks, and rightly. They had a horror of
some database schedule where coded names lay alongside
their true ones, like an invitation to kill. *Godzilla = Brian
Edward Aulus.* Clerks might be involved in making these
schedules. Who knew when a clerk was secure and
unbuyable? In fact, who knew when a very senior officer

holding the list was secure and unbuyable? That's how Godzilla would argue. Discs could get stolen. Remember that break-in at one of Northern Ireland's best-guarded police stations, Castlereagh. Informing carried horrific punishment by betrayed crook colleagues when discovered, or, if they'd been jailed because of it, by their brothers, fathers, uncles, aunties, chihuahuas, grandmothers, and pals. Godzilla and many like him would offer some limited trust to a detective they knew, and that detective only. Cooperation must be on a strictly spoken-word basis – no written record, or at least, none they knew about. And so, a frail and dangerous closeness developed. With this closeness came the risk of hints at corruption during cross-examination by a defence lawyer – and more than hints – if the detective presented information from a secret source in court. Traffic-copping could bring an easier life. Just the same, Sally hadn't fancied it. Here she was instead with the excitements and perils of managing a tout, and involved with that other kind of traffic and trafficking. For the present at least, Godzilla was paid no money for his tips. The official informant fund didn't know him. Sally could give his own operations a bit of blind-eye, though. This was a routine, illegal method of *quid pro quoism* for informants who would not register. Dave Brade had told her about that dirty, general, effective practice. It was probably worth more to Godzilla than fees. At any rate, he could afford a nice family home in Wordsworth Avenue.

The inside mirror showed her what could be a husband and wife returning from a shopping expedition, the woman pulling a largish tartan suitcase on trolley wheels, the man with two superior-looking pale-green carrier bags. They approached at a decent pace on the opposite pavement. These were the kind of local residents Sally could have done without. They would pass the house and come abreast of her car soon, almost certainly notice her, and probably wonder what she was doing there – casing the street for something later? If she hung around much longer, they might even report her, plus car details. Then Sally might have to explain back at the nick. She had a window part-open and the relentless sound of those small, hard wheels under the case sounded like sharp questions catching up. And yet this contraption looked so workaday and domestic.

Perhaps that was why she didn't connect it, or this pair, with what she was watching for. She might have been expecting a suitcase, but not one on cracklingly busy wheels, and not accompanied by two carrier bags, no matter how high-quality they might be – high-quality as carrier bags only, after all. But suddenly she started to wonder. Did people from this kind of street go shopping on foot? Where? Well, possibly they'd come from a bus. Now, though, while she tried to think of them as normal, she also found herself deciding this couple could be . . . could be on a buying spree, yes, though just starting it, not bringing the goods back, and with an interest in only one kind of commodity.

The uncertainty would be resolved very soon. Would they turn into the specified house? They came steadily on, untalking, blank-faced, framed nicely in the mirror. Perhaps they'd been told to make for the scarlet iron work. At any rate, they paused there and glanced towards a curtained upper window, as if clearing themselves with the anticipated, concealed lookout. The woman opened the gate. She went through first, turned, and with two hands yanked the trolley case over a small step. Then she moved up the very short tiled path to the black, possibly genuine wood front door, and the man shut the gate with a shove from one of the carrier bags and followed her. That might be a very rich way of closing a gate.

'What sort of money are we talking about, God?'

'Godzilla's one name that shouldn't be shortened. Or come from the other end and make it Zilla.'

'So, what sort of money?'

'Six, obviously.'

'Six what?'
'Figures.'
'What's the first?'
'Does it matter? Six figures is a lot.'
'Six figures when the first is eight or nine is a real lot.'
'This is a real lot.'
'I thought you knew about the money. You said, "Don't ask names – think about the money".'
'I do know about the money.'
'But not how many hundred thousand?'
'Does it matter?'
'If you don't know how many hundred grand, how do you know it's even one hundred grand?'
'These are people who wouldn't think a deal was a deal if it didn't make six figures.'
'How do you know that?'

This was the thing about informants, wasn't it? Godzilla as much as any. They'd edit what they told you. Most of them did it to up the fee . . . You got the first bit, which earned so much. Then they might come across with a fragment more, and this earned some extra. And another fragment eased the cost a notch or two higher. But greed did not entirely explain their skimpiness with offerings. After all, Godzilla didn't get fees. Constantly, though, all grasses guarded against handing out any slice of knowledge that could have come from one source only. This would be the same as getting their forehead hot-branded NARK. One way to break down this caginess was to do what Sally did at the garden-centre meeting – attack his credibility, so he had to give more to convince. The detective–nark relationship was complex. It could contain some friendship, and even a kind of love. But mainly it was commerce and followed that most sacred of free-market procedures – each side tried to screw the other, and not in the love sense.

* * *

'Obviously, this house in Schooner Way is rented. Seven hundred and forty pounds per calendar month'

'So you do know about money, Godzilla.'

'Three-month minimum tenancy paid for in advance – and cash, of course. Names of the tenants: Timothy Lestoque and Gordon W. Singlecomb. Alleged. They'll stay three or four days. It's a lovely letting for the owner. Next time they'll take somewhere else.'

'Do we know there'll be a next time?' Sally asked.

'Well, perhaps there won't, if you get them. We know there have been next times up till now. Several.'

'What are the real names?'

'That's how they sign themselves on the house documents. No indication of what the W. is supposed to stand for. Probably not Winston. They're both white, I gather.'

So were the two who went in with the wheelie case and stuffed carrier bags. Sally spoke descriptions of them into her pocket recorder. Yes, she had the training. 'Woman, white, thirty-three to thirty-eight, five feet five, hundred and thirty-five pounds, very upright, vigorous. Hair mousy-fair, to shoulders. Jeans that could be Calvin Klein or good mimic. Blue-grey plain GAP T-shirt. Leather flip-flops, no heel. Squarish, Slav-like face, high, pronounced cheekbones, oval eye sockets (too far for eye colour), tidy nose, deep forehead, surprisingly delicate chin. Brisk way with a carton of cash on wheels. Man, white, touching fifty, five-ten or eleven, hundred and sixty pounds, plentiful grey hair, worn anyhow, but a pride to him, lean face, strong straight nose, small mouth, beige two-piece lightweight suit, maybe custom-made, nice on the shoulders, open black or navy shirt, no medallion, brown slip-ons. Easy mover.'

'Have you been inside the house, Zill?'

'Yes, Zill's all right. I don't mind Zill, or Zilla. "God" as a shortening, no, but Zill, OK, interesting.'

'Have you been inside the house, Zill?'
'How would I have been inside the house?'
'Have you?'
'Is that important?'
'If there's a fracas and I have to tackle it, I want to know the layout, don't I?'
'Tackle it?'
'That's what police officers are paid to do with fracas, Zill, even with fracas bumped into by, as it were, accident. They tackle them. If not, it's dereliction of duty.'
'I wouldn't want you going into that house solo.'
'But you say it has to be solo. No team.'
'I say watch *solo. Some intelligent peeping.'*
'If I'm watching solo and there's an incident, I have to do something.'
'Yes, do something – call for aid.'
'While it's coming, I have to do something.'
'You can't go into a house like that alone, and I suppose unarmed.'
'Of course unarmed. I'm passing through Schooner Way by fluke when the entirely unexpected fracas starts. How would I be armed? This is Britain, not the Bronx.'
'Don't keep calling it a fracas, will you, for God's sake? It makes it sound like nothing – a punch-up at a pub. This is going to be intense.'
'An intense fracas, then,' Sally replied.
'Look, I don't want to push you into something like that, not by yourself. Not on at all.'

This was how things could go between a grass and a handler – a kind of mutual care that might get near to affection, or even something more. Sally didn't think it sexual on Godzilla's part, and it certainly was not on hers. She could recall no bodily contact at all between them –hand touching hand, hand touching arm, even unintentionally. There was closeness, but not this kind. She'd always been put off by thin, weak-looking necks.

11

David Craig

But everyone recognized that in running an informant a complex relationship might hatch out. A formidable link could develop, and not all to do with money and career. In fact, if the arrangement between detective and source really worked, the relationship was almost certain to get warm and tender. These were people who tried to deal with big risks together. They had to know each other, *really* know. The interdependence became even stronger when a relationship stayed secret and unofficial, as with Sally and Godzilla – or Zill. And it *would* stay secret and unofficial. That was the contract.

Naturally, Sally had her own dossier on him, but at home in microscopic script on half an octavo page kept in her copy of the Bible at the Second Book of Kings, chapter three. She used to kid herself she could eat the dossier if things went really rough. There were baby Godzillas – a girl, nearly two, called Serena, and Ambrose, a boy of four months. Ambrose Aulus – it sounded like a papal nuncio or circus high-wire star. Their mother, Ann Temperance Mayhew Donovan, had been in a steady partnership with Aulus for seven years, approaching eight. Sally could nowhere near match this stability – nor the children. Godzilla was born May 24 1975, in York, Ann Temperance Mayhew Donovan, January 30 1973, Dorchester. Someone with Godzilla's style of frail neck probably needed a woman older than himself. Both had education. Godzilla began an arts degree course at Leeds but dropped out in his first year. Ann graduated with a IIi in history at Exeter. They met on a carpet firm's management selection session in London. Each was offered a job. Neither took it up. They must have decided there were easier ways to make money, and Godzilla did all right, while Ann had the babies. Much of this background had, of course, been told her by Godzilla, so it could be lies. Also, of course, he did sound sometimes as if he had read a book, so the jettisoned arts degree might be a fact. She might check one day.

Sally worried now about what might happen to Anne and

12

the boy and girl if Godzilla were rumbled and his various useful incomes got suddenly and violently stopped. And – never mind the incomes – she worried what might happen to Ann Temperance Mayhew Donovan's life and limbs, and Ambrose's and Serena's, if Godzilla were rumbled and violently stopped. Reprisals didn't always end with the grass in person. Crook reasoning said that anyone who could put up with the odour of a fink in the house must be grievously sick and should be put down out of kindness. This included children/babies.

And, as to life and limbs, Sally saw that Godzilla worried about hers getting mucked up in a small but desirable Schooner Way villa because of something he'd heard and passed on. This was true concern, and she felt true gratitude. Oh, yes, garden-centre communing had its depths, bonds, obligations. There was a good, bracing stink from stacked fertilizer in white plastic sacks, which spoke of belief in assisted growth and a future. You could enlist yourself in that. And the chummy-looking ornamental gnomes and little pixies on offer, in their yellow, red and blue garments, made Sally feel taller, better dressed and more formidable than they were, less prone to those fucking please-all moronic grins. But, as to things moronic, it would certainly be that to keep on coming here, and she'd fix up somewhere else for next time.

'What are we talking about, Zill – four or five kilos of H?'

'Might be four or five kilos.'

'Street value? Towards a million? This is raw, unmixed stuff, is it?'

'You've been doing some research.'

'But this isn't street value. Wholesale. Say three hundred thousand quid at our Schooner Way meet? That much to be handed over? Is the first of your six figures three? Very bulky load of cash. Will the sellers take fifty-pound notes –ignore forgery warnings? Pubs won't.'

'*Who tries to fool people like these two?*'
'*Other people like these two.*'
'*There has to be trust.*'
'*Sweet.*'
'*The buyers can't test every packet of H to check it's uncut and not baby powder,*' he said. '*The sellers can't test every bit of currency. These people will want to deal again. They have to play decent. They've been trading together a while and have built up faith in one another. Reputation – so crucial in the higher commerce. Remember Iago?*'
'*Ah.*'
'*"Who steals my purse steals trash. But he that filches from me my good name . . ."*'
'*Literature's a treat.*'
'*Now and then it does get to—*'
'*Zill, I thought Turks ran H.*'
'*You have been doing some research.*'
'*Well, don't Turks run it?*'
'*In London. Especially North London. Harringay. Green Lanes. Battleground. But there are still sturdy Brit outposts around the country. Schooner Glorious Way, Cardiff Bay. For a day or two.*' Godzilla had hummed the start of '*Land of Hope and Glory*' and did a comic salute.

Sally readjusted herself in the driving seat. While those two, with trolley and carrier bags, approached the Schooner Way house, she'd slumped a little for better cover from the headrest. She loved the whole notion of self-concealment and watchfulness. It was crafty power. It could make you one-up. That's what she wanted to be, one-up. Didn't everyone? The Pope was one-up on the cardinals, and God was one-up on everybody. They must have parked their own vehicle somewhere near but out of sight. They wouldn't want it associated with this house, because . . . oh, because cars were often remembered much more precisely than people, and the fewer traceables the better, should there be slip-ups. They'd be jumpy, no matter how set their faces looked, and no matter how implacable and fruitily loaded the little wheels sounded.

From behind, Sally's Focus probably appeared empty. She straightened up and improved her mirror view now. She was jumpy herself. This stint must not last too long. She had to account for her time. Some vagueness was possible, but not infinitely. She'd use a trick picked up from other, more senior detectives who also ran personal, unregistered narks – a bit of know-how 'learned at Nellie's knee', as the phrase went. That meant it figured in no authorized manual, but was passed down by whisper, nod and wink from one generation of police to the next. Nice and simple. Sally had another informant, properly listed, officially payrolled, and, as far as her chiefs knew, she might be doing a delicate, prolonged chat and harvest with him today. Such conversations would drift, roam, take a while, or more. Narks jabbered. Their mouths were loose. That's what made them narks. Routinely, she kept back several snippets of knowledge he'd given, and could produce these in case a Godzilla tip needed some considerable, untimetabled work.

And now, here in Schooner Way, it did. Zill had always seemed more likely to come up with important stuff than Sally's statutory, properly fee-paid informant, Roger Basil Chancel, codenamed Coldfinger. To Godzilla, there was a radiantly bullshit side, flair side, joke and banter side, and Sally had always reasoned that to justify these he would know he must eventually provide something titanic – to justify them to himself, to Ann Temperance Mayhew Donovan, to the futures of Serena and Ambrose, and to Sally for the career hazards she accepted. Godzilla owned a trained mind – or partly trained, anyway, via that semester-and-a-bit with the arts at Leeds – and would know life occasionally needed to leave behind the bullshit and flair and jokes and banter and get to hard actuality. This was it now?

Terrifying, really. She had more to worry about than merely explaining a time gap to the management.

The Schooner Way 'town house' – meaning terraced – looked out upon a pleasant, rectangular, ornamental lake with swans, a working dock during Cardiff's big and grimy decades as a major port, now an environmental amenity, in marina smooch-talk. But the downstairs curtains, like those above, stayed closed to the spruced-up scene this afternoon. What was happening now, as the deal progressed? The woman would empty packets of notes from her case, would she, and the man might tip more from his carrier bags, the two of them creating a gorgeous, non-Euro hillock, probably on a fashionable, golden, hardwood floor?

'How will the raid party know when it's happening, Godzilla?'
  'What?'
  'What? The deal, of course.'
  I don't know how they'll know.'

And the stuff – the purchase? Would that be laid out nicely on a modernistic sideboard in transparent plastic bags, like ranked, podgy, giant maggots, and ready for random slitting and sampling? The only images Sally had for this kind of encounter came from the film *True Romance*, when Clarence, its hero, tricks his way into a drugs den, shoots up the foul gang and grabs a load of coke. Nothing as violent as that would take place in charming new marinaland, Cardiff, surely?

'But you're certain they will know, Zill?'
  'What my info says. Hard to set up that amount of cash and that amount of commodity without talk.'
  'And you heard the talk?'

* * *

On the far side, the lake had a pink and grey commemorative crane that once loaded cargo on to the world's ships – now a sedate, historical toy. The whole docks area had become sedate and pretty, a triumph of red cement brick and ancient stone warehouses gutted, done up and converted into flats. Sally had been born not far away, but was too young to remember the port busy. She sensed loss, though. Sentimental rubbish, probably. She knew the main sea trade had vanished with the decline of coal, and the docks had turned wasteland. Redevelopment made it bijou, an estate agent's romp. That was an improvement, wasn't it? Of course. Of course. 'Waterside', not 'docks', had become the revised name.

'I'm a good listener,' Godzilla had said. 'Some think I just spiel. But I can listen. That's what you want, isn't it?'
'And where, how, were—?'
'Don't ask any more. This is about me, isn't it, not about the hit?'
'But I need to know why you—'
'Don't ask any more.'

Sally's eatable dossier on Brian Edward Aulus, also Godzilla, also Zill or Zilla, but not God, said he made a substantial living as middle-league pusher, and as a local fixer and facilitator for all kinds of outside businesses with interests or potential interests in the Bay, some legal. Possibly even *most* of•them legal. He could often be seen around dockland streets in an Audi, wearing custom-made shirts. Grand to know a dud time at varsity did not mean a retard life. Sally gathered that occasionally he worked with or against the Bay's supreme middleman and chancer, Julian Corbett, who still stayed alive and out of jail. Aulus might run into all kinds of dodgy development folk and drugs-industry captains, and would hear smart fragments, if he listened. And, as he claimed, he really did listen.

Wherever the tip reached him from, she had to do what she could with it. If you ran a tout, you took what he touted, at least until you found you'd taken deepest rubbish. Naturally, what he touted would advantage him somehow, and not through pay, because there wasn't any, couldn't be any. But he had businesses to cultivate, interests to promote, activities to cloak, competitors to savage, or to have savaged on his behalf. Pointless to ask which of his sly games might profit from a leak about Schooner Way. So, she had asked.

'What's in it for you, Godzilla?'
  'In what?'
  'Killing the deal.'
  'A wish to help you. What else?'
  'Yes, what else?'
  'It taints the whole Bay project, something like this.'
  'Civic duty?'
  'Right.'
  'How many?' she replied.
  'What?'
  'The raid party.'
  'Unknown.'
  'How do they do it?'
  'What?' he said.
  'Get into the house.'
  'Unknown. Not subtly.'

No, not subtly. A gold metallic Lexus pushed itself grandly into Sally's mirror, stopped and cut from her sight the scarlet iron gate. Now, she found out how many. Three hooded men galloped up the little front path, another stayed at the Lexus's wheel. The hoods looked identical – black, going to a point at the top, eye slits, perhaps bought from a Halloween-gear shop. The fine, burly engine of the Lexus would be running, most probably. She couldn't hear at this

Hear Me Talking To You

distance. One of the running men carried a sledgehammer, the other two handguns, up and ready – big automatics, possibly .45 Colts. Sally was good on pistols – recognizing, not firing.

Sledgehammer Man went first. That made sense. Planning. Behind him, Colt Man One, about six feet, 170lbs, say twenty-four, like herself. He had only a few paces to run up the little front path, and yet, did the way he moved, the running style, remind her of someone, someone far back and vague in her memory? Too far back? Too vague? God, who?

Colt Man Two was shorter, fatter, older – maybe late thirties. He stirred no recollections. And Lexus Man? Balaclava-clad but probably white, round-faced, round-headed, dark eyebrows, heavy-lipped. It took two thumps with the hammer. People inside would be rather warned by the first, wouldn't they? Definitely not subtly.

'I don't see it.'
'What, Zill?'
'I don't see you have a duty to go in.'
'This will be an incident in a major street. What else are police for?' she said.
'This will be villains robbing villains. Who's bothered? You don't have to protect the innocent public, because there won't be any.'
'Possible violence, even shooting, Zill.'
'Violence on one another. Shooting one another. Who's bothered? Some natural cleansing.'
'Can't think of it like that.'

Now it had started happening, though, she found she could. Sally wanted a full offence carried out, or offences, not just attempted. Perhaps Godzilla had it right. What kind of crime would it be to steal crooked money and/or illegal drugs – maybe only *try* to steal? She must not intervene too soon.

It was a cruel thought, but Sally realized she and law and order needed some of that violence she spoke about to Godzilla, possibly even some of that shooting. This ruthlessness in herself shocked Sally, but not too much. Had the job begun to shape her? Did she think cop and nothing else? On the way to that, maybe. Best recognize it. Another factor: strangely, obsessively, she wanted a fresh look at Colt Man One, and his silky, gliding, effortless, left-leaning lope.

But when he reappears at a burst through the ruined front door, he is carrying in his right hand the woman's case, not pulling it on the wheels, and the weight seems to slow him and straighten him up, balance him, so this is hardly a lope at all any longer, and certainly not a tilt-to-left lope. It could be the laboured sprint of anyone loaded with boodle. No repeat chance to prompt her subconscious.

She has heard at least three shots and is almost out of her car, self-recriminating now, as the three get down the path. The Lexus driver leans over and pushes open both right-side doors for them. The Lexus is moving, only fractionally, but moving. He's full of nerves, probably – just sitting there. It might be easier to do the grab. Colt Man Two and Sledgehammer Man each have a green carrier bag in one hand, the Colt or the hammer in the other.

She was wrong, then, to imagine the money already out on the varnished boards. The deal must have been moving slower than that. Grand for these three to find the loot still neat and packaged. Only this seems to interest them, not the drugs. They're into the Lexus. It is coming towards her and will pass Barquentine Place, Halliard Court and Windlass Court and eventually reach Hemingway Road. This is nameplated additionally in Welsh as Heol Hemingway, pronounced Hail, or almost – like a tribute to the author of *The Old Man and the Sea*, a book Sally had made a try at once. Hemingway probably knew something of barquentines, halliards and windlasses. Crossing the road and running towards the scarlet gate and whatever's inside now, she radios for aid, just as Godzilla had thought wise. She's breathless as she talks, and wonders if she could be taught loping.

Two

This bad outrage in Schooner Way really rocked the city. Sally could understand that and felt quite a slice of the pain and shock herself – a sort of communal bruising. The violence seemed like an abrupt return to another, poorer, more savage, desperate time. After all, for nearly a century Cardiff dockland was notorious worldwide as Tiger Bay. Obviously, the name carried some silly melodrama and journalistic flashiness, but there *had* been race riots, pimp battles, tart murders, drugs turf wars, plus a lot of deprivation. Although Sally was too young to remember much of that, she'd heard her parents and grandparents speak of it. And she knew the pretty marina-izing of dockland was supposed to end this harsh reputation and bring good, professional-class behaviour – in pleasant line with madly jumped-up property values. Tiger Bay had certainly become an unsuitable title for this jolly spread. After all, the county council offices were here, and the meta-pricey, devolved Welsh Parliament building, with all those thoughtful assembly members on lovely pay and allowances. So, farewell Tiger Bay, hello *Cardiff* Bay. That was much more sellable to property investors. Logoland.

Then, suddenly, the Schooner Way incident. *Incident?* God, some dim and blank term for what happened! This was probably as bloody and rough as anything the docks had ever seen. Didn't it seem to mock the glamour aimed for in briny-fresh street names like Barquentine, Halliard,

Windlass and Schooner? These were farcical, of course, and Sally loved to visualize the giggles at a planners' meeting when some gifted Horatio Hornblower fan first came up with Barquentine. She could still approve the motives, though – transformation, rebirth, a boldly laundered image. But now, big drugs commerce, robbery, deaths and sledgehammer skull damage in Schooner Way made you wonder whether the old tiger really had died. Sally felt some guilt – felt some big guilt. Well, obviously. Hadn't she let it all go ahead? Why hadn't she blown the whistle? She knew why she hadn't, but was her answer good enough?

Raging Bullfinch himself arrived from headquarters almost as soon as the armed response vehicles. This attack had symbolism and he would feel he must appear in person. He wore uniform, including silver-leaf cap. 'DC Bithron?' he said. 'You made the call? A Lexus? And what's inside the house?' But Bullfinch, in that bustling, nervy, staff-rank way of his, did not wait to hear. Leadership required him to give a lead. He stepped past her. The wrecked front door had been pushed wide open when those three rushed in on their raid. The armed-response cars left to hunt the Lexus. Sally followed Bullfinch to the downstairs living room, off to the right of a short, narrow passage.

'Two men probably dead, sir,' Sally said from behind. 'The woman and another man alive, but hurt. Badly hurt.'

'Yes, badly hurt,' he said. 'Yes, probably dead.' He stayed just inside the room, staring at these four bodies and at about twenty cellophane bags laid out on five shelves of a free-standing pine bookcase. It had only three books, all at one end of the top shelf –a *Practical Home Doctor*, *Who's Who* for 1979, and what might be a novel, called *The Rich Pay Late*, in paperback. The bags looked untouched and free from the kind of blood spatters that swirl-stained two walls, painted a rich dark green, and had

soaked some furniture and floor rugs. The woman lay
unconscious and possibly on her last legs in front of those
stacked shelves, the left side of her head crushed and
oozing. It seemed so wrong for someone who'd been
pulling something as ordinary as a wheeled case not long
ago. But not ordinary. As they watched, she groaned or
sighed, a throaty, frail sound and half lifted an arm as if
seeking love or water or last rites. Her eyes stayed closed.
Bullfinch replied with a small, tender groan himself and
moved towards her.

Sally sensed he had paused near the doorway, because
this room should be left to properly kitted scenes of
crime people and medics, but the noises from the woman
had obviously troubled him, made him ditch the rules.
Bullfinch could be like that. Humanity was often one of
his things, when possible. He bent over her. 'We'll have
you away from here very soon, dear, very soon. Good
help is coming.' This was a mild, genuine voice. He
straightened. 'You've pulsed these others?' he asked
Sally.

Should she have touched the bodies? 'Well, yes, sir, I—'

'That's all right. I'd have done the same, I expect. What
answers?'

'These two nothing,' she said, pointing at one in an
armchair, another humped up on his front under the
curtained window. 'Him, maybe a flicker.' This man
seemed to have fallen, also face down, half on to a brown
leather sofa, his knees, lower legs and feet on the floor.
Blood from a chest or shoulder wound pooled on the leather
and dripped around his shoes. His left arm hung off the
sofa, and it was on this wrist that Sally had looked for a
pulse – possibly found it.

'Identities?' Bullfinch asked.

'I—'

'But you wouldn't know, of course. Didn't your call say
you were in the street by accident?'

'On my way through.' She had to hope no householder had reported a long-time lurking car with a driver in it pretending she wasn't. If you promised a grass you'd keep him right out of things, you did. This was one of life's holy and inflexible rules.

'And, obviously, you haven't searched them?' Raging Bullfinch said. His nickname came from the way he would flutter about in spasms of limitless self-pity and noisy, infantile fury when he thought a crisis had been dumped on him by someone's carelessness or malice. Sally considered the title harsh. Often, she felt sorry for Bullfinch. The job was probably too big. He couldn't have foreseen this when he applied. He believed in his abilities, and was entitled to. Didn't we all fool ourselves like that? How else to dodge the dumps? Blame the select arseholes who promoted him. They should have known – known what he was, and what the post needed. She hoped Bullfinch never heard the title people gave him. Today, in any case, he seemed all right so far, a bit hurried but basically calm and humane. He looked good in the gear: tall, solid, lithe. Just on appearance you could believe he had a future and would do things for the populace as well as they could be done. His breathing seemed steady, his movements about the room between the bodies and blood lakes carefully managed. There had always been times when he could escape bullfinchery.

'I thought probably an interrupted deal, sir,' Sally said.

'Yes. Three men into the Lexus after the attack, all loaded up, plus driver?'

'One carrying a trolley case, his arm around it, the others with full carrier bags. Two had Colts in the spare hand, one holding a sledgehammer.'

Bullfinch looked down at the woman. 'Yes,' he said. 'A sledgehammer. Was this necessary, d'you think, or simply . . . well, viciousness, evil exuberance? No identities for the three?'

'Hooded.' In her recollection, then, she vividly saw all of them, but it was on their way into the house, not the dash back to the Lexus with their prizes. And suddenly that easy, loping, gliding run of Colt Man One, unburdened by the trolley case, said something to her. But what it said – God, what it said was absurd, surely. It said . . . it said World War Two. World War Two? Absurd? Mad. Where did the notion come from? Her brain tried hopelessly to interpret while Bullfinch still picked his way delicately about the room. Someone runs up a garden path and she's back to a time . . . what, forty years before her birth? How could her mind, her imagination, do this? Was it the gun? Perhaps she'd seen pictures of street battles in the war, people carrying Colt pistols. Maybe. She didn't really think so, though. It had been the running style that got to her, only this, she was sure. Nearly sure.

The specialist teams arrived and Bullfinch and Sally went out on to the pavement. An ambulance waited, its rear doors already open. Bullfinch's Peugeot and other police vehicles were parked near. A small crowd of spectators had begun to form. He said: 'You did well. Naturally, I'll draw the chief's attention to it. You gave control a reg. number for the Lexus, yes? It might help. Stolen, naturally. Tell me the sequence. That's your car down the road a bit on the other side is it, facing away? You drive past the house and observe what? Was the Lexus already there? That alerted you? I'm trying to see things as you did, you know.' Childlike excitement and curiosity made his voice quiver. His blue eyes shone. Perhaps it was this enthusiasm that had swung the promotion panel. Obviously, the enthusiasm was haywire now, because things had not happened the way Sally told it. But he came over as fierce in his appetite for the job, and magnificently keen on detail.

'When I passed – nothing,' she said. 'No, the Lexus hadn't arrived.'

'You saw it in your mirror, then.'

'Yes.'

'You watched them pull across the road and stop at the house?'

'Yes. A man gets out at once. He's in a hood and carrying the sledgehammer. Then two more hooded men. I thought I saw handguns.'

'You stopped immediately?'

'I'm a distance away. I thought of reversing – for speed – but decided that would alert the driver.'

'Good. You park and begin running back,' Bullfinch said.

'I'm running and talking to the radio.' From here her account would be true. All the while as she'd told the first part of it she'd been scared he would suddenly see an inconsistency and ask something devilish. He could do that, as well as humaneness and temper. Nobody thought of Raging Bullfinch as stupid, just as Raging Bullfinch.

He said: 'They must only have been inside for a matter of seconds.'

'Yes.'

'They'd know the house layout and what they wanted. After the grab, they drive past you and your car and on towards Hemingway Road. But you still get no sight of faces?'

'The hoods and balaclavas hadn't been taken off.'

'Professional. They'd spotted you running, of course, and the handset.'

They brought the woman out on a stretcher. She'd had first aid, and a thick bandage around her head was already soaked red. Alongside her, a medic held a drip-feed blood flask aloft. They placed her in the ambulance and he climbed in afterwards. The man who'd been half on the sofa came out on a second stretcher and they put him on the other side of the ambulance. It drew away, led by a police Ford, its two-tone and blue light in play. Bullfinch said: 'My guess is none of these are local. They're major folk – that amount of gear and cash. So, we'd know the faces, wouldn't we? At least one or two of the faces. But the Lexus boys –they might be home-based. They get the whispers, and are possibly familiar with the terrain and properties.'

Yes, she thought, home-based. Or at least one of them home-based. How else would she know the running style? Another entirely unexplainable thought turned up from somewhere and nudged her: apparently, in the war, when the air-raid siren went because German aircraft were about, they would evacuate the elementary schools. Her grandfather was a child and had told her how pupils ran home in groups with a teacher and would get into their own Anderson shelters in their back gardens if a bombing attack developed. The teacher shared the shelter of the last child of the group to reach home.

But, for God's sake, how was this tied to complex villainy in Schooner Way, 2003?

Bullfinch said: 'We might get the Lexus before they swap. My bet is they'd go left on to Hemingway, up on the other side of the lake, left filter, then right towards Wentloog and the coast road. Not too much traffic. They'd have a switch vehicle waiting somewhere there. Shirenewton say or Outfall Lane.'

'Perhaps if I'd backed my car I could have blocked them in, even rammed them,' Sally replied. She knew she specialized in second thoughts.

'Yes, I'd considered that.' For a second she saw signs of one of his tantrums. *Why didn't this half-baked cow stop them before they could start? Didn't she realize what a ton of bother the heist would bring me? Did she care? Did anyone care? Am I – I, I, I – supposed to clear up the shit from every fucking crisis on this patch?* But amiability seemed to have a hold on Bullfinch today, so far. He said: 'But, no, you handled things perfectly. Cars are not weapons. You could have been killed. We need you.'

Kindness was as much him as the pettish bouts of paranoia and anger. She thought kindness exceptional in someone of his rank, and possibly a fault. Sally considered that if Bullfinch were even a fraction more capable he would be always settled and sunny, never slip into weird rages. He had to be pitied. That extra bit of capability could not be learned and added. Now, he must bluff his way until retirement, and in her view should go immediately he reached the date – a kindness to himself. Nobody would try to dissuade him. Certainly not the chief. For a while he stared at the shattered front door. 'Bithron, where, where was our intelligence?'

'If these are people from outside, sir, it's possible they could evade—'

'Something of this scale, yet we get no pre-knowledge? That's bad. That's frightening.'

'If it's the first time they've used this location we—'

'Only by fluke. We come upon it – *you* come upon it – only by fluke. Yet the word was around, wasn't it? Otherwise, how did the raid party manage the right time and place? Why didn't *we* hear the word, then?'

We did.

'We pay informants, you know,' Bullfinch said. 'What is referred to optimistically as a "network" of informants. Damned optimistically. D'you know the main quality of a net, Bithron?'

'Sir?'

'It's got holes in it. Ours is all holes. Where was the information from this expensive network? Am I supposed to run our domain like a fucking clairvoyant? Am I? Am I? People think I have a divining rod? Do they? Do they?' His face was boyish, fleshy, in search of comfort. 'Or has information been deliberately kept from me? Have you considered that? You're young in the service so probably don't realize the kind of self-interest that can get in the way of duty. I mean complicity by some of our own people in

29

a harvest like this. You'll find that impossible to believe, I expect. I'm sorry I have to tell you it could be so. Perhaps I shouldn't be telling you, in fact.'

No, he shouldn't.

'And who do you think must sort out such a dark mess, Bithron? Who? I. I. I. Tell me, is this reasonable when I'm starved of knowledge? Oh, is it?' His voice quivered again, but not with the sound of someone thrilled and eager, but someone nearly crushed by a mischievous fate.

His handset spoke. A control-room voice came over clear. Sally, alongside Bullfinch, could listen in. The Lexus had been stopped after a chase and five-car boxing on the coast road going east, a little beyond Shirenewton and near Outfall Lane, so perhaps Bullfinch *did* do clairvoyance. Three men were in custody.

'Three?' he said. 'Over.'

'Three. Over.'

'That should be four. I've an eyewitness.' He was in a hurry and now dropped the 'over'.

'Three. All known. And a quantity of cash, sir.'

'What quantity?'

'About ninety grand, sir, on a quick first scan.'

'It should be more.'

'About ninety, sir.'

'It *has* to be more.'

'Did your eyewitness have a chance to count it, then, sir?'

'What? What? Don't you get fucking lippy with me,' he told the handset. 'I'm the boy with this fucking lot on my shoulders. The city builds a sweet marina and then what? This. We're supposed to look after it. *I*, personally, am supposed to look after it. That's what rank means. You'll find out, suppose you ever get any. But do I get the slightest pre-intimation of such a disgusting event? Total nothing. All right, all right, you'll say my rank is big because I'm

OK for any task. That's undeniable, but I want proper recognition and no backchat.'

'About ninety, sir.'

Three men in the Lexus, three men only. Briefly, that troubled Sally as much as Bullfinch. She kicked her memory into another showing of the attack scene, scared that somehow she might have double-counted one of them. Such an error was impossible, and she knew it absolutely, but she still did the recheck. One: Balaclava Man, the driver. Two: Sledgehammer man, naturally first out of the car and up the path, because the door was his job, though he apparently lashed out with the hammer inside later. As Bullfinch asked, 'Necessary or simply viciousness, evil exuberance?' Three: Colt Man One, the lovely mover. Four: Colt Man Two, older, shorter, fatter.

And suddenly then, while running this replay in her head, she knew who Colt-Man One was. Of course. Of course. The lope. The lope. She could explain to herself now, also, the mysterious, flimsy, firm link with World War Two, and with the school-evacuation procedure.

'There'll have been a switch car near,' Bullfinch said to the handset. 'He might have reached that. With a stack of the money.'

'Who, sir?'

'The other man,' Bullfinch said.

'We have three only. Over.'

'Don't I know you have three only? Haven't you told me three only? One of them's got clear with the main takings.'

'No report on that, sir.'

'What about another vehicle?'

'No report on that, sir.'

'He's disappeared in it.'

'Who, sir?'

'The one unaccounted for.'

'No report on that, sir.'

31

'Plus very heavy swag,' Bullfinch replied.

'Ninety is the figure I hear, sir.'

'And ninety is the figure I hear from you. It's short.'

'Yes, ninety, sir, approx.'

'We trawl for another car,' Bullfinch said.

'Which, sir?'

'One man in it, probably unhooded now and with massive loot. A trolley case.'

'We can't stop every car with one unhooded man in it, sir. And there's no way of spotting which vehicle has funds aboard. Do you want roadblocks and a general search of vehicles on the coast road?'

'He'll be away from there by now.'

'We're without descriptions – man or any switch vehicle, sir.'

'Don't I *know* you're without descriptions? *Get* descriptions, for God's sake. The vehicle must have been parked there, waiting. Someone might have seen him transferring to it.'

'It's fairly rural. Few people about.'

'Don't I fucking *know* it's fairly rural and few people about?' Bullfinch replied. 'Why they picked the spot for the changeover.'

'We'll do some door-knocking in the farms.'

'Oh, brilliant,' Bullfinch replied.

'We might get a car description if it was parked there a while and noticed. Rural people do notice something like that.'

'Oh, brilliant. I'm going out there now, personally.'

'Oh.'

'What?'

'Right, sir.'

'And have we talked to the three we've got?'

'Sir?'

'About the other one and the vehicle.'

'I think we assumed we had them all, sir.'

32

'Don't I *know* you assumed you had them all? Adjust. These three will be pissed off if one lad's cornered the bulk and run. They might spill to spite him.'

'Are we sure there's another, sir?'

'*I'm* sure, so you get yourself sure and quick. Make sure everyone gets sure. You've seen *The Third Man* on telly, have you? Well, this is the *fourth* man. I want him. Must I do it all, all myself? Must I? Have we recovered weapons?'

'No report to that effect, sir.'

'We've got three men shot, two of them most likely dead, plus a woman pulped by hammer, but no weapons exist, do they?'

'No weapons reported, at this juncture.'

'Perhaps he's running with two pistols and a sledge-hammer, as well as the takings.'

'Who, sir? Over.'

'Four.'

'Should I put out an "Approach with care"?'

'Let's just get so we can approach at all, shall we? We'll think about "with care" later. At some other fucking juncture,' Bullfinch said.

'Which?'

'What?'

'Juncture, sir.'

'Find him. *That* juncture. And the money. All of it. No souvenirs.'

'Do we know what *all* is, sir?'

'*I* know,' Bullfinch replied. 'Let our cars know I know.'

'A figure, sir?'

'*You* know I know, so just let them know I know.'

'They won't understand how you *could* know.'

'They don't need to understand. Just let them know I know.'

'A figure?'

'You don't need to know the figure. You know I know

33

the figure, so let them know I know and they'll know then I want it all accounted for.'

'If there's no figure, they'll feel liable to accusations of skimming. Are we talking hundreds of thousands?'

'Like that, yes.'

'This is a ball-park figure, is it, sir? Not a *known* figure in the usual sense of known?'

'What does "usual sense of known" mean?' Bullfinch said.

'Known.'

'I *know* what it is.'

'This is like a guess, is it, sir? Obviously an *intelligent* guess, in view of whose it is, sir, but all the same a guess.'

'Just find the fucker, will you? What was the money in?'

'Which?'

'The ninety.'

'Carrier bags.'

'There should be the trolley case.'

'No report on that. What like, sir.'

'Tartan,' Sally said.

'Tartan,' Bullfinch said.

'I know the kind, sir.'

'Brilliant. He's gone with the case,' Bullfinch said. 'Hold on.' He lowered the handset and turned to Sally. 'The one with the case? Age? Build? Wearing?'

'Twenties. About six feet and a hundred and seventy pounds,' she said. 'Dark shirt, jeans, desert boots.' That would do for now.

Bullfinch put the radio back to his mouth and repeated the details. 'There could be a clothes change in the switch car.'

'Can we do better than twenties for age, sir?' the control room asked. 'Early? Late? Mid?'

Sally heard the questions. She could have given his age to within a month or two. It would match her own. But she shook her head when Bullfinch looked for a reply. 'It's the hood,' she said. 'Can't be exact.'

Exactness would be not just his age but his name. Exactness would be a betrayal. A betrayal of what? She was aware of what, but didn't define it to herself because she knew it would sound woolly, puffed up, sentimental. Especially that.

Bullfinch finished talking to headquarters. She felt he was the kind made for handsets. With it up to his face he looked resolute and very capable, regardless of what was actually being said. Suddenly, he turned away from Sally and sprinted up the front garden path and into the house, holding the radio down against his right thigh like a rested pistol. For about half a minute he stayed inside, then reappeared, sprinting again, but now the style was more laboured, as though he were carrying something hefty, say a trolley case with two hundred grand in it, fifties and twenties. He must have put the handset into one of his uniform's big side pockets and had both arms out in front at chest height and bent around nothing, which would be the money bag. Back on the pavement, he stooped to get into the Lexus – if it had been there. 'Whoosh!' he said, and waved one arm towards Hemingway Road and beyond, sign of a powerful getaway. 'So, like that, Bithron?' he said.

'Slightly different. He had the case in one hand, his right. The Colt was in his left.'

Bullfinch went back into the house and reappeared after a few seconds, this time the handset in his left hand, like a gun, and his right arm crooked, as if around the case. 'Like that, sir,' Sally said.

He walked down Schooner Way towards her car, then swung around and began to run back, the handset up to his mouth and ear. She could hear occasional words and phrases as he spoke to it, no gasping. Bullfinch did a lot of fitness training. The uniform cap must be a great fit and stayed absolutely secure. 'Schooner Way . . . Hooded . . . Two

35

handguns, possibly Colts . . . Shots . . . Three plus driver
. . . Gold Lexus saloon.' Bullfinch was obviously Sally
herself now, making her spurt, calling for aid. 'So – like
that, Bithron?' he said, reaching her.

'Like that, sir.'

'I believe in it, you see.'

'What?'

'Enacting.'

'It gives actuality,' she replied.

'At staff college I did a project on enactment. It was
appreciated, I think.'

'Immediacy. Often used by police to prompt public
memory.'

'I like to feel the concrete of the path under my feet –
the hardness, the grit. I indulge myself with an imitation of
the effort you made rushing to the incident while at the
same time so capably alerting support parties. I'd refer to
this experience as vicarious were I doing a paper on it –
meaning entering into something undergone by another.
Obviously, *only* vicarious. It cannot wholly match the
urgency and stress of your *actual* intervention. It mimics
merely. Merely mimics. Yet it enlightened, too, allowing
me to share and chart those key moments. I am enveloped
in them –not, of course, to the degree you were, but
enveloped nonetheless. You see, Bithron, I am not merely
a passive listener to your account. I reanimate that account.
I live it. And *their* experience – I live that, too, you see.
Or I live his, at least. Our missing lad's. Our lad with the
major holding. In so far as is possible, that is. Always, I'll
make this proviso. I live his experience *in so far as is
possible*. It is plainly not reality, or even *virtual* reality –
how, how could one claim that? But illuminating all the
same. Illuminating for me.'

'I think someone said there are many ways to the truth.'

'I don't see this as theatrical, more a kind of
communing, telepathy,' Bullfinch replied. 'An attempt at,

that is. A route to others' thoughts by, as it were, acting upon them.'

'Striking.'

'For instance, when I ran up the path, did it make you recall the original?'

'Certainly.' Except, of course, Bullfinch moved like Mr Super-Fit – very straight, elbows pistoning, long legs nicely flexing. How could he know he was supposed to lope?

Three

Yes, how could Bullfinch have realized he should lope and glide to fix the fourth man's identity? Answer: Bullfinch couldn't. The knowledge was special to Sally, and a grand privilege. The knowledge was special to Sally, and a vast pain. It sprang from fine old loyalties. It sprang from sloppy, sentimental loyalties that might have to be ditched. Ought to be ditched? Anyone could have felt such loyalties, and she did not consider them just a womanly weakness. Whatever they were, they had to be got rid of.

Bullfinch sent for her a couple of days after Schooner Way. 'You're going to be crucial, Bithron,' he said. Although his face was grave, it showed flecks of congratulation, too – in the upturn of his mouth corners and brilliantly shining blue eyes. Encourage, boost the troops. Here was leadership again. But his voice had a touch of tremor. Probably he feared what he forever feared in subordinates – that she would not shape up to the crucialness he had Sally storyboarded for, and would drop him in the cack.

This was true Bullfinch *angst* and Sally longed to help him, soothe him, buck him up. She yearned to satisfy his expectations, exceed them. It was a kind of duty: she suddenly understood what priests meant by a call, a vocation. *Her* vocation was to save Bullfinch from his doubts and terrors. She had come across people like this before – somewhere between genius and buffoon and beginning to tilt unstoppably towards the second. At general elections, this was the kind of judgement about candidates that often

38

had to be made. As she saw it, her mission was to shove Bullfinch back into the flair and confidence he must have owned when first fast-tracked. He'd obviously wowed people then. She must restore that power to him. She must save his police soul. Yes, mission. 'Crucial? That sounds good, sir,' she replied.

'We've nicked Schooner Way Number Four. A couple of hours ago.'

Shock hit Sally and its force amazed her, almost silenced her. 'Where?'

'Not his trolley case or money, though. A lad with piffling previous. Nothing on this scale.'

'The Lexus three talked, sir?' she asked. 'Is that how we got him?'

'Not a damn word. Why I sent for you.'

Now she became uneasy. Had he smelt something? Non-stop jitters like Bullfinch's brought high sensitivity. Bullfinch knew the world meant to get him, and he watched it, watched it with his cute genius/buffoon eyes. He was raw, his reactions instant. Sally said: 'I'm not sure what you—'

'As I see it, they need Number Four free and in credit,' Bullfinch replied. 'He hides the cash and will fund their families while they're locked up – long-time locked up. Villains think of such things. They can be remarkably strong on solidarity. When you've seen as many of them as I, you'll realize this. He's banker. They trust him. Well, what else can they do?'

'So, how did we find him?'

'Before this, only trivial bits of theft.'

'Sir, so how did—?'

'My feeling is, there were *two* switch cars, to confuse pursuit,' Bullfinch replied. 'That happens. A team splits then joins up again for the share-out when things are quiet. We caught the Lexus before it reached the second. He must have already left the Lexus and taken the first. Perhaps one

39

of the others in the Lexus was supposed to go with him,
but some difficulty came up. Wobbly legs, paralysis even,
after all the stress? That happens, too. Because Four had
the case, we assume he holds the main boodle. Ninety K
recovered. Where's the rest? Ninety has to be minor –
couldn't pay for even half the stuff on offer there. These
were very experienced dealers, as we now know. Avril
Kale, from one of the great South East London crook
dynasties. Her lover, Neville Nelmes Scott. These are
people who are brought up to know prices, and so were
the sellers, of course –Lestoque and Singlecomb, as those
two were calling themselves. We must be talking three
hundred K plus.'

'No trace?'

'You'll wonder if our pursuit people cornered the big
helping – like prize money in old Navy days.'

'No, I wouldn't for a moment think—'

'Say two hundred to two hundred and fifty K adrift. And
we've found no weaponry yet – the guns and hammer. No
switch car either. Burned out somewhere, I expect. The
Kale/Scott Mondeo in an hotel car park, yes – but it tells
us little we wouldn't have discovered anyway. We got
Number Four at home.'

'Does he admit it?'

'What?'

'He's the fourth.'

'Bithron, at this level people admit nothing. When you've
seen as many of them as I, you'll realize this. Even when
they do cough, they'll claim afterwards it was tortured out
of them or we made it up. He has a sort of alibi. *Claims*
he has an alibi. We'll pulp it, naturally. Apart from trying
to sell us that, he's a brick wall. Like the others. Interrogation
goes nowhere. So far.'

'Not even with the wobbly-legs one?'

'The body can fail while the mind stays tough,' Bullfinch
said. 'They might be new to this league but they've learned

shtum. Probably because of all that *omerta* shit in TV Mafia drama.'

'Without the money or armament or switch car as evidence, and if the Lexus people don't talk, it's going to be hard to—'

'That's what I mean, crucial. We'll need something outstanding from you as our witness. Solitary, gifted witness. We're confident you'll do it, Bith. We see you as very much part of the coming leadership generation, with an eye to cleansing our streets of outlaws and preserving the loveliness of the Bay.'

God. 'But even if he *is* Four—'

'No question. We're nearly ready to charge him.'

'With what?'

'Robbery, at present. We don't know who did what in the house. Not yet. Who carried the hammer and cracked the lady? You might be able to help with that – with a description of his physique. We can't match bullets to the guns because we haven't got the guns, and if we did we'd still be guessing who had which. Obviously, the driver is clear of the indoors violence.'

'How do we know, sir?'

'Well, he stayed with the Lexus, didn't he? You told us.'

'No, I didn't mean that. How do we know Four is Four?'

'Excellent detection work.'

'Who by?'

'Really excellent.'

'But how exactly?' Sally replied.

'Your evidence could be the clincher, though.'

'How?'

'How? *How?*' Bullfinch leaned forward across his desk to give her full staff-rank gaze, imperial but comradely. He was her chief. He depended on her. 'You were *there*, Bithron.'

'He had a hood on.'

'Height, build, age, and then anything additional. These

41

might seem small things, but they build a picture and help towards a verdict. Build. Build. Fragment by fragment. Eventually everything becomes evident to the court. You see, we're certain this is our boy. Its just a matter of parcelling him decently for some thick-as-sump-oil jury, in the fine tradition of thick-as-sump-oil Brit juries. It's our professional obligation to nail him good.'

The running style of Four and its precious history would probably get into Bullfinch's 'anything additional' category if Sally chose to mention it. She didn't. Those ancient, perhaps treacherous, loyalties restrained her, plus her conviction that how a man did six or seven steps across a pavement and up a path was not conclusive. And, there might be something in the alibi, though probably not.

'I want you to have a talk with Ray Regnal,' Bullfinch said. 'He's putting things together. Yes, have a word with Detective Superintendent Regnal, will you, Bithron? Ray's good at that – putting things together. For court. Parcelling. Obviously, you can't manufacture a description to fit our boy's face if it was not visible.' The preposterousness of this idea made him laugh for a time, though not a happy laugh, a furious, oh-fuck-my-fucking-fate laugh, a wouldn't-you-fucking-know-they'd-wear-fucking-hoods laugh. 'How could anyone expect that of you? But we're so fortunate to have yourself actually *in situ*, and *in situ* absolutely by accident. Absolutely.' He smiled, grew warm, grew reverential. 'I term it accident, *you* term it accident, but perhaps, too, there was a touch of inspiration, of prime detective instinct about it. You might have that unteachable, priceless intuition – call it luck, call it magic, call it telepathy – the intuition which ensures you're somehow on the spot when a crucial event is due. Synchronicity? That the word? The way Wellington had by chance looked at the lie of the land around Waterloo a year before. The way Graham Greene, the very famed author of many tales, wrote about the world's hot spots just before they got hot. I envy you that ability.

Such sublime *au fait-ness* can be the making of a career. You've done yourself tremendous good. I've heard several people mention this – influential people, I mean. And, of course, I've mentioned it myself.' He picked up a pen and, after a quiet, thoughtful pause, the corners of his mouth still hearteningly up, carefully wrote something on a memo pad – perhaps, *Kick shit out of her future if this bitch lets us down in court.*

Sally said: 'I'll describe physical type and possible age, yes, but—'

'Here's the extreme, indeed unique, beauty of it, Bithron –no snotty defence lawyer can claim we came up with this scenario, let it happen, so as to net people we'd targeted. This was not a planned operation – in no sense. All right, your presence might be in the magical, intuitive, telepathic realm we spoke of, but there was emphatically no set-up. Had there been, we would have prepared an ambush – not just one detective constable, but a real hit force, a regiment. You have given us a splendidly straight situation. I absolutely must *not* waste this fine good fortune! No. You'll agree, I know.'

Happiness conferred a real momentary glow on Bullfinch. She longed for the shaky sod to be always like this. He deserved some contentment now. This was humankind in constant agony. The wages could not compensate. He'd begun as a whizz-kid and it must be unbearably rough to feel your whizz was gone. Bullfinch said: 'Mr Regnal will let you have a leisurely look at him, to help confirm any distinguishing aspects noticed in Schooner Way. Ray's gift is for putting things together. Juries can comprehend that a villain *is* a villain and should be sent down for ever when it's Ray who prepared the case against. Our lawyers only have to unwrap the parcel he provides and give what's inside to the court. Ray is a model to us all in that respect, a lesson.'

'But isn't this going at it all—?'

43

'Backwards?' Bullfinch said. 'You mean, finding identification now and sticking it *post hoc* on to the event?'

Yes, that. 'I—'

Bullfinch nodded several times to indicate sympathy and
understanding. He said: 'No, I don't think so. Let me say,
I appreciate your scruples, esteem them. There can be no
question of placing him in the frame in hindsight. I feel you
know me better than that, Bithron. We owe honesty and
decency even to those who would never offer such commodi-
ties to us. But what I'm suggesting would mean only that
your memories of Four at Schooner Way might be recovered from deep within you – might be, as it were, rescued
– yes, rescued – reclaimed – impressions which, in the rush
on the day, you noticed but were not aware you noticed.'
He spoke with a mild but vivid teaching tone now. 'Yes,
rescue, *reclaim* such memories. They *deserve* it. This is
often necessary. For instance, finger decoration. On their
way in and out, hand jewellery might have been evident.'

Still seated at his desk, Bullfinch lifted one of his own
hands and held it in front of him in the shape it would take
for gripping the butt of a gun. He wore civilian clothes
today, shirt-sleeved, with plump, amber cuff links. They
seemed to give him dash. A little dash. His resident Bullfinch
jumpiness almost cancelled them. 'Backs of the hands very
much on view sporadically,' he said. 'Any adornments
would be apparent. I gather from Mr Regnal our lad wears
a quite heavy gold signet ring which might well have glinted,
mightn't it? Sunny? I think so. You could have easily
forgotten that glint. Entirely normal. You're hoofing it
desperately up Schooner Way in summer heat, confronted
by a wholly unexpected situation, while observing *and* trying
to talk into the handset – all these piling fierce demands on
your concentration. Something could easily get missed –
by the *conscious* mind, that is. But it will all be very much
there, stored in your head, believe me. When you've come
across as many experiences of this kind as I, you'll realize

this. Only a prompt might be needed. Think how the words of a supposedly long-forgotten song can come back when the music starts. Yet one would never have recalled them *cold.* Memory – a fascinating topic. Do *you* ever think about memory, ·Bithron – its power, its brilliant quirks and resonances?'

Yes, she did think about memory now and then. Now. And, yes, its power, its brilliant quirks, its resonances. Three doors away from Sally and her family when she was a child lived a boy of her age, Frank Latimer, and *his* family. They were in the same year at the local primary and junior school. She thought of Frank Latimer.

Bullfinch said: 'I'd like you to observe the signet ring when Ray shows you our prisoner. Achieve familiarity with it, as though you've been acquainted with this ring a while. This will bring poise and assurance, supreme assets in the witness box.'

'It's all going to depend on a ring, sir?'

'Not *only* a ring. The ring is a factor. A prosecution is an amalgam, a structure, a composite of many elements. As I said, build, build.'

Sally's and Frank's fathers and grandfathers had also attended the school. For a good part of the last century, Grangetown, Cardiff, was that sort of area, that sort of community. One generation of men succeeded another in Grange Council School – St Patrick's School for the Catholic O'Neills, Hickeys and McCarthys – then succeeded their fathers in the jobs nearby: factories and mills, or a bike ride over Clarence Bridge at the muddy mouth of the Taff to the docks. Although the district had begun to change by the time of Sally's childhood, some of the flavour remained, some of the old wonderful prole cohesiveness.

Bullfinch said: 'I know I hardly need to tell you this, Bith, but, forgive me, I will all the same – don't, don't on any account let him realize you're observing the ring, of course, or he'll tell his brief, who'll argue we're using subsequent knowledge. They're up to every dodge, these big-earning, bewigged bastards.'

'A ring? I wouldn't have been able to— Sir, I think in fact he might have had gloves on. Possibly they all did.'

'Gloves? A hot summer's day.'

'To defeat fingerprinting.'

'You *think* they had gloves on . . . that *he* had gloves on. "Possibly", you say,' Bullfinch replied. 'Not sure? Not at all sure.'

'I didn't concentrate on the hands, I suppose. I was trying to observe build, height, approximate age,' Sally replied.

'Of course you were, Bithron. And rightly. Entirely rightly.' He nodded several times. She felt empathy in these nods. He spoke gently: 'Look, I don't think gloves come into this, do you? No. We can reasonably forget gloves, I believe. A ring's ideal, you see. The jury can be shown that as an exhibit. They understand trinkets. Get a view of the ring right away, would you? We've let him keep it on while in police cells. Once he's charged it'll be put in a jail bag.'

Sally's family had shared their grandfather's Bargoed Street house with him. Her brother, Mark, and Frank Latimer were pals, and Frank would often call at the Bithrons' house. One day in the late 1980s, Sally's grandfather told Frank he'd seen him running along Corporation Road, and it was great – full of grace and energy, part lope, part glide. He did an imitation in slow motion across the room and the three children laughed. Sally hadn't known what 'lope' meant, but worked this out from her grandfather's perform- ance. He claimed it reminded him of a teacher at Grange Council they used to call Pop Daniels.

'Oh, certainly, powerful sun's rays that day in Schooner Way,' Bullfinch said. 'We've checked weather records. Think glint, Bithron.'

Instead, she went on thinking about the past – the past and then the further past. She remembered her grandfather had told them that, during the war, whenever an air-raid warning came in school hours, all Grange Council children were sent home at a trot in groups led by a teacher. He or she would drop each child off at their house where they could use the family's Anderson shelter in the garden. Pop Daniels, the Welsh language master, had charge of their group. They hurried, so as to be clear of the streets when the bombers turned up. Nearly fifty years later, it seemed Frank by some chance ran just like Pop Daniels in 1940. The teacher would be out ahead and the kids behind tried to keep up by copying his style – half mockery, half admiration. It was fast and looked effortless, just the way Frank moved, her grandfather said. He was one of the first to be deposited at home and Frank's grandfather the last of the group. Pop Daniels stayed in the Latimers' shelter until the all clear. Sally used to try to imagine it, these people huddled together, frightened together, half underground. She had heard of cavemen. That was how they seemed to her, but cavemen waiting for bombs. Because of the industry, and the Taff to navigate by, Grangetown did get bombed.

Bullfinch said: 'It would be natural for you, a trained, very observant detective, to focus on something like the ring during the Schooner Way fracas, given that the normal means of identification were concealed, i.e. face, head. All right, your *conscious* self would fix on the characteristics you mentioned – height, physique, etcetera. But there'd be other aspects to note. You'd do that automatically. Oh, yes, you'd be garnering giveways, though perhaps unaware.'

A joke came with her grandfather's tale, and this bit of humour had helped fix it for good in Sally's recollection. Bullfinch was right – memory could be odd. In 1940, the Latimers had lived a block or two away in a street called Coed Cae, named after a valleys mining town, like Bargoed Street. The proper pronunciation – the Welsh pronunciation – would be 'coy' plus the d, and 'eye' after the initial C. But Welsh was scarce or non-existent in Grangetown, a district of English, Irish, Scottish immigrants since Cardiff started to boom and need labour around 1880. In speech, Coed Cae Street was always strangely shuffled and anglicized by locals into Cockade Street, and when Pop Daniels asked Frank on their first evacuation run where he lived, this was how he said it. 'Spell that,' Daniels replied and Frank did. 'Coed Cae, boy!' Daniels cried in agony.

Bullfinch said: 'Then there's the way Number Four moved from the Lexus. Mr Regnal hasn't seen him actually run, but says our boy's walk is very loose-limbed – a kind of lope is how he puts it. A gliding action. Very individual, a bit balletic, a bit wolf-like. Mr Regnal gets to the theatre and cinema.'

Sally recalled how her grandfather had mimicked that yell of Pop Daniels for them with delight. His merriment meant something. Grangetown had developed its own distinct, aggressive, mongrel culture, probably a bit workaday and crude – and as a result somehow stronger, needier, more binding. It had no character, and was all character. Sally could still occasionally feel its grip, though she didn't live there these days – no longer spoke in that supremely jagged Grangetown version of the jagged Cardiff English accent. She felt this grip now as she half listened to Bullfinch, and it came with obligations, didn't it? Ties. Friendships. For outsiders, Grange was a puzzling, difficult section of the city. That must have been true for Pop Daniels. He probably came from a bilingual part of Wales, his surname Welsh – not like the Latimers or Freemans or Paisleys or Murisons or Smiths or Aitkens or Bowlings or Farrants or Halberts or Bravos or Elliots or Ridouts who sat in class with Sally Bithron and her father and grandfather. By 2003, of course, Grangetown was even more multiracial, the range of non-Welsh surnames bigger still.

Bullfinch stood and tried a slow-motion rendering, across his office, of Four's sprint mode, the way Sally's grandfather had a dozen or so years ago. 'Distinctive?' Bullfinch asked. He returned to his desk in a normal, non-lope way.

'You see, if you think back, perhaps you'll recall Numero Four moving like that, especially when he's on the way *in*, unloaded. Probably *only* on the way in. Some grandiose QC might query loping when a man's carrying a trolley case heavy with sterling. Yes, you should concentrate on your memories of their entry.'

Part absorbed as folk history, part actual from her own childhood, Sally's memory could still place that lope, that glide – had done so a good while before Bullfinch's demonstration. And so, Colt Man One under his hood was Frank Latimer, was he? The age would be right. She had no other evidence, only that and the way he moved. It was about fifteen years since she last saw him and Sally didn't know how he'd matured – tall, short, heavy, skinny – but there'd been tales he'd turned crooked. Some time late in Frank's and Sally's junior-school career his parents split up. The Bargoed Street house was re-let and he and his mother went to live in Adamsdown, another Cardiff working-class area. Mark and Sally lost touch with Frank, though occasionally they heard unhappy things about him. He'd been caught for small-time villainy and received police warnings and cautions. Later, when Sally joined the force, she found he was known as a minor nuisance. Now, she had to wonder whether, at going on twenty-five, he had suddenly decided to climb. Had he attempted a loping, gliding, daring, nicely organized move into a very considerable drug-dealing scene? Leave the stuff, take the money – quicker, easier. It hadn't been nicely organized enough, though. Or at least not secretly enough. Somehow, Godzilla heard.

'Bithron, I'd really hate to see our charges fail because of lack of mere formal identification,' Bullfinch said. 'We're talking two murders here, as well as the rest of it. Well, three murders now, of course. Our injured male has died – Neville Nelmes Scott. Accurate identification of people accused is important, obviously, but not when made the object of damned negative lawyerly quibbles. That depresses

49

me, makes one question the whole prospect for policing –
as if the legal system only exists to do us down. You know,
sometimes I ask myself why should these miserable irrita-
tions come to me? To me? To me? I wonder if the rest of
you in this building ever consider that? Oh, admittedly,
everyone in the force feels something of such anxieties right
up to the chief and down to . . . Yes, right down to . . . Oh,
yes, yes. But ultimately, conclusively, they come to *me* to
deal with, don't they?' He glanced away from Sally while
stomaching the affront and striving to regulate his bitter-
ness and anger. This struggle touched her. She would have
liked to stroke his shirt-sleeved arm so he might know his
sufferings were recognized and earned her pity. That would
be absurd with someone of his rank, though. He didn't
directly turn back to her, but looked down again to the
papers on his desk. 'Latimer, Frank, twenty-four,' he read.
'Age as identification is beside the point, obviously, given
the hood. It's the ring and his lope which could be helpful.
Bold capital F on the ring. Naturally, you don't mention
this in the witness box. You're too far away to make that
out. We need credibility. Just go for the glint.'

  'I—'

  'Yes, have a word with Regnal. We're proud of how you
managed matters on the day. He, myself, all of us. Your
behaviour then helps convince me policing can still achieve
much, despite everything – is not irrecoverably on the slide.
But that kind of accomplished work does need to be crowned
by getting all possible convictions, doesn't it? Fruition.
Completion. Yes, all possible. Four. The three are easy. It's
Number Four who is the challenge.' He leaned forward over
the desk again. 'Look, look, Bithron, isn't it patent he's the
one, this fucking Latimer, he's the one who thinks he can
mess me about, savage me through his ruses and selective
silence? He means to mess us *all* about, of course. I don't
want to sound egomaniac. Never that, I hope, never that.
But always it comes to this, you see – them against me, or

one of them in this case. It's *I* who have to carry it all, who is designated, and, all right, paid to carry it all, as Head of Detection. *I.I.I.* We must be competent. Our public duty. Get him put away for many a grand new millennium year or he'll plague me again, laughingly, relentlessly, oh, cruelly plague me. Let's see what a decade or two behind a fat steel door will do for the tight-lipped sod, shall we – his fucking flash signet ring with its fucking Frank F, kept in a safe for him in the junk room at some max security spot till he's too old and wasted to keep it on?'

Brian Edward Aulus, codenamed Godzilla, wanted another meeting. Well, of course he wanted a meeting. What happened at Schooner Way and afterwards made the news on TV and radio, and the national and local press. Even without all that, there was the street buzz, anyway, and someone like Godzilla heard every street buzz before it buzzed. Part of his trade skill. He would have been alert for this one. Things could not have turned out the way they did except for Godzilla and, naturally, he must realize it. How would he regard the outcome? Did grasses feel job satisfaction when their wise whispers got arrests?

At once she regretted this thought, or tried to regret it. If you used informants – depended on informants – it was disgusting to belittle them, mock them. Yes, disgusting, but informing could never be seen as a noble trade, even by those who sponsored it. She still wondered what was in the Schooner Way operation for him. She had asked, but there'd been no answer. No sane, credible answer – only some-thing half-baked about keeping the Bay's splendid image from taint.

'It seemed vital to see you right away,' he said, 'so I could let you know face to face that I have fierce contempt for these rumours about you, but—'
   'Which?'

'But, regrettably – so regrettably – I can't do anything to squash them. I'd be appalled if you thought I went along with—'

'Which?'

'I felt a real dread you might think I believed them.'

'Which?'

'What?'

'Which rumours?' she replied.

'I knew you'd have heard and might wonder whether I could do something to kill them off, Sally – through contacts and so on. That sort of thing. I can't. Can't. And this troubled me. I saw it as a sort of betrayal. I had to speak with you.'

Had he ever used her first name before? 'Which rumours?' she said.

'So damned hurtful. So damned malevolent and predictable.'

'Which rumours?' she said.

'Programmed response based on a kind of cynical folk belief – and stupid, inveterate distrust of all police, of course.'

'Which?'

'The money,' he replied.

'Which?'

'The big money. The trolley-case money. This is what – two hundred grand plus?'

'We don't know.'

'But a guess,' he said.

'It's missing.'

'Yes, I heard.'

'What's that mean?' she said.

'What?'

'"Yes, I heard."'

'It means yes, I heard, Sally.'

'But what does it—?'

'The rumours say what I'm sure you'd expect them to

say. Disgraceful, cruel. Believe me, I want to tell the folk spreading such stuff they're right off beam, because you're not like that. But can I? I'm sorry, Sal, but if I start defending you, where are we? Curtains on a fine arrangement. People are going to wonder why I'm on your side, and ask how do I know you so well. This is not long after "the incident". We'll call it that, shall we? You were a star of "the incident" – just happened to be there at the right time. That's the tale, accepted so far in the media and the buzz. Folk would begin doubting it, then, wouldn't they? This kind of suspicion spreads like foot and mouth. We might not be able to work together again. Plus, those four lads in the Lexus have chums and relations, I expect. The four in the house have chums and relations, I expect. I don't want them looking me up. It's not that I'm scared, yellow – nothing like that. But how do we function, you and I, if I get stalked?'

'What money rumours?' Sally replied. She had persuaded him they needed a fresh rendezvous spot and were on a pebble beach at Lavernock, a bit west of Cardiff. An historic spot. From here, Marconi sent the first radio message over water. Also, not long ago, a defaced body was washed up on the beach, result of some villain execution, probably in the Bay. And, for another bit of history, between these two dates, she knew her grandfather used to come to a field nearby for the Ebenezer Gospel Hall Whitsun Treats. Yes, permeated by the past. Sally liked the feel of that, was keen to be part of it. Or some of it, at any rate. They sat in hot sunshine on a big flat rock near the sea. Few people came here even in summer, because of the stones. He had brought a leather Sloane-Ranger-1990-style haversack, not harnessed on but carried by its straps in his right hand. This lay alongside him now on the rock.

'The rumours?' he said. 'Oh, you know how it is when crooked cash gets to be unfindable like that, although the crooks are taken.'

53

Yes, she knew how it was. She'd heard Bullfinch on prize money. 'No, I don't know.'

'This kind of situation often comes up.'

'Which?'

'Where the money goes missing,' he replied.

'But you think it hasn't really gone missing, do you?'

'Not me. The rumours.'

'So, the rumours say we've actually found the money and there's been a quiet share-out – me, Bullfinch, and whoever else got close enough?'

'Known as Booty Treatment.'

'And now you—?'

'Or Swag Recycling.'

'You believe I—?'

'As I said, it's the usual slur some make when they hear police announce so regretfully and with such puzzlement that crime proceeds are missing. No villain's going to complain his illegal stack has been incorporated. This is the thinking of people who start these rumours – if we can call it thinking. Clearly, a disgrace, the foulest of slanders.'

Sally tried to read from his frothy language and concerned face and kindly voice whether he did, in fact, assume she'd collected some of the big money, and wanted a slice for himself. Obviously, it wouldn't have to be accounted for and registered, like an official informant's fee. Did he have at least some of that born distrust of police, despite the arrangement with Sally? 'We're searching full out for this cash,' she said.

'Of course, of course. I know it.'

'Well, thanks. Zilla, I haven't got any of the money. Honestly, I can't cut you in on heavy funds.'

He put a hand gently on her shoulder. She was not sure about the use of her name, but this must definitely be the first time he had ever touched her. She found she wished he hadn't, and wouldn't, of course. It wasn't revulsion exactly, not quite that, but she wished he hadn't, and must make certain he wouldn't again. He said: 'You're not one to siphon off funds, not even crim funds.' He released her shoulder. She hoped her body had told him somehow that his hand should not be there, or anywhere else on her. 'Oh, please don't imagine I called this meeting to try a shake-down. Tell me that's not what you think, Sally. It would distress me.'

'You had something against the Lexus crew?' she said. 'Have they hurt you somehow in the past?'

'The Lexus crew?'

'A tit-for-tat thing?'

'How do you mean?' he said.

'Did you grass on the Lexus men because you've got a hatred going, a revenge motive? I'm trying to sort out the whys of it all.'

'A hatred? Revenge?'

'You owe a disaster to them –or some of them, or one of them?'

'The Lexus people are not important.'

'But—'

'Not important to me. They might be to you,' he said.

'I don't understand. You—'

'Or next to no importance,' he replied. 'They couldn't keep their plans quiet and I heard of them. Because of the four and their mouths, I found out about the Schooner Way house. That's my only interest in them.'

'Your objective was the dealers?'

'It's better not to be exact about—'

'Did you fear them as competitors, potential competitors? That what it's about – why you grassed on them? Big-time people moving about in the Bay, and you didn't like it? You felt crowded?'

'I don't want to be—'

'This is really strategic scheming. Oh, I see it now.' She had been part of his long-term commercial plans, had she, recruited to help smash possible trade opposition? He did not care about tipster fees. What he wanted was a kind of protection for his businesses. This she had given. Perhaps he was not even concerned about a lump of the trolley-case heavy wealth. His thinking was more long-term, more organizational, grander. Or perhaps he did actually believe, despite all the rumours and folk wisdom, that she had none of the Schooner Way Four's riches.

He said: 'The main reason I had to see you . . . Well, that Schooner Way coup had to be marked by a little prezzie, in my opinion.'

'Prezzie? Crazy.'

'I see your name everywhere. A heroine.'

'It's your success, and if we were running things right, you'd be due a real packet of recognition.'

'I had to guess,' he said.

'That wasn't a guess. Inspiration.'

'No, I mean I had to guess about your taste.'

'Taste?'

'As to a prezzie.' He opened the leather haversack and produced something thickly wrapped in tissue paper. 'I had to ask myself what would be the kind of thing you'd like. I was on my own in this. I couldn't consult Ann. Well, she doesn't know you, and she might not understand, anyway, if you see what I mean.'

No, she didn't want to see what he meant.

'I decided it should be something lovely and old and delicate,' Aulus said. 'I thought glass. Tell me, are you into glass? Victorian glass, that is.'

'Glass can be lovely, but—'

'I always feel fine glass can tell you something about the age when it was made. It speaks of a lifestyle –not necessarily a fancy lifestyle – glass items may be workaday or they can be superbly ornate and refined. Either way they allow us to, as it were, see through them to the time of their origin.'

56

Oh, Christ, some fucking crooked mate of his has robbed an antique shop and offloaded. Sally said: 'Almost always there's an elegance to glass, even when the article was, in its time, for quite ordinary use.'

Aulus carefully removed the tissue paper and exposed a vase about eighteen inches tall, of green tinted glass. It had a darker green central panel decorated with what looked to Sally like primroses. It was lovely. Sally knew nothing about glass or vases but felt sure this would cost. Christ, some fucking crooked mate of his had robbed an antique shop and offloaded. Did it feature on the stolen articles register?

'We think about 1860,' he said.

'Beautiful.'

'Hold it. Enjoy the shape.'

She took the vase and turned it slowly in her hand to gaze at the workmanship.

He said: 'I worried it might be too old.'

'Zilla, antiques are old.'

'No, I meant vases. I wondered if vases were not the sort of thing – kind of for middle-aged people, on their mantelpiece with the ormolu clock. Whereas, I obviously wanted something old but for someone young – someone young enough to do all that down Schooner Way, the real nitty-gritty, using first patience, then outstanding resolve.'

She held out the vase to him. 'No. A sweet idea, but impossible for me to accept this. Not because it's too old for me. Because I can't.'

He didn't take it. 'A token,' he said.

'No.'

'You helped me,' he replied.

'You helped me. Us.'

'All that waiting around. And then the running. You could have been shot or got hit by a Lexus.'

'Helped you how?' she said.

'Oh, yes, really helped me.'

57

'You mean the people dead or disabled? I've seen the names. All top dealers – all a menace to your firms.'

'Oh, yes, really helped me,' he said.

'I spectated, that's all. The Lexus Four – Lexus Three, in fact – did them all the necessary damage. I expect you counted on that.'

'If the raid hadn't taken them out, you'd have been able to scoop up those dealers afterwards. Gratitude for your presence there, regardless – that's what this glassware says,' he replied.

She put it back into the haversack. 'Not for me.'

'But, look—'

Oh, God, the primness, the churlishness. Impossible for me to accept. Bleak, trite, philistine cow. Dismal, ungrateful fuzz robot. Why not a bit of grace and elegance? Sally saw he was hurt. She took the vase back. 'I'll put it on the mantelpiece alongside the ormolu clock.'

'Grand.'

She drove home, stood the vase on a window sill for half an hour and enjoyed the sight of it with the sun behind. The subdued colouring thrilled her, and the wonderful, smug adequacy of a period that said, 'Right then, in case no blooms are around for vasing, we'll engrave some on the glass.' In the evening she walked to Cardiff Bridge with the vase in a duffel bag and when there was nobody about threw it into the Taff. She had pulled back from smashing it to bits for her black plastic rubbish sack. That could have seemed a bit unhinged. Aulus wasn't ever going to enter her flat to see how the vase looked there.

When a chance came, she did have a prowl through the 'Stolen Artefacts (Antique, Non-furniture)' schedule, but there were a lot of green glass vases ('floral-decorated'), and of about the size and period. The Victorian middle class would have been expanding and keen to beautify their sitting rooms in 1860. Godzilla's gift to her might be among the tally, might not. At any rate, for a piece of glass craft to survive almost a century and a half uncracked, unchipped, was damn good going. This vase had had a very reasonable run.

Four

Something like delight. Yes, delight. But she did what she could to keep a grin off her face. This was an interrogation suite, damn it, and the prospects for the gold-signet-ringed lad at the other side of the table were no joke. The ring had real width and weight, as well as its pert capital F. For Four? Bullfinch was right – right again: glint potential lay in that lumpy metal band, given a bit of summer sun. Even now, under the room's gentle bulbs, the gold glowed. Outside on a blazing afternoon, glow would definitely have sharpened into glint. For the first time, Sally tried to recall whether she was aware of a shine off his hand clutching the trolley case in Schooner Way.

She had given this idea top ignoral when Bullfinch floated it the other day. Far-fetched. Scenario whimsy. Also, of course, it was someone getting fitted up in a noble cause, a noble Bullfinch cause. Not just any someone. Didn't she have an enduring, vein-deep connection with this prisoner, a street connection, a granddad-World-War-Two-Pop-Daniels connection, a childish, park-hut, self-help, happy-sexual-learning connection? Against these memories, any supposed subconscious glimpses of a glint had seemed unworthy, sick – just Bullfinch, in his creative, frantic way, leaning on her, telling her to forget about gloves – that gloves were a figment. Although she wanted to help him, and tend and nurse his dodgy ego, restore his once-splendid spine, she had other calls on her feelings, too.

But now those other calls seemed to lose force. Across

60

the table, Frank Latimer, or Four, did nothing to show he recognized her. It was a grand, dismaying performance, epic eye-blankness. She felt certain he *did* recognize her, even after so long, but it was as if he wanted to kill off that lively past, annihilate it, forget it. This was what eventually came to delight her. Eventually, yes. At first she felt true disappointment and pain. Something good had been ditched, eliminated. He'd gone his way, she'd gone hers, and he obviously wanted the distance kept, not blurred by bygones. He was writing her off, and it bloody well hurt. For part of a second, she wanted to yell at him, 'What about Pop Daniels?'

Then her brain picked her up. All right, all right, if *he* could disown those memories and folk tales so could Sally. Perhaps it was good to get free from all the misty obligations dumped on her by a shared childhood and a shared family history. Their meeting here this afternoon became a confrontation between cop and likely villain, not a maudlin, Grangetown-mates-for-ever reunion. Yes, for the moment at least, it gave her something like relief – even delight – to emerge fully into the nowness of things, no daft old shadows.

And the nowness? Describe it. Deaths and brutality on Schooner Way, 2003, hijacking on Schooner Way, 2003, maybe a giveaway lope and jewellery gleam on Schooner Way, 2003. History was history. Grandfathers were scrapheaped, Pop Daniels most likely dead, World War Two's clean little bombs long superseded by fission monsters, smallpox scares, anthrax mail. The past was well out of date. Of course. Always, pasts would have been out of date, even looking at pasts in the past. That's what past meant – out-of-dateness. OK, but now, in 2003, didn't the past seem *especially* past, and *especially* non-relevant? It had become easy to feel cut off from it. Better like that? Much wiser like that? More mature like that? The tapes were running. Frank Latimer's lawyer sat alongside him.

Regnal chanted: 'Interview continued with Mr F. Latimer,

conducted by Detective Superintendent R. Regnal, Detective Constable S. Bithron present as an observer.' Regnal gave the date and time. Then he said: 'Frank, I want to ask some further questions in relation to the incident in Schooner Way, which we've already spoken about. Three men have been arrested in connection with that incident.'

'Yes, you told me.' Frank gave it weariness.

'I would like to tell you their names.'

'You already did.' He didn't yawn, but close.

'I'd like to give you these names again, in case you have remembered more clearly than you did previously about your relationship with any or all of them,' Regnal said.

'What I told you last time is what I'll tell you this time.'

'Repetition can become oppressive, Mr Regnal,' the lawyer said.

'The three men arrested are, Leyton George Candil, aged twenty-five, Simon Rex Mintwall, aged thirty-four, Carl Oliver Briedin, aged twenty-four,' Regnal replied. 'Frank, you told me during one of our previous interviews that Leyton George Candil and Simon Rex Mintwall are known to you. Is that correct?'

'I've met them.'

'You've never met Carl Oliver Briedin?'

'Not that I know of.'

'Could you explain what you mean by that?'

'I don't know the name of everyone I meet every day, do I? Do you?'

'So it's possible you *have* met Carl Oliver Briedin?' Regnal replied.

'Not in . . . not as you mean "met".'

'I'm sorry, what do I mean, "met"?'

'In the sense of knowing him, really knowing him.'

'So you're saying you might have come into contact with him without knowing his name?' Regnal asked.

'I think my client's point is quite obvious, Mr Regnal,' the lawyer said. 'A casual, possibly brief acquaintance where names did not figure.' She spoke in a flat, brisk style, as if the matter were so clear it hardly needed argument.

'It could be, then, that you know all three of the men, Frank?' Regnal said.

'Is he a barman? I might have asked him for a pint. Is he a taxi driver? I might have asked him to take me home. Is he a policeman? I might have asked him how come he chose that.'

'I don't know if he ever had a taxi, but you're correct, he *is* a driver.'

'My client was simply illustrating the kind of basic exchange that might have taken place between him and some entirely imaginary acquaintance. He did not say or imply he knew this man was a driver.'

'We know Carl Oliver Briedin drove a Lexus,' Regnal replied.

'Nice car,' Frank said.

'It is,' Regnal said. 'This one is back with its proper owner now, and cleaned up. He grieved when it was stolen.'

'I expect he would. This is a luxury car.'

'And fast,' Regnal said. 'Big but still quick off the mark.'

'These days some of these big cars are. for Presidents and Royals who get shot at,' Frank Latimer said.

'Have you ever been in a Lexus?'

'I'd remember if I'd driven something like that.'

'I don't mean driving it yourself. Being driven. Like being in the taxi you mentioned. A *professional* driver taking you somewhere.'

'They used a Lexus at Schooner Way, didn't they?' Frank replied. 'That's what they said on the TV News.'

'Gold.'

'Many of them go in for these classy colours now – silver-grey or gold. It's to imitate the Mercs and Rolls. A selling point.'

'Have you ever been in a Lexus?' Regnal replied.

'I'd remember if I'd been in something like that.'

63

'You said you'd remember if you'd *driven* something like that. But what if you were only a passenger?'

'Yes, I'd still remember if I'd been in something like that. I expect I'd recall the leg room. I should think it has leg room. People shelling out big money for a car, that's one of the first things they ask about – leg room. I don't mean leg-*over* room. I shouldn't think people with that sort of wealth shag in cars. They have penthouses and what's known as *pied à terres* or love nests. But leg room as leg room. Short people with a lot of money like to feel they walk tall.'

'We believe there were four people in the Lexus originally. By "originally" I mean when it arrived at and left Schooner Way.'

'Yes, you told me.'

'But only three when we stopped it.'

'So, you've got a real problem there,' Frank replied. 'Anyone could see that.' Square-faced, deep brow, square-chinned, dark eyes, dark, cropped hair – she thought she would have recognized him from how he was as a child.

'Although the Lexus is such a fine car, we believe these three were going to change it,' Regnal said.

'Trade it in?' Frank said.

'In a way, yes. They would leave it and switch to another vehicle, to make pursuit more difficult. Getaways are often managed like that.'

'Remember that great film with Steve McQueen – *The Getaway*?' Frank replied. 'And then a remake, *without* McQueen, because he died.'

'Luckily, we intercepted them before it happened.'

'I should think your boys were proud of that.'

'We were at the scene quickly. We had a witness at Schooner Way.'

'Yes, I heard,' Frank replied. 'In the news.' He switched the blankness of those eyes to Sally for half a moment. 'This lady detective. I think I saw her on TV after that incident.

And her name. You said her name, and I seemed to remember it from the TV. Brandon?' It was as if he wanted to tell her a pact bound them not to let on they knew each other. Perhaps he had some purpose. She couldn't see it. Frank was always a clever, forward kid – precocious, she realized now. Did he hope she might favour him as a one-time pal when she eventually gave her evidence in court, and so think it would be better the connection were concealed?

'This is how we know there were originally four,' Regnal said. 'Our witness.'

'A true conundrum.'

'We're lucky to have an experienced observer counting people on their way up and back down the little front path, plus the driver who stayed behind the wheel.'

'Remember those TV clips from the history of the Falklands War – the BBC reporter on an aircraft carrier talking about our planes completing a mission? "I counted them all out. I counted them all in." Those words have become famous. This would be like your witness, would it?' It was at about this stage she started to feel satisfaction – delight – at the break that time had caused between them. These smart-arse, cheap, gabby digressions – Steve McQueen, the Falklands War. She didn't want to be bound to someone so fucking laboriously obvious, such a carica-ture of slipperiness. She preferred the other side of the table, even with Ray Regnal.

'The driver was Carl Oliver Briedin,' Regnal said.

'I think the news reported the driver had a balaclava on.'

'And was still driving when we picked up the Lexus,' Regnal said.

'This was quite an operation.'

'Our cars had to box him in.'

'Without damaging the Lexus? This was quite an oper-ation.'

'Obviously, the fourth man had left the Lexus before we stopped it.'

'That would seem to be the answer,' Frank replied. 'Anyone could see that. If it starts off with four and this four becomes three – well, one has left.'

'Yet why would a car doing a high-speed escape – attempted escape – from a murder scene – and bodily harm and robbery scene – stop to let one of the gang get out?'

'This is a true conundrum.'

'Could their plan have involved the use of not just the one switch car – which the Lexus never reached – but another, also, which the Lexus *did* reach?'

'This is what you ask yourselves, is it?' Frank said. 'It's only a guess, but you *have* to guess, don't you, because you've got no real information on that aspect? As a guess it might not be a bad guess – I mean, as guesses go. Probably you'll come back at me and say, "One guess is as good as another," and I wouldn't argue. But, of course, what police *usually* have to go for is evidence. I heard judges can be fussy about this.'

'Sometimes when a driver's brought in for a raid, he – or she – doesn't let their name get known, and they're just called "Wheels", or "Motor", or along those lines,' Regnal answered. 'They are not integral members of the gang, who would probably know each other well. Drivers may be outside specialists. They conceal identity as a security thing, in case of cock-up, meaning people can't blab on him/her. I wondered if this might be why you don't recognize the name Carl Oliver Briedin?'

The lawyer said: 'An improper question, a blatant leading question. It presumes what you are not entitled to presume. My client was not with the Lexus party. That is why he has no knowledge of the Lexus driver. It's simple.' She sounded a bit nearer to spitting now.

'In the same way that, as you mentioned, Frank, you might not know the name of a taxi driver who took you here or there, although you had a kind of business arrangement with him – that business arrangement being, of course, to get chauffered.'

'My client was not chauffered by anyone during the Schooner Way incident, because he was not present at the Schooner Way incident. I give notice that this is a formal objection, Mr Regnal, to the way you are conducting parts of the interview.'

Regnal said: 'It could well be, Frank, that one of the other two in the Lexus – Leyton George Candil, Simon Rex Mintwall – knew Carl Oliver Briedin previously and engaged him as driver for the Schooner Way raid without ever informing you of his real name, simply "Wheels" or "Motor" or some such, because there was no requirement for you to know his real name. "Need-to-know" basis. That's a security category in ministries. I expect you and your friends have heard of it.'

'I wish to record a further formal objection to the assumptions contained in your questions,' the lawyer said.

'Did you play along with Briedin's security obsession and agree he'd be simply "Wheels" or "Motor" or similar, Frank?'

'His mother would have hated that – I mean, when she's picked out fancy first names like Carl and Oliver, and then someone comes along and calls him "Motor",' Frank replied. 'It's not human, is it, and most mothers like to think of their sons as human? Nicknames can be cruel. At school there was a boy christened Beauregard, but he had a gammy foot and built-up boot and all the kids called him "Clog".'

'Which someone?' Regnal replied.

'Which someone what?'

'Which someone called Carl Oliver Briedin "Motor"?'

'Just the general idea,' Frank said. '*If* someone called him "Motor".'

'But which someone?'

'Anyone,' Frank replied.

'You?'

'What?'

'Called him "Motor".'

'When I say "anyone", I mean anyone who's met him, obviously.'

'This is merely a plucked-from-the-air illustration,' the lawyer said. She was round-faced, a bit podgy, very bright-looking and in a terrific dark, silk suit. Sally thought probably not legal aid. How did Frank pay for this?

'Or "Tail Light",' Regnal replied. 'This is another name drivers like, suggesting that, in a night caper, all the pursuit will see of them is the car's disappearing rear. It would interest me to know if you've come across the name "Tail Light", Frank. The usage might be in a phrase like, "Hit the pedal, Tail Light." Most likely it would be spoken by Simon Rex Mintwall.'

'I believe many trades have their own private language and way with titles,' Frank said, 'such as "Gaffer" and "Best Boy" in cinema credits. Funny terms to those outside, don't you think?'

'Did the other two, or one of them – Leyton George Candil, Simon Rex Mintwall – tell you Tail Light or Motor or Wheels was the Best Boy you could get for that kind of job? Word of mouth is so important in your work, isn't it? You don't ask a management-selection firm to find a driver for a tricky blag with three hundred grand lying around.' Regnal smiled a while. 'I can hear a friendly conversation like, "Tail Light knows big cars, Frank. He'll get us there and he'll be waiting when we come out – never goes yellow and bolts, regardless. This one can do street corners and straighten faster than he went in. And he prepares – knows the ground. He'll find the switch car."' Now Regnal sighed. 'Of course, he didn't, or didn't have time to. Or only the first switch. I don't consider this makes him a dud, do you, Frank? He couldn't know DC Bithron would by chance, by absolute chance, be in Schooner Way and able to get the back-up at once.'

'As a career, it must be quite dodgy,' Frank replied.

'What?'

'Getaway driver. Not like more usual occupations, such as a greengrocer.'

She'd heard his alibi was a woman – one of those standard ploys, depending on somebody close and only on somebody close: '*Just the two of us, home in bed or about the flat together, never mind it was such a gloriously sunny afternoon.*' Regnal would get to the alibi eventually, of course. Sally was not sure she wanted to hear this. She found herself curious about the woman and somehow a little resentful. So, perhaps the past couldn't be altogether chucked. Her delight turned shaky. On the other hand, did she imagine kid stuff in a park hut could signify something for the rest of his life or hers? The alibi might be false, anyway – almost certainly was. In a way, though, that troubled her more. He had a woman who would lie for him, did he, not just a sleep-around? She'd do perjury? This turned the relationship spiritual. He'd found someone really right for him? She envied Frank that. She'd envy anybody that.

Regnal said: 'We would categorize this crime as a *planned* crime.'

'Ah. I've heard of that kind. The Great Train Robbery. If they didn't plan that, they wouldn't be in the right spot and the right time to intercept.'

'With a planned robbery you need a planner.'

'I can see that.'

'Now, someone like you – shoplifting, taking and driving away, train without a ticket – you couldn't put together such a hit. I don't want to be insulting, it's just fact. You're miniature.'

The lawyer said: 'We have been telling you that since—'

'Whereas Simon Rex Mintwall is very capable of setting up Schooner Way,' Regnal replied. 'An older man with that sort of form. Was *he* gaffer? I should think so. How did you meet Simon Rex Mintwall, Frank?'

69

The lawyer said: 'From the beginning my client has maintained that he knows nothing of the Schooner Way incident, nor of crime on this scale at all. Yes, we accept, he is "miniature". We don't – can't – dispute he has a record, but a record on which the offences are . . . very well, miniature. No precedent suggests he could be party to something major.'

Cow. Dismal, cruel, treacherous, royal cow. Sally felt a torching rage, wanted to yell at this legalistic piece, on the record, that she was supposed to stand up for Frank not fucking well shrink him.

Regnal said: 'I've checked and you were not behind the same high walls at the time Simon Rex Mintwall was behind them. In fact, you were never behind the kind of high walls that Simon Rex Mintwall was behind, because Simon Rex Mintwall went, as of rotten right, to high-security spots. You were in young offenders' and opens. So, you didn't meet in any exercise yard and discuss the future.'

'Of course not, of course not,' the lawyer said.

Her job. Sally did see that. The lawyer's game was to get him off – make him look no Lexus man, make him look not up to it, trivialize him. But did she need to rush so gratefully to grab Regnal's rating of Frank as low-level low life, comically small small potatoes, an also-ran of also-rans? Sally loathed hearing someone she had known and shared a childhood with slighted like this. All right, Frank had chosen to go crooked, and that must be bad. But there was crooked and crooked. To go crooked and get no status as crooked in the august crook rankings – Christ, pathetic. It reflected not just on him but on people who had been part of the same background and sweet, rough culture. Sally felt humiliated hearing him crushed. If someone she'd run the pavements with, and listened to folk yarns with, and larked in evening parks with, turned hood, it ought to be at Al Capone level, or at least Simon Rex Mintwall level. Thinking of Frank picked only as a run-of-the-mill Simon Rex

Mintwall aide sickened her. Why, though? Hadn't she
ditched the Memory Lane stuff? She was, after all, a cop.
And Frank . . . Frank probably robbed, possibly killed.
Almost certainly killed. *Couldn't* she ditch the Memory
Lane stuff? No? Not altogether. Just the same, she didn't
yell at the lawyer and the tape.
'This lad is not local,' Regnal said.
'Who?'
'Simon Rex Mintwall. That's what I mean. How would
you meet him?'
'I'm really interested in the way you work, you know,'
Frank replied.
'Is that right?'
'Such as trying to make links.'
'Is there a link between you and Simon Rex Mintwall?
When you told me you knew him, is that what you meant
– a link?'
'Guess what – for a time, when I was younger, I wanted
to be in the police myself,' Frank replied.
'Is that right?'
'My father and my grandfather, they both thought it would
be an idea. I was tall enough.'
'But you said you couldn't understand why anyone picked
a police career.'
'That's now. Not then.'
'When you mention a link between you and Simon Rex
Mintwall, what kind of link are you referring to?' Regnal
asked.
'No, he did not mention a link,' the lawyer replied. '*You*
mentioned a link. My client suggested you were trying to
make links and you then asked if there were a link between
him and Simon Rex Mintwall.'
'Yes, I'd be really interested in knowing what *kind* of
link with Simon Rex Mintwall he had in mind,' Regnal
said.
'He did *not* say a link between himself and Simon Rex

Mintwall,' the lawyer replied. 'He spoke generally of the attempt to prove links as a standard police method.'

'Frank, this was why I inquired how you and Simon Rex Mintwall met,' Regnal said. 'It would help define the nature of the link.'

'My client has not said there is a link in the sense that you use the word link, Mr Regnal. The contrary. I wish that to be understood.' She turned her head towards the tape. This was another now-hear-this, for-the-record pronouncement.

Frank said: 'You get someone like Simon Rex Mintwall, and then, because you think you've *really* got him – say, boxed in in a Lexus right after the offences – once you've got him like that, then you start looking around and trying to find out who he knows, because you think they could be in it as well. Is that how it works? Is this what the training's about? Such an education to watch it operating, I can tell you!' He nodded a few times, like admiration.

'I don't say it means anything about grades within the team, but sometimes the places people occupy in a car – say, in a Lexus – these places are significant,' Regnal replied. 'When we stopped the Lexus, Carl Oliver Briedin was driving, obviously, and Simon Rex Mintwall in the front passenger seat. This, to us, would, on the face of it, at least, indicate leadership – the fact that, even in the scramble of exiting the house loaded up and getting aboard the Lexus, he had the discipline to take this apparently commanding spot. Only one rear seat was occupied – by Leyton George Candil. We assume that the fourth man in the Lexus – that is, the one who left it – we assume he would also have been in a rear seat, and that this would indicate the kind of link existing between him and Simon Rex Mintwall, i.e., between a subordinate and a chief, a honcho, a planner. Would you agree with this, I wonder, Frank?'

'But then things didn't exactly go that way and the scheme for joining the police got lost a bit, I don't know how,'

Frank replied. 'My grandfather used to sound off about the pension – how great it was, and when you were still quite young. Grandfathers *would* think a lot about pensions, I suppose. But a kid can't consider so far ahead, can he?'

Regnal said: 'Someone like Simon Rex Mintwall – truly large-scale and operating on a national basis – someone like that gets a murmur about heavy possibilities in an area he doesn't know, and he might put out a call for a lad who lives near and can give him and, say, a driver like Carl Oliver Briedin – can give them the geography, plus a picture of the particular police set-up – tough or a pushover, officers armed or not as routine, number of rapid-response chariots, that kind of special info. A liaison role. Subordinate, yes, but a genuine chance for someone down the infant end of lawlessness so far, and keen to develop. This is what I meant by the nature of the link, you see. This is why I'd like to know the circumstances of your meeting.'

'Some kids around where I lived did,' Frank replied.

'What?'

'Join the police. But I don't know if they got on.' He kept looking at Regnal.

'It was a really interesting word for you to bring up,' Regnal said.

'Which?'

'Link.'

'Plain clothes,' Frank said.

'What?'

'If I'd gone in I'd have wanted plain clothes. Well, like you.'

'As we see it, Frank, when the Lexus reaches switch car one – as per the plan – Simon Rex Mintwall already realizes things have turned bad. The brave perception of a gifted bossman. He saw our witness in the street, obviously doing an aid call, and he's worried the cavalry's going to get there faster than he planned for. Faster than he could conceivably have planned for – no slur on him. He's buffeted by

73

random accident. So he readjusts. He must extemporize. He has that ability. This is your British Expeditionary Force in France, 1940. They find they can't beat Jerry, so think again and do Dunkirk instead. Simon Rex Mintwall stops only long enough for the fourth man to get out, and tells him to take most of the money. That's true leadership talking. He's saying to Number Four he must look after the dependants, in case the Lexus gets caught.

'Maybe, in the plan, Leyton George Candil was supposed to go with Four, but, of course, Leyton George Candil has a lot of blood on him – cranial – and he's shaky, anyway, following his time with the sledgehammer. Why didn't they *all* leave the Lexus and get to the first switch car, knowing as they did that the Lexus had become a target? I'm not clear on that. Perhaps dividing the risk still looked better to Simon Rex Mintwall.

'Anyway, he decides number Four must go alone, because he's their insurance. Four can hide the trolley case in the boot of the switch car, but he would not be able to hide someone red all over like Leyton George Candil, even if Leyton George Candil were fit enough to get out and make the switch. Possibly Four was the only one not bloodstained and conspicuous. Simon Rex Mintwall says Four should go alone. Decisive. The Lexus owner felt pleased to get it back, yes, but quite a bit of valeting was necessary, especially around where Leyton George Candil sat with his sledge-hammer. We might have trouble proving long-term intent by Leyton George Candil to smash heads with the hammer, because, clearly, the original purpose of carrying it was to break down the front door, but we'll try. This is what we have to show in court, you see, Frank – known in Latin as *mens rea,* meaning guilty mind. Obviously Leyton George Candil had a guilty mind when it comes to damaging the door and helping steal the funds. But did he *intend* to do the head job also, or was this just an off-the-cuff impulse? Tricky.'

Sally thought this had ceased to be an interrogation, more a piece of scene-construction by Regnal. He seemed to realize this himself suddenly and went back to questions, but still drifting into a ramble. *Seeming* to drift into a ramble. She was not sure she could keep pace with Regnal's brain. 'How did you come to meet Leyton George Candil, Frank? Probably, when your father and grandfather agreed you should try for the police, they thought not simply you were tall enough and would collect a nice pension, but that if you *didn't* join you might get to associate with people like Simon Rex Mintwall and Leyton George Candil, plus, via them, Carl Oliver Briedin. Fathers and grandfathers – they've learned how the world is. What use are they otherwise?'

'Dunkirk?' Frank replied. 'My grandfather used to talk about that. He was too young to be there, of course, but he said you'd see soldiers around the town just after, bits of uniform gone missing, boots filthy, no rifle, their eyes hopeless.'

'Hopeless,' Regnal said. 'That's what your grandfather and father would have had in mind when they said choose the police, Frank. They didn't want you in the kind of hopeless situation that might come from knowing folk such as Simon Rex Mintwall and Leyton George Candil, plus, via them, Carl Oliver Briedin. How did the links with Simon Rex Mintwall and Leyton George Candil establish themselves, I wonder?'

Five

They called on her, just appeared at Sally's place one evening, all giggles, flowers and champagne, he and the tall, big-framed, cheery-faced girl she'd seen newspaper and television pictures of during the weeks of the Schooner Way shindig trial – and had heard plenty about before that, during Interrogations Three and Four by Ray Regnal. Sally didn't want to see them – couldn't have said very intelligibly why she didn't, just knew she didn't.

In a moment, he would mutter to her secretly: *Sal, can we manage a private word at some stage?* She wanted to answer, *Not fucking likely*, and at plenty more than a mutter – say towards a scream – but she stayed silent.

They had voice-boxed from the porch, the giggles already going: 'Sally, it's Frank and Lydia. Can we come up?'

Oh, God, oh God. 'Frank? Frank Latimer?'

'Which other Frank? And Lydia. You know Lydia? Or you know *about* Lydia? You didn't think we'd let it go without saying thank you, surely?' he replied.

'Never!' Lydia chortled.

'Thank you?' Sally asked.

'Naturally,' Frank said.

'I don't know what you mean,' Sally said.

'Of course you do. But, in any case, we're here to tell you what I mean,' Frank replied.

'Oh, yes, we'll tell you and tell you,' Lydia said.

In a moment, he would mutter to her secretly: Sal, can we manage a private word at some stage? *She wanted to*

76

answer, Not fucking likely, *and at plenty more than a mutter – say towards a scream – but she stayed silent.*

'All right, come on up,' Sally said. 'Third floor. The lift's been sticking today. Best use the stairs.'

'Some impressive place – even with a stuck lift,' Frank said.

'Oh, by the way, I've got company,' Sally replied.

There was a pause. 'Not . . . not colleague company?' Frank asked. 'I wouldn't be keen on meeting any of them, especially Regnal – not after all those lovely interrogation sessions in the summer. And not now the trial's over. They must be very, very disappointed – and vindictive.'

'No, not police. Just company,' Sally said.

'Great,' he replied.

'Great,' Lydia said.

Sally pressed the street door release button and switched off the intercom. When on, it spoke to the room. 'They're some friends, Pete,' she said. 'Or *he's* a sort of friend. I don't know his partner.'

'Which sort of friend?' Pete said.

'Dubious. But long-time.'

'How long-time?'

'Long. Since I was a small child.'

'How dubious?'

'Quite,' Sally replied.

'So, he's bothered in case I'm police?'

'Probably.'

'You kept in touch?'

'Something happened. We re-met.'

'There's a novel called *Something Happened.* When it happened it wasn't good.'

'This wasn't good.'

'Am I going to like him, them?' Pete said.

'Am *I* going to?'

'Why not?'

'Why?'

'But if you've known him so long?'

'He's different now, isn't he?'

'Different how?' Pete said.

'And *I'm* different.'

'You would be, obviously, if we're talking about something from childhood, but—'

'Really *very* different. Both.'

'So why are they here?'

'It's silly. It could be embarrassing. I think he's misreading things.'

'Which things?' Pete said.

'You'll probably recognize him. Or the name.'

'Famous? To do with your work?'

'In a way famous.' Sally went out from her flat to greet these two on the landing. She was glad the lift had troubles. She wanted the time. Why didn't Pete wait out there with her? It would have made them look a unit. He did not live in, but they were surely a unit, weren't they, after . . . what . . . four, nearly five, months? Five *months*! Or *five* months. On the whole, she liked being part of a unit, as long as the other part was OK, naturally, and when something had gone on for nearly five months – *months*, for God's sake, *five* – it must mean she felt more or less content with Pete, mustn't it? A bit of visible support now might have been useful. He stayed in the armchair but crouched forward a little when she went out, so as not to seem completely uninterested. She'd admit he looked good like that – lean, very still, eye bright, as if poised to spring. He often looked good. She would have liked him to look good alongside her, welcoming Frank and Lydia.

Perhaps he objected to the job poking into their life. She had big objections herself. Enormous objections herself. Or Pete might resent an intrusion from the past, an area of her life he knew not much about and probably didn't want to. Pete thought the past should stay in its place – past. He'd told her that from time to time. He believed in what he called 'the moment'. That was fine. But what to do if she answers the buzzer and the voice, voices, downstairs sound so happy and eager? It would have been cold to refuse them, a sort of denial. Perhaps they were 'the moment' at this moment. Pete must see that. Generally he could be quite sensitive and acute. Definitely. Would they have gone on for nearly five months otherwise? This approached half a year!

He hadn't even asked the name when she said he might recognize it. A sulk? Childishness always bored her, though she could fall into it herself now and then, and knew that. Would this turn out a strained, miserable night? Their arrival must bring tension, but she could also see real charm in it. After all, here was someone who felt duty bound to celebrate with Sally his acquittal in a murder, wounding and robbery trial, when, of course, he should have been sent down for ever with his three fucking hijack Lexus mates.

Tonight, he appeared at the top of the stair flight carrying a magnum of Krug in one hand, what looked like a couple of dozen white lilies in the other, a smile reaching right across his face and across fifteen years and dissimilar careers, when he'd probably expected to be in the opening weeks of something behind the sort of high walls Ray Regnal mentioned during the first interrogation she sat in on. Pete wouldn't have run across any situation like it. He ought to be fascinated. Sally could more or less put up with lilies, although the smell off a gross bunch like Frank's made her long for a bit of armpit to lower the sweetness.

In a moment, he would mutter to her secretly: Sal, can we manage a private word at some stage? *She wanted to answer*, Not fucking likely, *and at plenty more than a mutter – say towards a scream – but she stayed silent.*

The ring glinted with all its F-ness on a finger around the magnum neck. And it *was* a glint, even here, under the low-watt landing light. This present glint she could certainly have sworn to, if their arrival had been important to a case. Raging Bullfinch might have been proud of her then. She'd

79

like that. She still longed to help him, because, overall, Raging was such a pathetic prat and needed support, poor love. There should be a sub-division of the Royal Society for the Protection of Birds – the Royal Society for the Protection of Bullfinch. She'd accept the presidency.

Frank, 170lbs, six feet tall, no hood, stretched his arms as wide as they would go, champagne in his left hand, the flowers right, a stance reeking of conviviality, as though he were host. She thought he might try an embrace, holding her, the bottle and the bouquet. He didn't – just stood there for a while, beaming, a lesson in how to signal delayed happiness through body language. 'So, here's my salvation, Lydia. Sally, Lydia, Lydia, Sally. But what a relief to be able to recognize you, Sal! Recognize, that is, in the fullest way – recognize and *show* I recognize. Not like the interrogations. Not like court. And, of course, it was the same for you. Worse? Weren't you scared some nuisance voice from the past would suddenly pipe up, "Hey, these two know each other, used to be neighbours in Bargoed Street? Fond, fond neighbours."'

'It wouldn't have been so very serious.'

'Not serious?' he said. 'Courts don't like stuff hidden, especially not stuff hidden by cops.'

'Let's go inside, shall we?' she replied.

He dropped his arms. 'Of course, of course, you won't want to be seen talking to—'

'Its cold on the landing,' she said. In fact, the lift seemed to be all right now and was called downstairs from one of the floors above. She'd like them out of sight before it returned. Him out of sight.

'Was this a bad idea, coming here?' he asked.

'Let's go inside,' she replied.

'He's *so* grateful,' Lydia said. 'Well, *we*, obviously. I don't think they believed *me*. But I'm sure they believed *you*.'

'Who?' Sally said.

'The court, the jury.'

'Certainly they believed you, Lyd,' Frank said. 'They

believed you because what you said was true. Would I be here if they didn't believe you?'

'*Really* believed me, not benefit of the doubt believed,' Lydia replied.

'Come in and meet Pete,' Sally said. The lift was climbing.

'That'll be *really* great,' Frank said. 'Excuse me, Sal, but does he . . . well . . . know . . . ?'

'What? Just be normal,' she replied.

'Normal,' Frank said. 'Right, normal. Remember Laurence Olivier in that film *The Entertainer,* on TV singing "Thank God we're normal, normal, normal?" Wonderful.' Frank stood back to let Lydia go in first, and turned to stick his face close: 'Sal, can we manage a private word at some stage?' She wanted to answer, *Not fucking likely!* – and at plenty more than a mutter – say towards a scream – but she stayed silent.

Pete did stand and smile when they came in. Perhaps, after all, he had played it right. These were *her* guests, not his, and it might be more suitable that she should go out alone and greet them. Frank was from the past and Pete wasn't into the past. He had been on management courses and believed in right procedures. He was fond of fine points, though not really to a footling degree. That would have got her down. But, obviously, he was entitled to his ways.

She made introductions. Frank said in a happy, warm voice: 'We go far back, Sally and I. Childhood. Mates. Lyd and I were just passing, so we thought, look in. The bubbly's only just out of the quick freeze at the offie. We should do some serious reunion drinking right away. You'll wonder, and quite reasonably, how come we knew she lived in this building and this flat. These things are discoverable if they're important to discover, aren't they, Pete? And this did seem important.'

'Well, more like an obsession,' Lydia said.

'*Very s*mart place,' Frank said, looking around. 'Central.'

'My brother stays sometimes when he's in these parts on business,' Sally said. 'The firm he runs pays part of the rent.'

'Your brother.' He did a frown for concentration: 'Mark?' Frank said.

'Mark.'

'He's part of our past, too, isn't he?' Frank replied. 'Mark, yes, older.' He put the magnum on the sideboard and laid the lilies alongside it. He wanted to free up his arms for full gestures. He waved his left in a circle. 'All right, Lyd's word – an obsession. I believe in *expressing* things – good things, bad things. Give them air.' She saw that the wave of the left arm was intended to mark out the air he referred to. 'Give them *form*,' he said. 'This time it's a *good* thing. Undoubtedly. It's the power of long-ago friendship.'

'Jealous,' Lydia said. 'Yes, I could almost feel jealous.'

'This friendship, unique, and yet not unique,' Frank replied. 'Not at all.'

'Oh, God, he's gone mysterious,' Lydia said. 'He'll do that sometimes. Don't anyone panic!'

'It's just the old muckers thing, isn't it?' Frank said. He put both arms forward, his palms outwards, to suggest obviousness. 'Many could tell of it.'

'So, how come unique – and then the opposite of unique?' Lydia asked.

'I always see life as complicated,' Frank replied. 'That's one of my central beliefs. There'll be two sides to every coin, and even more than two.'

'That would be some coin, and useless for slot machines,' Lydia said. Nobody had sat down. Sally wanted them to, but there wasn't much relaxation about.

Frank said: 'Complicated and even contradictory. Unique, you see, because although friendship is known to many, *this* friendship had a special way of working, of revealing itself.' He spoke mainly to Pete, as if aware he must be won over. And Pete was good – kept boredom and distaste off his face. Perhaps those management courses weren't entire horse shit.

'Well, yes, that was definitely unique – how it revealed itself,' Lydia said.

Sally went into the kitchen and found a vase and some glasses. Godzilla's handsome green gift wouldn't have been big enough to cope with the plague of lilies. Its proper place was the bottom of the Taff. Pete would have asked where she'd got the piece, anyway. He might not have liked it. Pete thought Victorian stuff came from a smug, triumphalist epoch and always had these qualities built in. He'd probably read this somewhere. It could be right. Triumphalism he despised. To be told Godzilla only had the glassware because some pal did an antique shop and flogged off bits cheap to get rid quick would not have altered Pete's view.

She put water in the vase and then returned with it and the glasses on a tray. The three of them were talking about upbringings and their impact. 'Friendship – it's a difficult one,' Pete said. He sounded precise but amiable, not scratchy. 'Definition. Unlike, say, a love affair. I don't think I have any—'

'It's difficult and yet it isn't,' Frank replied.

'Oh God this multi-sided coin again,' Lydia said.

Sally took the flowers and arranged them in the vase. God, the obnoxious, fine whiteness of the petals, like virtue or a dead face. She stood back, admiring. 'Gorgeous, aren't they? How did you guess I love lilies?'

'They seemed right, that's all,' Frank replied.

'An impression,' Lydia said.

'I see them reaching out and up for something,' Frank said. 'Symbolic.'

'Wow,' Lydia replied.

Frank popped the champagne cork and handed her the magnum. She placed the glasses near the lilies and poured. She made sure the glass she'd take for herself was furthest from the creepy fucking blooms. She handed the drinks around. 'To justice,' Frank said. Lydia repeated the words. Pete picked up the magnum and looked at the label. He prized definitions, not just of friendship – wine, anything. Definitions were land-

83

marks, life a wasteland, difficult to navigate through. He set the bottle down again. They all drank. Then they did take seats.

'I don't think I have any friends from right back in childhood,' Pete said. 'In fact, I'm not sure I've any *real* friends.' His tone now was matter of fact, no self-pity. Sally knew he loathed self-pity. Once or twice he'd told her. No, more often than that. This was all right, though. Everyone had themes and wanted to repeat them. He said: 'Not friends as *simply* friends, I mean—'

'I suppose Sally doesn't talk to you much about her work,' Frank said. 'That's how it should be, obviously. Confidential. Like a priest or doctor.'

'To clarify terms,' Pete replied. 'I'd say a true friendship means you can call on him/her – no sex element in it, of course –call on him/her for help and know it will be available. *Know* it.'

'I'll buy that, Pete,' Frank said.

She began to think things might turn out peaceful.

Frank said: '*Our* friendship – Sal's and mine – is unique in two ways. One, how it revealed itself, yes. But, two, the fact that for a long while it couldn't reveal itself at all. A really great acting performance from both of us. I mentioned Laurence Olivier just now, Pete! Mind, we had great practice fooling people. Her grandfather and my grandfather used to bore us barmy with tales about the war, but we had to look fascinated – politeness. Politeness did matter then, even politeness to the old. Its departure has to be regretted – a symptom of decline in GB 2003, I fear. Remember that story about running home from school when the warning went, Sal?'

'They ran home?' Sally replied. 'Dangerous? In the open streets?'

'They both went on about that. And went on,' Frank said.

'Really?' Sally said.

'And then the bakery. How often did we hear about the bakery, Sal?' Frank asked.

'I *do* recall the bakery,' Sally said.

'Direct hit. I don't know how many sheltering in the cellar. January 1941,' Frank said. 'I forget the name.'

'Often the past is something we need actively to free ourselves from, in my view,' Pete said.

'Henry Ford – "history is bunk",' Lydia replied.

'Billy Hollyman's!' Sally cried.

'Hollyman's! Right. The baker,' Frank said. 'I couldn't have got it. See, you remember some things better than I do.'

Of course. But she meant to smash his idea of joint recollections. So, she'd play dumb about the home run but leave him behind on the bakery. Hell, though, 'a private word'. Could she dodge that?

Frank said: 'Clearly the past should never *dominate*, but some thing or things are fixed there in our two heads, Sal's and mine. We'd hear about the Gospel Hall Whitsun Treat at Lavernock. A chartered train. The Sunday school processing through the streets to Grangetown station. Marquees. Two brothers from the school drowned when the ship evacuating them was torpedoed. Then the stuff about the way people said Coed Cae Street. Supposed to be a laugh.'

'Said it how?' Sally replied.

'Cockade Street.'

'Cockade Street? Did they?'

'Still do, I expect. Pete, these things might look to you like fragments of the past and only that, but then suddenly, in a certain situation – say, for example, a court situation – suddenly then they *mean* something. Bound to. This is nothing to do with jealousy or no jealousy, Lyd. This is just influences. This is heritage.'

'Court?' Pete replied.

'What – she really *doesn't* talk to you about her work!' Frank said. 'But the Press? TV and radio?'

Pete said: 'Oh, you're not the one who – three guilty, one got off? Schooner Way? The drugs money? Sorry to be slow. Yes, of course.'

'And so a celebration,' Frank replied, holding up his glass.

Pete said: 'I knew Sally was involved in that, obviously, but I hadn't—'

'This was a true example of high-calibre justice,' Frank said, with definite emotion. Again, he gave that minor, unflashy wave with both arms in front of him, one hand holding his glass. The fact he was seated did not weaken the gesture very much. The movement spoke approval and praise. 'And the thing is, Pete, justice might have failed but for Sal.'

'Would *certainly* have failed,' Lydia said.

'All right, I made fun of our grandfathers and their war stories, but the point is, one reason we fought that war was to preserve famed British justice,' Frank replied. 'It was a just war and a war for justice. This is what I was trying to get at – Sal and I are, like, connected, not just through growing up together, but via some of the best aspects of this country, also. This is what I mean by friendship.'

'Friendship,' Pete said. 'Friendship?'

Immediately, Sally thought she heard a change. It worried her. His intonation now had that touch of snarl and managerial sneer which could sneak out occasionally. She stood and did some refills. Occasionally, Pete liked to 'reach the nitty-gritty'. All the management courses had apparently insisted this could often become vital, regardless of the need also for courtesy. Edge. Managers needed edge. 'Do you know what I wonder, Frank – I mean as to the friendship idea? I wonder how it felt to go free from court like that when three friends are jailed – big-sentence jailed, weren't they? Well, life for two of them. Justifiably. People murdered and terribly injured.'

Frank thought about it. Then he said: 'How do you mean, friends – in what respect?'

'We were talking about friendship,' he said.

'Yes, I know,' Frank said. 'But what's that got to do with those three from the Schooner Way matter, Pete? You see, I'm getting some confusion here. Who's whose friend?'

86

'Just a business arrangement you'd say, would you, Frank?' Pete asked. '*Not* friendship. People coming together for a purpose, only that purpose, rather than a continuing relationship?'

'What business arrangement, Pete?' Frank replied.

Pete said: 'Well, the—'

'Frank's defence was that he didn't go with the three to Schooner Way,' Sally said. 'That he was not present. Lydia gave the alibi.'

Pete said: 'Yes, I think I read that in reports of the trial, but—'

'This is the whole point, isn't it?' Lydia said, chuckling. Perhaps she felt the change, too, and aimed in a womanly, placator's way to lighten things. 'Frank was at home with me.' She speeded up and giggled some more. 'Look, I felt *really* self-conscious – well, you can imagine, I expect, Pete – having to talk about our sex life to a courtroom full of people, and the reporters, but it was *so* necessary. Bed. Bed in the afternoon! Bed on a summery afternoon? Duration. The timetabling. They *really* wanted to get Frank. Sorry, Sally, I know I'm talking about your work associates, but it was obvious – they were determined to turn Frank into Number Four.'

'There *were* four in the attack, weren't there?' Pete said.

'I believe so,' Frank said.

'Didn't Sally testify to this herself?' Pete said.

'Let's leave that side of things, shall we?' Sally said. 'And talk about the future, now Frank has—'

'When Pete asks what it felt like when those three were convicted and I wasn't – what I sense is, he thinks I should have gone down with them, but somehow dodged out of it. That's how I hear it. I hope I'm wrong. But, yes, how I hear it.'

'No, I didn't get that idea at all,' Sally said.

'It seemed to fit into our chat on friendship,' Peter said.

'Yes, you told us,' Frank replied.

'I looked for a sort of *instance* where friendship was tested,' Pete said. 'I have to see things as it were concretely. I'm not good just on the conceptual. It's a failing.'

'Sad,' Frank replied.

'Frank's defence was that he knew two of the men slightly, in other circumstances, Pete, and the third, the driver, not at all,' Sally said. 'I can't see what you're getting at.'

'You're suggesting those three and myself were friends, and I should have gone to jail with them, aren't you, Pete?' Frank said. He had the glass up to his face, just below his eyes, as if sighting Pete through a fortress gun-slit. Sally yearned to get him back to eloquent, bullshit arm wagging and meditations on the Brit way of life. He tried a poncy send-up of Pete's voice: '"How did you feel when they were taken down?"'

Sally said: 'I don't believe that's—'

'What are you asking, Pete – was I ashamed?' Frank said.

'I think you're reading all sorts into Pete's question,' Sally replied. Probably Frank's interpretation was spot on. Pete would detest the woolly, worthy, sentimentalized notion of friendship, and be keen to test it, possibly knock a hole in it. As well as the nitty-gritty, Pete believed in what he termed 'intellectual rigour'. He had told her this, also, from time to time. Usually, Sally found it fairly OK. She thought he'd found the phrase in an obituary of a Cambridge University chief who'd been hot on intellectual rigour, apparently. She'd heard you couldn't move for intellectual rigour at Cambridge.

'Identification, you see, Pete,' Lydia said. 'They didn't have any for the fourth man. They didn't have identification for any of them, but three were caught in the car. The fourth man had a hood, like the rest – or a balaclava. The high-ups in Sally's lot obviously wanted her to say on oath things about the fourth man that would make the jury think it was Frank. You could tell this from the way your lawyer asked the questions, Sally – about how did the fourth man move, was there anything special to it, and were there any unusual items, like, say, jewellery, that would help. I wasn't let into the court while she gave evidence, because I'd be appearing as a witness later, but I read the newspapers. And Frank told me afterwards. Sally wouldn't go with what that lawyer tried to make her say. They're smart and ruthless. When I was in the box and cross-examined this lawyer – this is the same one, the sod – he tried to make me sound like a liar for saying Frank was home with me that afternoon. He asked who could verify this. I said did he have someone watching when he and his wife or partner were at it together. The jury got a good laugh at that. And then he wanted to know, did we make or answer any phone calls that might be traceable – their times to show we were in the flat when the incident occurred? I said there were some occasions when we did not make or answer calls. And the jury had another little giggle.'

Yes, apparently they did. Sally had read descriptions of the exchanges in the *South Wales Echo*. 'People crowding the public gallery, and even members of the jury, laughed at these replies to counsel by Lydia Mastille.' Sally had not been in court herself when Lydia gave evidence. Raging Bullfinch told Sally to keep away. He'd decided she would have nothing more to do with the case. As Lydia said, Sally's own prosecution testimony had been given earlier, and, of course, Bullfinch and Ray Regnal loathed her for it. Bullfinch, in one of his most prolonged rages, told her he felt 'wantonly, viciously betrayed'. Sally did understand his disappointment and sympathized. As ever, she agonized over Raging's raging agony. It upset Sally to think this high-flier would fly no higher. Had she helped spike him? Or perhaps he was at his right level – even beyond it. Maybe his wings were not good enough to go nearer the sun. At school she'd always been repelled by those dopey classical tales, but possibly one or two of them said something. Anyway, she could never have doctored her account of the Schooner Way raid to suit Raging's nice script.

* * *

David Craig

'*Detective Constable Bithron, I'd like you to tell us about the man whom you saw at the Schooner Way house, and who has been referred to throughout the trial as Four. You have said that all the men had covered their faces with hoods or a balaclava helmet. Would you describe particularly now the hood worn by Four?*

'*It was of some kind of beige or tan material with eye slits.*'

'*What length?*'

'*The bottom of it rested on his shoulders.*'

'*So, no part of his face, neck or hair was visible?*'

'*His eyes.*'

'*If you please. How far away were you when he ran from the house carrying the trolley case and entered the car?*'

'*About twenty yards.*'

'*About twenty yards. And you would be approaching from his left side, would you?*'

'*Yes.*'

'*You were never closer than twenty yards and you were never observing him other than from the side. Is that correct?*'

'*Yes.*'

'*So that, even though the beige or tan hood had eye slits, you were never near enough or well placed enough to determine the colour of his eyes?*'

'*No.*'

'*Thank you. Now, if the hood came to his shoulders and he was dressed as you described so graphically during your evidence in chief – long-sleeved dark shirt, jeans, desert boots – there would, in fact, be no area of his skin exposed to your view. Is that so?*'

'*I'm not sure.*'

'*Not sure? But if the hood comes to his shoulders and—*'

'*Perhaps the witness means his hands, Mr Galty,*' the judge said.

'*Thank you, My Lord. Detective Constable Bithron, did you notice the hands of Four?*'

90

'*I'm not sure.*'

'*I don't understand. Why are you not sure?*'

'*He was holding the trolley case but I can't remember whether he wore gloves.*'

'*Thank you. Criminals undertaking this kind of attack might well wear gloves regardless of the weather, so as to avoid leaving fingerprints. Is that your experience?*'

'*They might.*'

'*They might. Let us put it this way, then, shall we? Whether or not he was wearing gloves, nothing about his hands struck you as distinctive, or you would have remembered. Is that so?*'

'*Probably.*'

'*Surely it must be so, mustn't it, Detective Constable.*'

'*Probably.*'

'*If you please. What your description amounts to, then, as given earlier, is an estimate of height, weight, age, plus details about clothes and shoes and the beige or tan hood. Is that so?*'

'*Yes.*'

'*And would you agree that your estimates of height, weight, age could fit any of tens of thousands of young men, perhaps more?*'

'*Probably.*'

'*Yes, probably. I submit there is nothing in your description of Four to identify him as my client Francis Roy Latimer.*'

Bullfinch had not been in court. Ray Regnal was, sitting with the prosecution lawyers. He turned to stare at her twice during the cross examination, his features blank, unreadable – as a gifted interrogator's features should be. From the dock, Frank had stared at her, too, more or less continuously. He tried to keep his features blank and unreadable, also, but she saw flickers of friendliness there towards the end of her time in the box.

91

And he seemed to have grown more friendly now, as well
– more friendly towards Pete, thank God. She didn't want
the noise of a fight, or worse than a fight, here. 'But, all right,
I can see why anyone might wonder about my acquittal,'
Frank said. 'The police, the prosecution, piled on the dirt –
the police except for Sal, that is, naturally. People *want* to
believe the police, *want* to trust the police. If they can't . . .
well, if they can't they get scared because it looks as if . . .
looks like chaos. There's nobody they can have faith in to
protect them, and to guard society and the state. That's most
likely how you feel, Pete. In this case, it's wrong, so wrong.
But I can respect that point of view. I was brought up to
believe in the police – even thought about joining.'

Sally picked up the magnum again and did refills. Christ,
she wished they'd leave – all of them, including Pete. Once
they'd gone she could waste-dispose the lilies. She wished
they'd leave, all of them, including Pete, and there'd be no
opportunity for a dodgy tête-à-tête with Frank. She had the
idea he might have softened his behaviour because a rough
house could kill all chances of a talk alone with her. As a
kid he was devious, too – devious as well as precocious.

And when it came, the private word was *very* private. Or
private from Pete, at least. Lydia would be in on most of
it, wouldn't she? 'So important to see you alone, Sal,' Frank
told her. 'I can *really* give you my thanks now – in detail.
For you to say, and keep saying, you were down there by
accident – terrific. Brilliant.'

'Yes, driving through.'

'No need to stick with that tale – not while it's just the
two of us.'

'Tremendous luck.'

'Oh, come on, Sal. Why would you?'

'What?'

'Drive through Schooner Way.'

'I often do.'

'It's not on your route home,' he said.

'I have to see people in the Bay.'

'Flukes don't happen.'

'Timing. Place. If that's not fluke, what is?'

'You had a whisper, yes? You were watching.'

'We have cases in the Bay all the time. I drive around there a lot.'

'Someone somewhere opened his gob and somebody listened and then somebody talked to you. How detection works. It's called intelligence. Who leaked? George Candil? Has to be. Neither of the others – they'd know about silence.'

'We should go back to the sitting room now, Frank,' Sally replied. 'This is not good. It will unsettle the other two. It unsettles *me*.'

They were in the kitchen. Frank had suddenly and simply said to Lydia and Pete: 'Excuse us, you two, for a minute, all right? Sally and I have to swap a few confidences, deep but nothing saucy, believe me.' Pete looked astonished and perhaps . . . perhaps what? Scared? Frank had ignored him and walked towards the door into the kitchen. Pete's management courses probably didn't cover situations like this, or people like Frank – people like Frank had become. Sally was not sure herself how to cope with *this* Frank.

'I'll just see what on earth he's on about,' she said, and followed.

Frank was sitting at the breakfast bar. Sally kept on her feet. There would be no settling down. This had to be brief – full of tip-top lies and brief.

'You've got a good grass, Sal,' he said. 'That's a prime talent. I'd have guessed you'd do well in the police. Or anywhere.'

'Oh, yeah!'

'You're the sort people would *want* to talk to.'

'Well, *you* do. Time we rejoined them.'

'They'd want to impress you. And they'd trust you.'

He was turned away from the breakfast bar to face her,

his right arm resting bent on it. Half a swede and an empty baked-beans tin stood near his elbow. It seemed wrong for him to be among ordinary domestic items. He was from somewhere else. But he'd let his hair grow a bit since she saw him in the interrogations. A mistake. Now and then, it made him look clerky – used to getting becked and called on piffling pay. She said: 'If there was a whisper, do you imagine I'd have been at the house alone – to deal with eight people? Egomania? I'd be risking lives. It would rate an all-round stake-out.'

'Protecting the grass? He made conditions? You could call up aid fast – *did* call up aid fast once it started. "Stop and apprehend all in metallic gold Lexus."'

'Absurd, Frank.'

'You knew it was me, didn't you?'

'The trial decided absolutely conclusively you were not there. Congratulations.'

'You knew it was me, didn't you?'

'It wasn't,' she replied. 'The jury said. That's what juries are for. If I did know, and, of course, I didn't, because it wasn't, how *could* I have known?'

'Search me. You did, though. Intuition's one of my things these days. In my kind of life, you learn to sort out the signals. But you wouldn't let them see it – that you knew. They sent you to sit in on three interrogations so you'd get familiar with how I'm made now, maybe how I moved when I was brought in and out. The old lope? The Pop Daniels glide? You *do* remember it, don't you? Why did you deny it just now? Is that what told you it was me?'

'Lope? Pop Daniels? Who's he?'

'All right, then, all right.' He gave the half swede a frustrated mock punch. 'Obviously, I've done some wondering.'

'About what?' she replied.

'The grass.'

'There isn't one. Grasses deal in information, not luck.

94

There's a whole regulated structure for grasses, you know. I'm much too junior to be let in yet.'

'George Candil gets around, bumps into all sorts, all sorts, but there's a lad called Aulus, Brian Edward Aulus. A dealer – a dealer with big hopes. Heard of him?'

'Aulus. Yes, of course. A dealer with *very* big hopes. All of us have heard of him.'

'Big hopes that could have been hammered if a new outfit got going in Schooner Way. So he picks up a hint about the cash raid, discovers an address, and decides you can scoop them all up. He's concerned about the dealers only. Rivals. Queering the pitch. The raiders point him to the meeting spot. That's the sole interest he has in them. As it turned out, though, they obliterated or disabled the new trade opposition for him. Does he talk to you, Sal?'

'Aulus? How would I get contact with him? He's on the way to being a biggy. *Too* big for me.'

'Someone like Aulus – partner, kids to support, he'd be truly bothered about another firm nudging in. He says to himself, "Detective Bithron could splatter them for me, and no peril to self. I'll have a discreet word."'

'He doesn't talk to me, nor to anyone else, I'd think.'

'Let's forget anyone else.'

She got some *fuck-off-now-would-you-please?* into her voice. 'This is enough, Frank. Pete won't like it. We've had our private talk. It dazes me.'

'"Pete won't like it." Oh, dear. How do you get to be with him, Sal? How does he get to be with you?'

'I don't have to discuss Pete or—'

'Just . . . he seems strange for you.'

'You haven't seen Pete at his best,' she said. 'I mean, you wouldn't, not in this kind of situation.' God, the defensiveness. Pete didn't need her protection, did he?'

'Which kind of situation?'

'Echoes of the job. Echoes of the past. He's disturbed. It's natural. I wouldn't like it.'

'Does he think you've got some of the money?'
'Which money?'
'There's a buzz around that you and colleagues—'
'The usual slander,' she replied.
'Yes, well—'
'You mean, is Pete—?'
'Does he hang around because he thinks you've got—'
'Fuck off, Frank.' She could speak it outright now.
'*I* know you haven't got it,' he said.
'He's a good man.'
'Well, perhaps he is. You picked him, stick with him, so perhaps he is. I heard months. Getting on for half a year. But what I'm saying – he'd never be able to understand what makes you go into the box and look after me the way you did, Sal. That was *so* brilliant. That was . . . that was, like, holy.' He lifted his elbow off the breakfast bar and started a two-arm gesture, then stopped, as though seeing she would find it a farce. He said: 'Yes. This goes right into the fabric of life. I don't mean just the park hut, all that. I mean something really important and worthwhile. Now, listen, why I spoke about the money – All right, yes, I've got people to look after, but there's plenty and—'
'I'm going back to the others.'
'I owe you, Sal. I'm not one to ignore that. You mentioned you had to have help for the rent here. If things are tight, why not let me . . . ? This would in no way set up obligations. You wouldn't be on the take. You're not one who would ever fall into that. I know it. This would be thanks for cooperation by you, cooperation that has already occurred, not a matter of me trying to buy the future.'
'Are you going to stay in the kitchen by yourself?'
'Did he actually give you *names*, Sal?'
'Who?'
'Aulus. I mean, not just Candil's. All of us. You *really* knew? And yet that fine refusal to say.'
When Frank and Lydia left, Sally did not kick Pete out

as she'd intended, after all, but she did get the lilies to the masher in the kitchen sink. It would take three at a time – possibly more, but she started with three and stayed on that as satisfactory. She fed them to it upright. Probably it would have swallowed the flower heads first if she'd wanted that, but she liked to watch the blooms pulled down inescapably by their lengths of green towards the teeth and then gobbled, not just shoved in like a Mars Bar into a mouth. This way it was a process. This way it was the opposite of what Frank said – the reaching up bit. This way was sinking . . . sinking . . . petals safe and horrible still . . . munch . . . gone. Pete stayed in the sitting room, though he watched her take the vase from the sideboard and must have wondered why. As processes went, it might be one outside his understanding. He'd be able to define the lilies as lilies and do a count, but wouldn't realize there could be an attitude to them.

She felt he needed some comforting and it would have been harsh to make him go. That was a bad couple of hours for Pete. He'd spent so much time working out a frame-work for his personality, card-indexing then clarioning all his attitudes, but along comes an encounter like this tonight and he's suddenly nothing and nowhere. She must look after his dignity. He deserved that. *She* deserved it. Hadn't they been together nearly five months? They took more Krug. She didn't object to drinking it. She was nauseated by the lilies not because they came as a present from Frank but because they were lilies and so deeply white and sweet.

Pete said: 'He *was* at Schooner Way, was he?'

'Of course.'

'You knew it?'

'Of course.'

'But you helped him get off. Old loyalties?' Pete asked. 'They must be really something.'

'They're meaningless. To me they're meaningless. He tried to make something of them. A gambit, that's all. No, I didn't help him get off. I knew he was there, but I didn't have any evidence he was there. Nothing that would have lasted a second in court. I'd have been slaughtered by his lawyer.'

'Frank thinks you helped him.'

'Of course he thinks I helped him. He wants to. It's a triumph.'

'*Would* you have helped him if—?'

'Oh, Pete. This is not you. You're not a what-if person.'

'Would you have helped?'

'He says you're only still around because you think I landed a share of the takings,' Sally replied. She wondered whether she should be arguing this bollocks with Pete, instead of getting to Brian Edward Aulus now, tonight, to tell him his name had surfaced – *his* name, not Godzilla's, and with his name, and almost spoken, the names of those linked to him, Ann Temperance Mayhew Donovan, his partner for seven, almost eight, *years*, and the children Ambrose and Serena. But Sally felt Pete was entitled to her for the present. He *was* a good man. He had rights. He deserved priority sometimes. There'd been one or two moments when he might believe she took Frank and Lydia's side against him just now. He hadn't said so, but he didn't always say everything. She would hate him to be hurt. 'Let's go to bed, Pete.'

'I ought to get back,' he replied, and stood up. 'I've things to do.'

It made her happy he could say this, and not just because she'd wanted earlier to be by herself. It showed he resented the crudeness of her suggestion that everything could be put right between them by an emergency love session. She'd been stupid, flip, insulting. He'd stay dick-zipped. His answer had flecks of that dignity she must guard in him, or what was he? She'd fight Frank's verdict on him – not spelled out but evident. 'Yes. Right, Pete,' she said.

However, the idea of some closeness and comradeship lingered and was strong. After he went, she walked to the

98

Pal Joey club off Queen Street, near the Catholic cathedral. Great to be so central. In the morning she would certainly get to Aulus. Although she often found them a bit sniffy at the club about women on their own arriving late, she negotiated that. As always, she gambled that nobody here would know her. For a decent while, she stayed at the bar, putting only tonic on top of the Krug, so as not to get more tiddly, and ready for conversation if anyone on his own looked conversational. Occasionally you could come across a man quite worthwhile and amiable. But tonight she saw mainly couples and bigger groups. They were friendly enough, yet not to the point. Now and then, this brand of disgustingly unaffectionate evening would come. She'd try to stop it depressing her. Around two a.m. she went back to the flat. Such disappointments always made her realize how valuable someone like Pete might be, regardless, and the plus aspects of a unit, union, that could survive months. All right, he had turned negative tonight, but she knew why and felt more or less sure it would not last. Pete was what she'd told Frank, a good man, as long as he got the kind of good conditions Pete would regard as good. At the flat earlier, conditions had been what he – and most others for that matter – in fact, what anyone reasonable would see as poor, and it was natural for someone of Pete's ideology to bring out coldness in reply. Did he have much else for a scene like that? Like what? Well, someone arrives out of Sally's far-off past claiming an inimitable, near-magical connection with her, and he's revealed to be a killer and robber who has dodged the law, fooled a jury, and fancies a walk-free celebration party. No management course could teach someone how to manage that.

Because he was as he was, Pete most probably really did return home after that bleak episode, not try a club for comforting, though Sally would never have phoned his place to check. She hated intrusiveness. He might not have answered, anyway, so as to keep up the punishment and feed his valuable selfhood, as he saw it. There was still some Krug left, warmish and flattish now, but Krug just the same, and vintage and authentically brut, a zing trip after tonic. For a while she sat on the settee beneath one of her framed Andy Warhol prints, enjoying the champagne and the blessed absence of people and flowers. Christ, those voices and petals. Slowly, though, this contentment ebbed. Her mind sharpened. Drink could do that to Sally sometimes, and especially better-grade drink. Krug was a quality sup, even in this condition. She began to think it wrong to be lounging here taking dud bubbles aboard when Godzilla ought to be warned secrecy was finished and he'd made it to someone's celebrity list. She had been wrong to go to Pal Joey's, also, and to have considered turning in for compensation sex with Pete. Time-wasters – especially as there'd been nothing at Pal Joey's, nothing but tonic, and not the kind of tonic she was after. It could become a pain, this need for contact.

The point was, wasn't it, Frank had taken the trouble to dig out her address and then call here, not just to party, but because he wanted to know whether she'd had a tip on Schooner Way, and whether it came from Brian Edward Aulus. Oh, he'd do all the ardent fucking pleasantries and corny reminiscing, because they got him into the flat. The Krug, flowers and show of gratitude might be nothing but cover for the visit. Had her face and tone of voice and jumpy calls to close their private kitchen talk told him he had it right, and stuff the denials? Someone able to choose vintage brut Krug might have all sorts of other sophisticated skills, like how to get rid of a grass who helped sink three of Frank's mates, and would have sunk Frank himself if the timetable had been a fraction different. Frank was not just a Bargoed Street kid plus some years. He had polish and responsibilities, although he could mess up on lilies.

She feared he would act fast, or fast now he had the acquittal and freedom. Presumably he'd thought of Aulus from the start. The visit might have been the last move – a search for formal confirmation. It might also have been Frank telling her what was going to happen, without actually telling her, and letting her know, without actually letting her know, that he expected the old solidarity to work again, as he thought it had worked in court. This kind of brazenness, this kind of arrogant idiocy, were at his centre now. In conventional business it might rank as chutzpah or creative boldness. In Frank it was brazenness and arrogant idiocy, and dangerous.

Could he really believe she'd sympathize with vengeance by him or his against Brian Edward Aulus? Yes, he might. Frank seemed convinced he and she were for ever blood-bound together by the past. A unit. Frank thought she had saved him at the trial because one ex-kid-about-the-streets-and-park-hut had to look after another ex-kid-about-the-streets-and-park-hut. From somewhere, since those years, he had picked up a fine helping of crazed faith in his destiny. Escaping from the Lexus in time and with the big loot would boost this mad perkiness. He considered himself unstoppably in charge of that future he'd talked about. Frank assumed she would help, even if it involved her blind-eyeing reprisals against the informant who gave Sally the Schooner Way tip-off in the first place. Frank made errors. He misread her behaviour at the trial. All right, he brilliantly bought Krug, but he bought a brutal throng of lilies, too.

And how the hell did he expect to reactivate all that children-together stuff if he appeared with a chortling, devoted, obviously live-in woman? Yes, yes, OK, Sally was also with a partner at the time. But Pete just *happened* to be at her place. Frank actually *chose* to bring Lydia. In Sally's face. Hurtful? But why should it be? He didn't signify in that way, did he? Did he? Hurtful.

Although it was a breach of their established contact drill, Sally rang Godzilla at home. Like all grasses, he distrusted telephones, especially his own. Sally distrusted it, too, but she thought present urgency excused the risk. She did not call from home, of course, nor from the nearest payphone. The one after that. It was a bit of a walk, but perhaps necessary. Tracing had improved, and kept improving. If Godzilla's line *were* tapped and he received a late message in a woman's voice from the box right outside Sally's apartment block, deductions might be made. Now, an answer machine at Godzilla's invited her to say her piece or leave a call-back number. Probably they switched over to that at night. She did not contribute but returned to the flat. In the bathroom, she stood over the lavatory and put a finger down her throat, trying to throw up at least the most recently swallowed Krug, and so get near the breathalyser OK limit. She must slip over to Godzilla's house in the Newport Road area of the city. Must? Sally knew this decision had no logic. She wouldn't be able to tell from outside whether he was all right, and she did not intend banging on the door and waking everyone, everyone in the street, as well as Godzilla's family. That would really highlight him and finish their word-in-your-police-ear affiliation.

Godzilla lived in Wordsworth Avenue, a quiet side road of handsome Edwardian or late-Victorian houses, very near to what, more than half a century ago, had been her grandfather's grammar school after he passed the eleven-plus examination – 'the snob school', as he'd often told her it was called. All Sally would be able to do was satisfy herself the Aulus house still stood, its doors on the hinges, windows intact and not bloodied, no torching, no corpses on the basement steps. Her plan was a kind of tic, nothing better than that – a demonstration that her loyalties, her current, adult professional loyalties, were where they should be: to her grass. A demonstration? Who for? For herself. As part of his buttering, Frank used the word 'holy' about all the memory stuff and its continuing impact.

Cop and grass – *that* relationship was holy, created in cop heaven.

Vomiting didn't seem to produce much, and the alcohol might already be into her bloodstream, anyway. Almost certainly no drink tasted as good when dredged up like that as it did originally, but Krug-based puke seemed especially vile, even in small amounts. The heavy-duty wine columns probably never mentioned this. She bit off half an inch of toothpaste from the tube to restore her mouth, then went to the car. She didn't expect to be kissing anyone, just wanted relief from her insides. She meant to get to Godzilla's fast, but would drive temperately. Few vehicles were about at three a.m., and any that were might rate interest from police patrols. Bullfinch would love to see her name on the drunk-driving charge sheet. When raging, he could see this as payback for her court treachery. Regnal would also delight. In fact, especially Regnal. Or especially Bullfinch. But poor, poor Bullfinch. His malice was so frail. It grieved her to wound him. He had soared high, but now his wings were truly moulting. She would not be among those giggling when the splash came.

On her first approach, she did not turn into Wordsworth Avenue but passed the junction and then the building that once housed Cardiff High – the snob school. She took a quick glance left into the avenue as she went on up Newport Road. It looked quiet. Well, for God's sake, of course it looked quiet. She stopped, reversed into Partridge Road then returned and was making a right into Wordsworth Avenue when she saw in her mirror, far back on Newport Road, an approaching vehicle. She had time for only a glimpse before taking the corner. It seemed dark-coloured – say black or navy – and driving on sidelights. Both impressions would mark it as no patrol: Traffic Division cars were off-white with bright-coloured, very visible stripes and rectangles, and they used dipped headlights in town. She found parking near Godzilla's house and waited to see whether the car behind also came into the Avenue. Had her instincts been right and things were urgent? Was someone, or more than one, on their way to deal with Brian Edward Aulus? Thank heavens she had decided to come here at once.

Apparently, pupils from other grammars gave the snob school that nickname back in the thirties and forties because it tried to build unique status by refusing to play any of them at rugby or cricket, but had fixtures instead with English public schools – meaning, of course, not public but private. In fact, Cardiff High for Boys regarded itself altogether as a cut above – understated black and white uniform, lessons on Saturday mornings. Sally's grandfather had later written a poem about his school years, and recited this so often she had it by heart. Called '1941', the verses dealt with the aftermath of a big Cardiff air raid:

This was a school where pupils walked about
the yard at break, no running, fighting, games
of tag; no shouting and, except in almost
unimaginable moments of
emergency, no vulgar signalling
with arms and hands, like – as the Head once sharply
told us after prayers – men tick-tacking
a change of odds to on-course bookmakers.
Another school just down the road got blitzed
one night and lost a slab of classroom space.
Three lower forms were refugeed and took
accommodation for a while with us.
Amazed, we noticed that at break time they
would often run and chase and scrap, and once
or twice we'd spot kids wave to other kids
across the yard and not get struck down
by agents of the Schools Inspectorate,

or vengeful thunderbolts dispatched by God.
Enchantedly we saw world war had helpful
aspects after all, and brilliantly
brought handy hints of insurrection to
our ape-the-strutting-gentry ordered ways.

Sally was doing another bit of mirror watch. The approaching vehicle did not turn into Wordsworth Avenue but passed the junction and went on down Newport Road towards the city centre. She'd been right about the colour – navy or black. It was a Citroën, no patrol.

Because of security, she'd never been to Godzilla's house. But she knew the address, from her personal dossier on him, including frontage pictures. She had sat and watched it for a while now. The place showed no lights and was undamaged. Naturally, undamaged. Her self-congratulation faded slowly and she began to wonder whether this expedition had been stupid – melodramatic, provoked by champagne in quantities more or less non-returnable from her insides. At about four thirty she gave up and drove home. Additional traffic stirred as the day got into its stride. Normality would resume. The booze buzz died. That might be for the best.

Although the outflow had been trivial and had been flushed away, she could smell up-chuck as soon as she entered the flat. This was easily her chief sensation. She registered no feel of someone else already inside and waiting. Perhaps the invincible stench distracted her from him. But Sally knew she was rarely good on intuitive stuff, anyway. She needed to see or hear – or smell. Even when she did spot him there, sitting flinty in the dark, she made a mistake and thought it was Frank again. Maybe Frank and the complications he brought had the main place in her brain for now. *What the fuck, Frank?* she nearly said, and became very glad almost immediately that she hadn't. There'd been some juvenile carrying on in the park hut, but that didn't give

105

him a right to her now, for God's sake, did it – well over a decade later, and he a crook and probable killer? Probable? Oh, come on. She didn't actually *want* him to have a right to her now, did she? No, surely. Impossible. No. *What the fuck, Frank?* would have meant not just what the fuck are you up to coming back here, Frank, and how did you get in, but *what the fuck, Frank,* is the whole fucking thing to do with – the earlier visit, the blather about the past, the naming of Brian Edward Aulus, the offer of reward cash, the flaunting of that bloody in-possession bitch?

'Pete,' she said. 'I thought you'd be tucked up.' He had keys to her flat, was entitled to keys, was possibly entitled to return, so it would have been pointless asking, *What the fuck, Pete?* – meaning what the fuck are you up to coming back here, Pete, and how did you get in? She switched on the lights, found the air freshener and did an all-round squirt, though avoiding Pete. The air-freshener pong was disgusting but not quite as disgusting as recycled Krug.

'I phoned,' he replied. 'I didn't feel right about what had happened.'

'Why in the dark?'

'I feel like that sometimes.'

Oh, God, God. He had a tremor to him. His feelings were busy and due for show. Sally said, 'I needed to get out. Some air.' She did a couple more good squirts.

'I thought, best come over. I mean, there being no reply.'

'That was considerate, Pete.'

'This was . . . well, a *difficult* evening. I think that's a reasonable word for it, in the circumstances. I decided it would be wrong to leave things like that.'

'Thanks.'

'Did *you* feel it?'

'Difficult?'

'A tension. Unresolved,' he replied.

'I'm not used to expensive drink. I was sick.' She used the freshener up towards the ceiling.

106

'But relationships.'

'Which?'

'You–him. Him–you. Him–me. You–the woman.'

'Relationships? They were like strangers, Pete. She *was* a stranger. And he – obviously not the person I'd known.'

'I mean the *vis-à-vis* situation.'

'*Vis-à-vis?*'

'Interplay,' Pete replied.

'She seemed fine. I don't mind clothes like that on someone tallish. A nose job would take away her individuality.'

'You seemed excited by it all.'

'Krug. And then impatience with lilies,' she said.

'On a high.'

'Such a relief when they left.'

'A real uneasiness – I felt a real uneasiness. Yes, I felt that. Why I went.'

'It was all right. I understood. In the circumstances.'

'You on a high, and in a sense . . . in a sense *needy*. I knew I shouldn't have—'

'Really, it was all right, Pete.'

'So, eventually I rang. No answer. Disquieting. Did you do your *Looking for Mr Goodbar* thing? You, on a high, and possibly resentful – I thought, she'll do her *Looking for Mr Goodbar* thing. Pal Joey's? Cruising?'

'Resentful? I told you, Pete, I understood why you wanted to go.'

'I meant were you resentful of the woman?'

'Lydia?'

'This is why I mentioned the *vis-à-vis* aspect.'

'Does she know what she's taken on with him? That's what I wonder. Poor kid,' Sally replied.

'I just read a review of a book about women cruising, called *Not Just Friends,* by someone called Glass. She reckons there's been a kind of reversal of how things used to be, and now it's women who go looking for sex as sex and only sex, whereas men want something more – affection.'

'Books can be quite useful in my view,' Sally replied.

'All the same, you ought to ask yourself if it's wise.'

'What?'

'I don't want to preach, Sally, but *Looking for Mr Goodbar* came out when health considerations were quite different from what they are today.'

'*Looking for Mr Goodbar* was a book, too, wasn't it?' In her view, the air freshener had started to win, but she found now that even a glance at the empty magnum gave her queasiness. 'You should have gone to bed, Pete, not sat out here.'

'And just announcing you two were off to the kitchen for a private conversation, and calling you Sal,' he replied. 'In a sense, confrontational. Would you say confrontational? Is that his style?'

'What did you and Lydia talk about?'

'Aren't I bound to wonder about the *vis-à-vis* developments when there's this kind of . . .'

'But, obviously, the bounciness of him, the belief he can get it all worked out – that's an anxiety,' she said. 'There were other people in the Schooner Way case.'

'You think he feels an obligation somehow to those three? That's what I was asking him, I suppose.'

'And the trouble is, he *has* got it all worked out.'

'All being what?'

'The kitchen chat was important,' she replied.

'In what way important? This is not prying, but—'

'Important.'

'Does he frighten you?' Pete asked.

'And you and Lydia – how was *your* chat? The jewellery looked real.'

'I suppose what I'm referring to could be called a change in the dynamics suddenly. I *felt* that.'

'If you'd gone to bed you could have warmed it. Come on.'

'I wondered if . . . I wondered if you'd want that, after I'd refused before. I didn't feel it was . . . well, didn't feel it was my due, in the circumstances.'

Christ. 'Look,' she said. 'If you like, we shag each other senseless and then get a couple of hours sleep. It's nearly five thirty.'

'Yes, but sometimes, you see, I feel I'm only—'

'Nearly five thirty.'

Six

The alarm woke them at seven forty. There was a comfortable, homely procedure when Pete slept here. He would leave bed first, dress, put the kettle on and then go into Queen Street and buy a couple of warm croissants from a shop with micro-baking gear. On his way back, he picked up one or two newspapers, always chosen for what he considered the 'grab' quality of the front page. In his view it lowered selfhood to take regularly any particular paper or papers for doctrinaire or habit reasons. Knee-jerk attitudes he despised, and dreaded. He would hate to be known as 'a *Guardian* man'. He would hate to be called 'a *Daily Mail* reader'.

But sometimes he'd have one or both of these, sometimes any of the others. He said he didn't mind being seen carrying the *Guardian or* the *Daily Mail.* That was the point. He'd told her he felt 'not necessarily a duty but a built-in, natural yen to be eclectic'. Pete had all sorts of phrases, the bulk original. So far, she could put up with them more or less all right.

On return, he used to make coffee in a big jug and bring breakfast to her on a tray. Sally stayed in bed. He'd sit on the edge and lay the tray on the duvet, newspapers nicely folded alongside the crockery. He was like a butler who more than buttled for the widow marchioness. Sally didn't mind that role off and on. Pete liked to do all the preparation – spreading butter but not too thickly on the croissants, pouring the coffee and adding a touch of milk to hers,

110

refilling the cups when needed. Although both of them would eventually go to work, they could be leisurely with the meal, skimming the newspapers, reading interesting bits aloud, especially items that one or the other, and sometimes each of them, found funny. Also, they commented on the quality of that day's croissants, Pete having noticed they were variable as to lightness. Sally believed these meals together probably helped make them a unit, at least as much as more serious conversations or the fierce, adequate fucking. Sally could not imagine pleasant a.m. comradeship and domesticity with someone from what Pete described as her *Looking For Mr Goodbar* interludes. People like that hardly ever hung on till morning, and she didn't want them to. Mr Goodbars were good for bars and après bars – immediately après only. That's what that book he'd mentioned must be about. Women had learned sexual casualness. Women were the new men. Sally didn't understand why a woman should want to write such a book. Theory could sink something which ought to be instinctive, natural.

She longed to try another phone-booth call to Godzilla, but knew that if she rushed the breakfast and newspapers it would be a slight to Pete and, in fact, to their relationship. There had been enough slights lately and Sally felt a real obligation to go on with repairs, if she meant the relationship to pick up and survive a while. Frank and the damage he so casually caused to the atmosphere here were mostly her fault. In a way, she was glad he seemed established with Lydia. That should mean he wouldn't get stupidly resentful and jealous about Sally and Pete and imagine the past had lasting, important power. She thought Pete had been quite brave dealing with him. Pete was not all eyewash. She wondered now, for the first time, whether Frank was carrying something last night. Obviously, the Colt had been efficiently ditched right after Schooner Way. He'd know where to find a replacement, though. Maintaining Pete's safety now, as well as Godzilla's, made her very anxious.

111

Pete always kept a change of clothing here, and the clean shirt he had on, with blue background and white lines, gave him a fine, settled appearance. He did not look like someone liable to get shot or otherwise wiped out because of a woman. This was a graduate of a totally genuine university up North, and he had followed that success with a master's degree in business administration and several very valid management courses – that is, valid among people who were interested in management courses. She smiled as he sucked marmalade from his fingers. Inevitably, someone of Frank's sort would totally fail to understand the meaning in these croissants and newspapers. He liked flashiness and antagonisms, not such pleasantly mild, plateau moments. He'd been part of a team that fired twenty-three rounds in the Schooner Way house, eleven of them recovered from the dead and injured – a team which included one playmate who'd smash a woman's skull with a sledgehammer. Never was Frank going to provide for Lydia something seemingly ordinary, yet full of meaning, like this continental breakfast and the papers . . .

But, God, the thought that he *couldn't* do this brought with it the freakish counter idea that he *might*. She visualized Lydia sitting up in *their* damn bed and grinning her sleepy thanks at him from under the nose, while exulting that their loot pile had been no dream after all. This picture knocked Sally speechless for a few seconds, unable to offer Pete one of her amused readings from the paper, or to concentrate on his about the Portuguese health service. It infuriated her to think of Frank discussing the texture of croissants with Lydia. He was just a jumped-up nit from Bargoed Street and would not have even known what a sodding croissant *was* then. Probably that thing in the park with Frank had been a real long-term error. He would have it in mind. They were only kids, but he would have it in mind. He thought this counted with her still. It didn't count with *him*, of course, except in the sense that he thought it counted with *her* and so he could use it. She would have liked to warn Pete, just as she wanted to warn Godzilla. But speaking to Pete about all that would entail saying too much and perhaps troubling him. Although her occasional bouts with Mr Goodbars made Pete ratty, and concerned about her health and his, he knew these were only single-night adventures and apparently given the OK in a book by someone called Glass. A connection from the deep past was different. For now she wanted to enjoy the assured, striped-shirt Image of Pete, not see him all fretful and disorientated.

As soon as he'd washed up the dishes and gone, she quickly dressed and walked to the same payphone. Calling the Aulus house remained against their agreed rules, but even when not wined up, she considered it necessary. Normally, their way of getting in touch if he thought he had something was for him to phone her, either at the flat, or on her direct line at work, and *only* on her direct line, cutting out the switchboard. That was vital.

'I want to speak to Detective Constable Sally Bithron.'
'Speaking.'
'That's Detective Constable Sally Bithron?'
'Speaking.'
'This is Godzilla.'

He would be unable to use his codename to the operator, because officially Godzilla did not exist, and he and Sally had contracted that's how it should for ever be. He'd made it a condition. They must not risk gossip around the building about this name. Such chit-chat might reach Raging Bullfinch. However high he fluttered in one of his panics, he could always hear corridor talk. He had the wingbeat of a scared little bird, but the ears of a bat. Word might reach even those *over* Bullfinch.

Occasionally when Sally had to reverse things and reach

Godzilla rather than waiting for his call, she would send by
post, not email, a single-word letter on otherwise blank paper
– 'Ringo', and a twenty-four-hour-clock time. Ringo meant
Ring office. He'd usually come through. But she believed
this too slow now. He must protect himself and his family
at once. A police guard was impossible. *Officially, Godzilla
did not exist*. Also officially, no informant had any part in
the Schooner Way set-to. Intervention was all on account
of Detective Constable Sally Bithron's brilliant luck. Hadn't
the court believed this? She'd told Aulus that if anyone else
ever picked up her direct-line phone he should cut the call
without speaking, *not* give his codename and ask for her.
Officially, Godzilla did not exist. Really, the name lacked
much purpose. But by police tradition a grass's true identity stayed concealed – as seen in TV crime drama – which
was what had impressed Aulus. And so he recreated
Godzilla, half a century after the original first appeared in
those Japanese monster films.

   Again she reached only answer-speak, Ann Temperance
Mayhew Donovan in an extremely vibrant, fucking useless
recorded voice. Sally could hear the greasy, plonking tones
of a seven or eight *year* relationship. 'Neither Ann nor Brian
is able to come to the phone just at this moment. But,
congrats, you *have* reached us, and if you would leave your
number, she or he will be delighted to return your kind
call.' Sally redialled, hoping this time a bit of actuality –
him or her – would cut in, but only got the tape again.
Absurd to let anxiety mount, surely. They might be away
– were obviously away. A winter break with the kids somewhere? Visiting? Generally, though, Godzilla let her know
when they wouldn't be around. He was vain about the social
and travel sorties he could afford.

   Sally waited. She'd try another call in five minutes. God,
she should have rapped the door in the early hours or at
least gone closer on foot, perhaps popped down the steps
and taken a squint through the basement window, trying to

spot any evidence of trouble. That Citroën had made her pathetically overcareful, timid. She could have done a close-up examination for signs of a break-in. What did that mean, 'evidence of trouble'? It meant a body – bodies – didn't it? Was this a daft, overheated notion, too?

Would Frank risk something like that when he'd only just dodged eternal jail? But this was Frank, wasn't it? He'd think himself magic and that nothing could ever touch him now. Impossible to do him again for the Schooner Way offences. That was only a bit of it, though. He'd feel fireproof, all-round fireproof. If he could sidestep the Schooner Way charges, he thought he'd get away with murder. He *had* got away with murder. Some of that arrogance she'd already noticed. In any case, he was probably rich enough to buy people who'd do Aulus, keeping Frank sweetly uninvolved – do Aulus and perhaps those who lived with him. Live with him, die with him. As everybody knew, among villains grassing was the supreme villainy, and the elimination of grasses, and maybe their dependants, a privilege, a grail. Possibly Frank felt he had a cast-iron responsibility to the three in the Lexus, not just to look after their families, but to carry out or commission vengeance. Honour. Frank would be into all that. It would make him feel worthwhile – worthwhile by the stinking standards of the stinking life he'd picked for himself.

That woman, Lydia, wouldn't worry where the money came from. She could argue, anyway, it was only crook money and fair game, pirates robbing pirates. Her kind would love fancy logic like that. She probably considered herself entitled to a good wedge of the Schooner Way cash, as thanks for non-stop alibi lies. You were bound to question the jury system when twelve people could believe a man would want to spend a lovely summer afternoon in bed with her. Shoulders like Tyson. She thought she had Frank tied up for ever through gratitude. No wonder she chortled. Although Lydia knew he'd been on a killing spree, she and the jury said he hadn't, so that was all right then, wasn't it? She still wanted him.

Sally dialled Godzilla once more, and once more listened to the Ann spiel. Sally would keep trying, when she could, for the rest of the day. And what if still no answer, no *live* answer. Would she need to get across to Wordsworth Avenue again, but this time discover the state of things inside? How discover the state of things inside if nobody opened when she knocked? Get a peep through one of the windows, two of the windows? One window or two showed only one or two rooms. What about the rest? Would she have to break in?

She left the phone booth and went back for her car in the apartment-block basement. As she made her way past other garaged vehicles towards the Focus, she heard somebody, half saw somebody – a man, large but nimble – saw him flit about one foot behind one of the big BMWs, someone not obviously on his way to one of the cars himself. She kept going and felt for her mobile. Indoor car parks were unfriendly – too many shadows, even early in the morning, too much concealment on offer behind too many pillars and too much metal. Remember Deep Throat in *All The President's Men* on TV? Remember that rape in *The Sopranos*? Pete said indoor car parks could be seen as symbols of the modern urban condition. They were capacious temples to mobility, they were bare, concrete jailhouses, locking us into a life of menace, fumes, violence, theft. She had her free hand on the door handle of her car. Get aboard, then central lock and drive.

But in a patch of shadow to the left of the BMW she made out a profile now and recognized it, a belly profile plus the nose and chin profile. This was another of her dossier folk, though minor. Her very second-string, very officially registered informant, Roger Basil Chancel, his cover name Coldfinger. Occasionally he'd come up with a fragment, something marginally more than bike theft. She kept him going because a detective was supposed to have a grass, and she could not disclose her main one. 'Sally,' Coldfinger said, across the wide, silver roof. 'I know I shouldn't be here.'

'In the back and lie down. I'll drive somewhere.'

She got behind the wheel and started the engine. Quickly, he came to the Focus, opened a rear door, pulled it shut behind him and lay down, face up. Almost as soon as they were out into the traffic he said: 'Personal.'

'What?'

'This is why I thought, come immediate.'

'Right. It's probably OK.'

'And then Aulus.'

'What?' she replied.

'Brian Edward Aulus. You know him – Aulus?'

'What's happened?'

'Runs a drugs firm. Middling size.'

'Yes.'

'That's got to be tied in to it. Somehow.'

'What?' she asked.

'Why I got over to you immediate.'

'Thanks.'

'I wanted to be sure I caught you. There's some *occasion* this morning, isn't there? Something at the Schooner Way house. I read about it in the *Echo*.'

'People are moving in there today. An ordinary, law-abiding family. We're making . . . yes, an occasion of it. A public-relations effort – to show the Bay's image is intact, not permanently damaged by the carnage and the drugs. Its image is important. Logoland. We don't want investors frightened off.'

He stayed silent.

'How long had you been waiting?' she asked. 'I—'

'Worry not. I'd say I was not observed. That's in the car park. When others came for their vehicles, I kept unobserved. It's a gift I got, able to blend with the background, like, same as troops in camouflage or a chameleon. I knew it could be bad to be seen.'

'CCTV.'

'I spotted the cameras. I out-angled them.'

She wondered. 'Great. Personal how, Rog? You've got trouble? Or Aulus?'

'You,' he replied.

'What?'

'When I said personal, it's you.'

'What's me?'

'The personal side.'

'About me?' she said.

'That's what I mean, personal.'

She drove him to the big open-air car park for King of Leather, Comet and Curry stores at Culverhouse Cross on the city's west edge. It would be reasonably safe for him to get into the passenger seat and sit up here, although he was fat and large-headed – very visible through a windscreen. She pulled down the vanity mirror in front of him but it could only conceal a fraction of that hefty face. He had on an anorak of blue and yellow rectangles, not chameleon gear.

He turned the hefty face to her, sympathy spread in quite good amounts across its acres, his voice considerate: 'As if, like, wanting to get you,' Coldfinger said. 'Why I thought, come immediate. I thought, Sally will want to hear this immediate, to protect herself. There's the questions. Then Aulus. These are things that . . . well, put them together, they indicate. In my view. When I say out-angling them cameras, do you know what I mean by out-angling? These are words much around in this day and age, but you might not know them because you yourself probably never have to out-angle on a personal basis. Cameras got what's known as a field of vision. I should think you *have* already heard of that. What you got to do by out-angling is out-angle them by guessing their field of vision and staying out of it, or

118

only your back. First thing, spot the camera. Then you can work out the field of vision and do the out-angling.'

'Sounds difficult.'

'Difficult, but I done a lot of it, so it's like a habit now. A habit, and like an instinct. You heard of a *métier* at all? That's French, meaning a way of life to do with the trade you got. In my *métier*, you got to master out-angling – the way, say, a tightrope walker masters the balancing pole, or a girl on the cappuccino machine masters getting a deep froth.'

'Who?' Sally replied.

'Who what?'

'Who wanting to get me?'

'You got some enemies.'

'Who?'

'It's natural in your work,' he said. 'You can get up noses.'

'Whose?'

'When I say "natural in your work" – well, obviously, if people get sent down because of you, it means enemies.'

'Which people sent down?'

'Yes, that's natural. But this is *not* natural, what I'm talking about. Not as I regard it, anyway, which is why I said to myself, come immediate.'

'What's not natural?'

'You tell me, Sally – is it natural for police to ask questions about police? This is colleagues. Usually, they got their eyes on villains and their villainy and that's natural. I can understand that. That's their job. You got police on one side, villains on the other. You know where you are with that. But when police got their eyes on other police – do I find that natural? No, Sally. Do anyone? Spying on mates, dirty plotting against mates.'

'Which other police?' she replied.

'You.'

'*I'm* the other police?'

'That's what I mean, see? Why I said to myself, come

119

immediate, regardless – though being careful, of course –
out-angling the cameras and getting right down in the back.
Look, I'm not trying to be funny, but what's a mystery to
me is, you got no rank – I mean, no rank to speak of – and
yet these big people are asking questions.' He leaned towards
her. With that body, he could do a lot of body language. It
said, *Please clarify, explain.*

'Asking about me?' she replied.

'When I say asking, they're not just asking the way
people usually ask – because they want to find out something. No, they're asking because they already think something, and they're asking so they can get stuff to prop up
what they think anyway.'

'Asking what?' she said.

'Once there's money, people start asking.'

'What money?'

'Once there's real *big* money, people start really asking.'

'Asking what?' Sally replied.

'Not asking me in my personal state. Of course not. They
know I'm in the arrangement with you. I'm on the list,
aren't I – Coldfinger? They'd be scared I'd come and tell
you, as, like, a friend, if they asked me in my personal state.
Well, like I *am* telling you now, as, like, a friend.'

'Thanks, Roger.'

'It's only natural I want to tell you – if we got an arrangement. This is like friends, co-workers, which is why I
decided, come immediate. The questions. Then Aulus.'

'Thanks, Roger. Is he all right?'

'Who?'

'Aulus.'

'He important? I mean, important to you?'

'You mentioned him,' she replied.

'They wouldn't ask me in my personal state, but I heard
from some of the ones they did ask. This is the kind of thing
that gets mentioned, police asking about police. It's like what
reporters say – a dog bites a man is not news, although it's

definitely an incident, yes, and bad for the man, his trousers and leg, but it's too *normal*, because dogs *do* bite people sometimes. But a man bites a dog – that *is* news, owing to the unusual side of it, because usually men do not bite dogs. Well, police asking about villains – that's not news, because it's the way things go, but police asking about *police*, that's news, and folk talk about it. They ask themselves, *Whence this social, legal turmoil?* Oh, yes, whence, whence?'

'Thanks for listening, Rog. On my behalf.'

'I would, wouldn't I? This is like responsibility. This is why I said to myself, come immediate.'

'It's a terrific skill,' Sally replied.

'What – out-angling them cameras?'

'That. But also knowing at once what might be important to me,' she said. You let grasses tell things how they wanted to tell them. This sliver of guidance she'd collected early on from Dave Brade in the Bay. Most of them were not trained in terseness and would be poor at writing a one-page memo for the Foreign Secretary on the future for Africa. She would have liked to get Coldfinger going faster with some spotlighting, of course she would, and especially some spotlighting on Brian Edward Aulus, but the way an informant laid out his tales – the stop-starts, the cloudy bits, the omitted bits, the round-the-houses bits, the whences – they could help you decide what was believable, if anything, what was guesswork, what was packaging, what was salesmanship. Every grass had a style. It was a way to know him, really know him. Go with it. Also, a grass's ego must be nursed. Informing probably made him feel important. He thinks he's part of a great organization and gets paid by it. Don't shake that by suggesting he can't put two words together – or that he can put a lot more than two together but say fuck all. These people had very hazardous lives. *Christ, tell me about Aulus, Rog.* All right, they were paid for it and not paid too badly, although you wouldn't know it from that anorak.

121

But they needed the notion of status, as well, Brade said. Although grassing gave them importance, they also knew it was treacherous and vile. Esteem. They longed to believe they had your esteem. Someone with a great slab of a face like this, and the gross body – he'd be really grateful for nice treatment, and she was prepared to give it, but short of putting her hand on his crotch.

'Mr Regnal,' he said.

'What?' She looked about urgently at other parked vehicles.

'No, it's all right, not here. I meant, asking the questions. Mr Regnal himself asking the questions. Usually, you'd never see someone like that, someone with that rank, out asking questions. It scares people. Maybe it scared Aulus. This is why I said I don't understand. You, just a DC – bright, yes, no offence – but just a DC, and someone like Mr Regnal, someone with that rank, out asking questions about you. This is what I mean when I say big money. It can cause all sorts.'

'Which big money are we—?'

'Childhood,' he said.

'Childhood?'

'Digging for information re that.'

'Asking about *my* childhood?'

'To me, when I look at this, I see two ways of looking at it,' Chancel replied. 'There's the arrangement, you and me, so I come over to your place immediate. But then there's Mr Regnal. He's head of detectives, yes, and he has the list with me on it, Coldfinger, like a joke. "Coldfinger = Roger Basil Chancel." So in a way I got an arrangement with him, too. Do you see what I mean?' He nodded a few times, like saying *he* knew what he meant even if Sally didn't, and that was what counted. 'You and me, we got the arrangement, Sal, and this comes inside a bigger arrangement, which is Mr Regnal, with all the grasses, because he got rank. What I got to think a bit about – he's not going

to like it, me coming over to tell you what he been asking.'
Now he shook the huge head, like a mountain-rescue St
Bernard shifting blizzard snow from its ear.

'This conversation is private, Rog.'

'One officer hiding things from another. But I suppose
that's what policing *is*.'

'Always I have to choose what material I pass on. It needs
sorting.'

'And then I think about the pay,' Chancel said.

'What?'

'He's in charge of paying out, right, Mr Regnal? Runs the
fund. You can't tell him I got to be paid for telling you he
been asking questions about you. That's supposed to be secret,
he been asking questions about you, so he's going to be pissed
off if you say to him Coldfinger got to be paid for telling you
about what he been trying to keep secret from you.'

That was a tough one. She'd thought of it. 'Now and then
the accounting can be left vague. I don't have to be exact
about what I'm getting from you – not until it starts an
actual operation.'

'I don't want to upset Mr Regnal. Like I said, no offence,
but he got the rank. He can mess people about.'

'We'll be careful.'

'Or perhaps you could pay me out of the money, so Mr
Regnal don't have to come into it at all – don't have to
come into it at all this once, I mean.'

'What money?' she replied.

'This is what I mean about the questions. The childhood
questions.'

'Or, if you agree, we could postpone payment on this
item until you come up with something else which is not
so sensitive, and then I could give you extra – to cover
both. It's only an accounting matter. Or fill me in on
Brian Edward Aulus. That might be something I can use,
something I can show and request your fee for. He's a
significant dealer. Any information about him rates.'

'Significant?'

'Middling, in your word, but significant.'

'When I say childhood, what I mean is where you lived, that sort of thing, during that period – your childhood,' he replied. 'This is how the money ties up with it – with your childhood.'

'Which money is that?'

'Asking questions – asking older folk in Grangetown about your childhood and the families,' he replied. 'This is what I mean about asking. He's asking but he wouldn't be asking if he didn't already know the answers, or *think* he knows the answers, because he wouldn't know what to ask. This is why I come straight over when I heard. That and Aulus.'

'Thanks, Roger.'

'Frank Latimer. Schooner Way. This is what I mean about tying up – tying up the childhood and the money. Or the childhoods – with an s.'

'Which answers?'

'To what?' he replied.

'You said he already knows the answers. Mr Regnal already knows the answers. Which?'

'This is the way it goes, yes?' he said. 'There's a trial and they don't like how it ends. Oh, they like *some* of how it ends – the Lexus three gone for ever. But they don't like Frank Latimer walking away. And they don't like Frank Latimer walking away with nearly all the money. Oh, they hate that – the last bit. What I mean when I say big money. They got a true interest in that. I don't make no reflections, but they got a true interest in that. So, they start digging. How did that part of it – the Frank part and the money – how did that part of it go wrong? They're wondering. They get a whisper from somewhere, don't ask me where, they get a whisper from somewhere about childhood. Or childhoods with an s, like I said. Mr Regnal decides he better ask some questions – really get that picture of the childhoods in his head, neighbours, playing in the street, families going right back, the school, all of it. So, as he sees it, when the trial comes, one of them ex-kids looks after the other. And when the trial's over and there's a not guilty, one of them ex-kids looks after the other, only the other way around now. When I say "one looks after the other" – this is how it's all tied together, as Mr Regnal sees it. There's the childhoods together and the kid closeness and family stuff, there's Schooner Way and the trial, there's the money. That's what Mr Regnal thinks. I can tell that's what he thinks because I heard about the questions he asks. What's referred to as deduction.'

'How about you, Roger?'

'I could not of been more sure you would want to hear this right off,' he said. 'I come over immediate for that reason. What you said about the payment would be all right for me, either way – give it to me now out of the bulk money, which is obviously private to you, your share, or wait until we got other items for purchase through the official fund and smuggle in some extra at that juncture. If there's one thing I am it's reasonable. Flexibility. In business, flexibility got to operate or where are we, Sal?'

'Or if there's stuff about Aulus,' she replied. 'I can raise a payment for you on that from Regnal and the fund.'

'Aulus?'

'As head of a firm.'

'Only middling.'

'But significant. He's worth a fee.'

'Aulus? He rates big with you?'

'I'm scrabbling around, looking for something to justify a payment.'

'Aulus? Oh, what's he done but a bunk,' he replied. 'Gone. Him and all the family. That's the tale around, and I done some checking. There's kids, you know.'

'That right?'

'Two. Some droopy names.'

'Where?'

'What?'

'Done a bunk where?'

'Not known. He's too smart for that. Plus his woman, obviously. A long-time thing.'

'That right?'

'Seven, maybe eight years.'

'That right?'

'Education. Both of them. But too smart to let that get in the way of business.'

'Done a bunk why?' she replied.

'It got to tie in.'

'What with?'

'The questions.'

'Mr Regnal's questions?'

'Got to. That's why I come over immediate.'

'Thanks, Rog.'

'What's scared him?' he replied.

'Aulus? You think he's scared of something.'

'He got a good house, Wordsworth Avenue – very nice, quiet area,' Chancel said.

'That right?'

'Why's he so scared he runs from a nice house like that? It's poor for a family – all the shock and rushing about getting stuff in cases, and special baby food. Finding the passports.'

'They've gone abroad?'

'One of them big Audis. All right, a lot of luggage space, but they'd need it. Nappies – they take up space, unless they're disposables, which some don't like. So, Aulus hears about the questions and says to his woman, "Get out, immediate." You ring up his home now, all you get is their tape, with his woman on being lovely and civil.'

'That right?'

'When I heard he done a bunk, I had to be sure, didn't I, because I had this idea it's all tied up? That's my profession, yes? Or also described as a *métier,* as I mentioned.'

126

'Which?'

'Making sure.'

'Right,' Sally replied.

'Obviously, Aulus is ex-directory, but numbers of people like that, like higher-level people – these are numbers I got to have – in a professional role. Or call it a *métier* role.'

'Right.'

He fluted his voice and put a ladylike little tremor into his lumpy cheeks. '"Neither Ann nor Brian can come to the touchpad blower at this specific moment in time, owing to other highly crucial engagements of a highly crucial nature, but should you be willing to leave your number, name and tailor's address for identification and proof of status, one or other of us might be able to fit in a call to you around Mothering Sunday." She been with him seven, maybe eight years, so she gets *so* hoity-toity.'

'I know, it's—'

'What I see it as – Brian Edward Aulus hears about Regnal and his questions and he thinks there got to be some link between Frank Latimer and you. Well, that's what we all got to think. Why I came over immediate. All right, then we got to ask the question, why do it scare Aulus so much he thinks he and his must exit?'

'That's quite a question.'

'Ambrose.'

'Ambrose?'

'The name of one of the kids. This is a kid only a few months old. That's a kind of cruelty, calling a kid only a few months old Ambrose. My idea is, Aulus got the frights because of Frank Latimer. He's around, you know.'

'That right?'

'He's around with the woman who said in court he could not of done the Schooner Way carry-on because he was in bed giving her one at the time, despite the sun. There's quite a bit of that about.'

'What?'

127

'Couples sticking together.'

'I suppose so,' Sally replied.

'You into anything like that?'

'Frank Latimer would be so pleased to have got off that—'

'Frank might look like Mr Revenge to Brian Edward Aulus. I expect you're going to ask why.' He gave her some brown-eyed stare. 'Or maybe you're not.'

'Why, Rog?' she replied.

'Aulus gets scared as soon as he finds out you knew Frank when you were kids – something going way, way back. Strong. Now we obviously got to ask why would that make Aulus scared.'

'Why would it make him scared, Rog?'

'So scared he bales out from his fine property.'

'Why, Rog?'

'Now and then a whisper goes around that Brian Edward Aulus whispers.'

'Whispers?'

'Grasses.'

'Aulus? I never heard that.'

'No?' he replied. 'I don't mean on the register, so no good looking there.'

'Only Mr Regnal sees the register.'

'This might be, like, unofficial.'

'All informants have to be registered. An absolute, nation-wide rule, Rog.'

He gazed ahead, upset, his voice sad now: 'I'd be hurt, you know, if I found Aulus was grassing to you, Sally. That would make me look . . . I'd be like a fucking nobody if you had Aulus talking to you, talking big matters like Schooner Way. I mean, this is hundreds of grand, plus the slaughter etcetera.'

'I was lucky to be in Schooner Way, that's all. I told the court this.'

'And Frank Latimer's woman told the court she was shagging him at the time.'

'Correct. And the jury accepted what each of us said.'

'If Aulus was talking to you and then he finds out you were once such a pal of Frank Latimer, he's going to be so scared. He talked to you but now he thinks you might talk to Frank, mention Aulus's name as tipster. Serena's the other one. That's not so bad.'

'Which other one?'

'Aulus's kids. All of them, into the Audi, down to a ferry port. Ann's shouting at him, "Why, why?" And he says: "Because fucking Sally Bithron will tell Frank Latimer I put him and his Lexus pals on a plate for her." And Ann thereupon will mutter, "Oh, God!" then snatch up dear little Ambrose and scream, "Serena, into the car. *Now!*"'

'They say about the great detective that what he or of course she has above all is luck, Rog. But the trouble is, when he, or of course she, gets some luck, like driving through Schooner Way at the right time, all sorts thereupon refuse to believe it *was* luck. This couldn't be more thereupon, Rog. It's because mummies and daddies are afraid we'll trust to chance too much in life, and they tell us, "You have to make your own luck."'

'Did your mummy and daddy tell you you had to make your own luck, when you were growing up with Frank? Did Brian Edward Aulus help you make your own luck?'

'As rendezvous spots go, this is not bad,' Sally replied. 'Good space between cars most of the time. People eager to get into the stores and spend. They don't bother to look around much. We can come here again. I must go now – nearly time for me to star at Schooner Way.'

'Again.'

She drove him back for his car. It was in a multi-storey symbol of urban living not far from her flat. He lay out on the rear seat again for the trip. She didn't have to ask him. He transferred from the front automatically when she started the Focus. He'd see it as a way to prove professionalism and/or *métier*. He had to show he was as complete an informant as any of her other voices, including Brian Edward Aulus – assuming Aulus did leak to her – even if Aulus *had* come up with big loot cues and blood cues like Schooner Way. Coldfinger would insist that although his physique and features looked slack, his brain stayed always smart, aware, disciplined. Let her realize that one day he'd produce items of unmatchably glorious grassing. She had better stick with him. This was his message.

He said: 'Sal, when I mentioned paying me out of the money, this being your share of the incident gains and therefore private, this don't indicate I think you definitely got that money, even if Mr Regnal and others believe it on account of childhood – you and Frank Latimer. When I mentioned paying me out of the money, what I was suggesting was, *if* Frank Latimer cut you in for a share of the takings on account of childhood and your clever, loyal cooperation subsequent – *if* you collected like that, and, it's obvious, only *if* – but *if* you did, it would be a simple way to deal with the fee matter. I was what could be called *mooting* this idea. I know you'll know that word, the mooting aspect. In life many ideas can be mooted, can't they, but the point is it's *only* mooting and maybe not at all in the area of the definite, only moot? On the other hand, if Frank Latimer did *not* slip you a tidy wad – which would be ungrateful but quite believable, knowing the way some villains hang on to the lot from greed, and would take no notice of past connections . . . and then me, knowing you for being extremely unbent as an officer, never on the take, no, never to my knowledge, anyway – *if* that's how it is, then what you said – a bit of delay and then rolling fees together for, like, disguise – this got to be the most sensible. We wait. I'm all right for funds at present.'

'Yes, we'll scheme it, Rog,' she replied. Another advice item Dave Brade had given her was never ask a grass what he was driving now. They'd regard that as a way of nosing out their life level and knocking the fee down lower if they had something old or small or both, because they'd be ready to grab whatever. The pay they collected was important as money, obviously, but it also defined their league position, like the salaries and share options of company chairmen. Mind, the anorak didn't indicate a brilliant income. 'I can always rely on you to be reasonable,' she said.

'Reasonableness I love. It could not be more vital in this kind of arrangement, our kind. This is not like buying fish and chips over the counter, for God's sake – the newspaper packet coming this way, the money for it handed that way, and "Thank you very much." We got factors to deal with, some of them factors awkward – no other word for it.'

'When I say reasonable – well, it's surely a sign of the reasonableness that we can have a sensible and good conversation like this, you on your back and me talking over my left shoulder,' Sally replied.

'As I see it, it's the spirit of agreement that counts, not the conditions.'

'True.'

'What I got to think is . . . what I'm going to say . . . this is only an idea again – what could be called a doomsday scenario – I'm sure you heard of that . . . What I got to think is, if they do you—'

'Who?'

'Mr Regnal. Plus whoever sent Mr Regnal to ask them questions. You thought of that? All right, Mr Regnal is high, but there are some higher. What I got to think is, if they do you, where's this arrangement then? Do you see what I mean?'

'How do you mean, "do" me?'

'Get rid of you.'

'Get rid?'

'Out of the job.'

Sally laughed: 'People seeing me must think I'm talking to myself at the wheel, and now giggling to myself, as well. Nuts.'

'Destruction of anyone who fucks things up for them – that's how they operate. That's how they get to the top, which is important for their pension. When I say "fucks things up", what have I got in mind? They got three out of four put away, which many would regard as not a bad rate. Plus the four who was dealing in the house, either dead or beautifully disabled. One way or the other, no future problem. Plus, again, a lot of commodity. But not the money, not the major money. That's what I got in mind when I say "fucks things up for them". They can be unforgiving, especially about big money. But you know all this. You might never of been on the end of it, though, not until Regnal began asking like that. This is what I mean – if they get a real hunt going for you. This could make things rough for the arrangement.'

'We're coming into Dumfries Place. When I stop, just disappear, Rog. I'll contact you.'

He made a sound midway between a sob and a groan, a big-bellied man's sound. 'Do I come over as bloody selfish, Sal?'

'How?'

'You got trouble and all I can think is what about me? Like, "Oh, where is dear little Coldfinger if Sally gets squashed?"'

'I'll be all right. *We'll* be all right,' she said.

'You know, I'd just like to give you a kiss, that's on the cheek, I mean, as, like, a token, and hoping things will *really* be all right for you, even if the shit is flying. Like a good luck kiss.'

'I'll imagine it – imagine you did, Rog. It's a sweet thought.'

He sat up and she sensed him lean forward. He did not kiss her, though. He said: 'I wish now I'd picked a more serious codename, not a laugh, like Coldfinger. It's got no stature to it. Say, more like Puma or Django. Goldfinger was already a joke, so Coldfinger is a joke on a joke. Do you see me as a joke, Sal?'

'Go, go, go, Rog,' she replied.

Seven

They met in Raging Bullfinch's suite before the trip to the Schooner Way house. 'This will be an occasion,' he said. 'Television, radio and the press. An opportunity for us.'

'Bringing out the positive,' Regnal said.

'I hope so, hope so,' Bullfinch replied.

'With Detective Constable Bithron our star,' Regnal said.

'Absolutely,' Bullfinch said. 'A picture of you talking to the new inhabitants of the house, Sally, will give the message we want. Yes, positive.'

'A plus is certainly how I would see it,' Regnal said. 'Although Sally may have been forced by Fate into becoming an inadvertent part of that terrible, disgraceful Schooner Way episode in the past, she, like the people taking over this property, is also full of substantial and vibrant hope for the future.'

'Not to get fancy, ' Bullfinch said, 'but she's a symbol.' In uniform he looked really good – reliable, fit, almost majestic. Sally always thought that. At these times the nickname seemed not just cruel but a slander. The fine wool cloth lay beautifully around his big shoulders, as if these were the kind of leadership shoulders it had been meant for while it was still on the sheep. Frank's Lydia had shoulders, but shoulders on Bullfinch seemed more suitable, though, obviously, a bullfinch had negligible shoulders.

But there was more than this. Although Sally observed physical strength, she felt also the power of presence, and

134

of mind. His smooth skin and snub nose made him seem boyish, yet there was also a reassuring worldliness to him. Here was someone who knew how to meet life and make the best of it. She could for quite longish spells think him trustworthy. This was remarkable, given his staff rank in the police.

Regnal said: 'Sally links the two aspects of Schooner Way, but with the emphasis very much on now and tomorrow for the Bay. She is young, she is – that excellent, inescapable word again! – positive.'

Sally listened and watched as this fancy stuff floated from him like spores from a puffball, and tried to detect what other, slimier thoughts Regnal might have – thoughts that sent him sniffing like a hungry hound into her far past. Did Bullfinch know about these inquiries? Did Bullfinch authorize them, initiate them? He might be rock-like and comforting in his uniform, but he remained Raging Bullfinch also – paranoid, feeble, vindictive. That was the sadness. Surely no stranger who first saw Bullfinch, grand in his gear, would realize what non-stop dreads of betrayal and victimization often gripped him and produced those nursery-school surges of why-why-me temper? Oh, God, if there were only a counsellor or psychologist who could do for his essence what the tailor did for his frame. Not long ago that essence must have been brilliant. How did it trickle away? This was appalling loss, heartbreaking waste. Once in a while, she even longed to scream at him a famous line from the poet Dylan Thomas, 'Rage, rage, against the dying of the light' – that is, rage against the death of Raging's own confidence and flair. He did rage now and then, of course, but it was playpen rage, and not against the dying of the light but against his belief that things had turned maliciously rough for him, him alone, and would get rougher. She saw tragedy buttoned into that grand uniform and wished to save him, or at least reduce the pain.

Regnal went on with his glorification commentary. Of

course, Sally could pick up nothing in his voice or face but what he wanted her to pick up. There was no deader deadpan. Gradually, as would sometimes happen, Bullfinch began to slip into doubt. 'I trust the media will not treat this in ghoulish fashion – dwelling on the deaths and injuries. The unfortunate past. Essential, as you say, Raymond, to look forward.'

'I've briefed them quite thoroughly, sir,' Regnal replied. 'They do see our thinking. They love the Sally angle. That link. The sort of circular nature of things – she was there then, she is there today. That's the kind of simple thought they can cope with, thanks to post-grad journalism training courses. Practise your smile, Sally.'

'Renewal,' Bullfinch said. 'The motif.'

'This is a theme I've stressed,' Regnal said. 'Renewal.'

'Renewal . . . renewal?' Bullfinch shook his head slightly twice. 'Yet I'm not sure this is the most appropriate word. When I say renewal, I don't want to suggest that the Schooner Way incident set back the Bay's reputation and that it therefore *needs* renewal. This would be to concede more than we need to concede.'

'The Bay project is more robust than that, sir,' Regnal replied. 'Nobody would be in any doubt of this. The Bay is a *concept*. Its integrity cannot be destroyed by a few thugs and villains, by hijacking or the foul trade in drugs.'

'Renewal in the sense that the Bay's image has always remained intact and full of promise, regardless, but today's rather pleasing little ceremony – well, hardly anything as glamorous as that – today's rather pleasing little *function* gives us a new chance to demonstrate the success of this project,' Bullfinch said. 'To demonstrate it once again. The continuing, uninterrupted success.'

'People will get this, sir, I'm sure, even thick-as-shit local journalists,' Regnal replied.

'I'll speak along those lines to the cameras and reporters,' Bullfinch said.

136

'This is a means of turning that dark episode into an asset,' Regnal replied. 'Again, the positive.'

'The Home Office looks to us to give the public reassurance and to maintain social cohesion,' Bullfinch said. 'Reassurance. Social cohesion. All right, that can sound like the purest Whitehall blah, but I do see what is happening today as a contribution to both those objectives. You rightly speak of the Bay as a concept, Ray. Well, in a more modest style, I see and have shaped this occasion today as a concept.'

Regnal said: 'Certainly this is—'

'And the poor woman at the University of Wales hospital with the head wounds?' Bullfinch asked. He stood up from his desk and began to pace, with small, agitated steps. 'Still there, and now I damn well gather some fears are about that she might not . . . So terribly unfortunate. But perhaps typical – I prepare an event of this kind – something meaningful and . . . yes, *positive* – and on the exact same day, she . . . In bed for months, bad, well obviously, when hammered like that, bad but stable, and now, this same morning, a crisis, I'm told, and the possibility she . . .' His voice thinned and became all edge. He was somewhere between self-pity and rage, that territory he had annexed and made his own long ago. His colonist's flag hung limp and shredded there.

Now, though, he had to dredge for decent formal tact about the woman's plight. 'It wouldn't be good if she were to die at all, obviously – at any time, poor thing. This has been a tragedy. We all, I know, understand that.' But Bullfinch had to be *positive* and not let sympathy take over totally. 'If it were to happen today – the death of Avril Kale – this could destroy entirely the message from our planned enactment at the house. Don't you see? Don't you?' The questions came in a miserable, beaten-sounding whisper, but a whisper which still filled the room. 'The media would make a damn meal of something like that. You know how they are, Ray.' He went back to full voice. 'They don't care

137

about the positive, as you so rightly call our effort. They
don't worry about the image of the Bay. What they live for
is the sensational. Violent death – it's a tonic for them, a
high. They'd have no respect for what I'm trying to achieve
by this Schooner Way exercise. None. If that pusher woman
were to slip under today, the media would make it an excuse
to go over again all the other deaths and violence associated with the incident. We'd get the hammer job, the shoot-
ings, the escape of Number Four, the missing money. I pity
her – major trafficking bitch though she, of course, was –
grasping, profiteering cow, with her damned innocent-
seeming, foully deceitful wheelie case – but it could cause
us undoubted embarrassment if on the precise day I've
arranged this, as it were, house-warming, she . . . Oh, I
hope I would never speak uncaringly about someone with
their brains bashed in, but . . .'

Regnal said: 'The very latest at the hospital, sir, is they
don't believe anything to be imminent, not *immediately*
imminent, in her regard. Oxygen. Devoted nursing, regardless of her rampant, innate crookedness. Drip feeds cease-
lessly monitored.'

'Months laid out there, life only a flicker, and yet the
critical downturn *has* to be today, hasn't it, hasn't it?'
Bullfinch replied.

'Not *immediately* imminent, sir. That was the word. I
couldn't get the consultant himself, but I spoke to his secretary, who seemed up on things all right. She knew the woman
I was talking about more or less straight away.'

'*Constructive* policing is my aim,' Bullfinch replied. 'I
don't think I need apologize for that.' He stopped pacing
but did not resume his chair. 'As we've all heard so often,
British policing is "by consent" – by and with the consent
and cooperation of the populace. Yet, I always think this
makes us sound passive – dependent on a lead from the
public and on their approval. Who the fucking hell are
they to imagine they can give us, or withhold from us,

138

their lousy consent? But, very well, it *sounds* good – the supposed democracy of it, the civic aspect. However, I, I seek a more *creative* role for us. Initiatives. Proactive – in the jargon.'

'Exactly what Sally makes possible,' Regnal said. 'We should be so thankful she was there by marvellous luck at the time of the incident – almost incredible luck, mind-boggling fluke – and that here she is today, undamaged, buoyant, and keen to help welcome these folk into their new home and share their delight.'

'An invaluable member of the force,' Bullfinch said. 'Where would we be without you, Sally?'

She wondered how he'd answer that one to himself. He probably thought that without her and her fucking failures at the trial, as he'd regard them, he'd be one up on convictions, and aglow with major recovered loot.

'Where indeed?' Regnal replied.

At the Schooner Way house, things seemed to go sweetly according to script. Bullfinch said his words and said them well. His voice had timbre now. This was a voice that matched the uniform. She could feel the creative, the constructive, the positive in it. If he spoke like this at promotion boards earlier in his career, it was plain how he must have impressed. Sally went into the house on a small tour with the new occupants, then posed on the front path for television and newspaper pictures with them. As always when the cameras were around, a small crowd gathered. The television reporter asked Sally to describe her feelings on the day of the incident and now.

'On the day of the incident, shock, some fear, but also a determination that these Lexus people must be caught. Just a range of standard police-officer reactions, I suppose. And my feelings now? Happiness for the family. Happiness that the house is no longer a kind of criminal-trial exhibit, but a home. And then . . . oh, and then, just general happiness for them and for the project.' God, get it over. If she had wanted to work in advertising, would she have joined the police?

At the end of formalities, there was a tiny spatter of applause and the meeting broke up. Bullfinch said: 'Positive, heartfelt, Sally.'

'Thank you, sir.'

'It obviously came easily – because it was genuine,' Bullfinch said.

'Unquestionably my impression,' Regnal said.

Sally walked quickly to her car and was about to drive off when an Astra parked along Schooner Way, a good distance off, flashed its lights once. As far as Sally could make out, a woman sat behind the wheel alone. She didn't wave or make any other sign. Sally waited. After a while, when everyone around the reclaimed house had dispersed or gone inside, the Astra moved towards her. She saw now that the driver was Frank's Lydia, long-backed and straight behind the wheel. As she passed the Focus, she smiled across at Sally and pointed a finger forward. The Astra crawled, obviously inviting Sally to follow. She u-turned and caught up. Lydia went right at the end of Schooner Way, then into Bute Street and bore left after that. Eventually, she pulled up on Windsor Esplanade.

This was the northern edge of a wide, freshwater lagoon formed lately by the Bay barrage between Penarth Head and the Queen's Dock. These lagoony, vista days, terraced Victorian houses here had an asking price of £400,000. At the end of the esplanade was Cardiff Yacht Club and a smart new brick-and-glass apartment block called Lacuna, with balconies overlooking the water. Lacuna, lacunae, could mean lakes, could mean emptinesses. Rocco Forte's St David's Hotel and Spa gleamed just beyond the other end of the esplanade.

Lydia walked back to the Focus and climbed into the front. She had on a businesswoman's sleek, dark suit and carried an executive-style briefcase. 'I hope you don't mind,

Sally. I had to get to you – a talk. I saw in the paper you'd be at the house. It seemed a chance.'

'Bit elaborate. Why didn't you—?'

'Private. Entirely private.'

'The house. We have to do these bits of theatre now and then,' Sally said.

'It must have been . . . oh, I don't know . . . eerie – yes, eerie for you, going back to the place like that.'

'We're trying to look to the future now.'

'Oh, sure. But recollections – they're bound to be strong, aren't they? The images are still in your mind, I expect. The skull-banger cometh. To be walking over the same ground, touring rooms previously filled by so much carnage.'

'I've put all that away.'

'Really? Can you?'

Could she? 'It's a drill you learn in this job. How to forget.' Oh, yeah?

'And then Frank hoofing it. Were they bloodied, those three, on the day? Or two of them, certainly. Frank stayed clean. He does stay clean, doesn't he? If the other two hadn't been so stained, I suppose they might all have gone to the first switch car and there'd have been no convictions at all. But the sight of them on the day – awful. So damn vivid – the memory. Bound to be.'

'Frank?' Sally replied.

'Holding that notable stuffed case.'

'Frank wasn't there.'

Lydia sighed. 'No, of course not. In bed with me. Pardon me, I forgot. I was the notable stuffed case.'

'Very notable.'

'Thank you.'

'Notable enough to sway a trial,' Sally said.

'Not on its own.'

'Pretty vital.'

'Not as vital as the nice, comradely vagueness of your evidence,' Lydia said.

141

'I don't see it like that.'

'Which – not comradely or not vague?'

'Neither.' Sally disliked the enmity, the point-scoring in their conversation. It seemed foolish. They would not be seeing each other any more. But the tone had become inescapable. 'So, what's this about?' Sally asked.

'This meeting? Oh, safety.'

'Whose?'

'Frank's. Mine.'

'Did Frank send you?'

'Would he? I told you – private, entirely private.'She had lost some of her jolliness and poise. Her body seemed tense, her mouth clenched. She could be called beautiful if you didn't mind biggish features, and some men didn't. Oh, not fair, not fair. Sally corrected. Lydia was beautiful, no question. Perhaps slightly statuesque, and probably not pretty, but definitely beautiful. Unarguably, a nose job would have detracted. Sally still thought that. 'I had to stay well back, and in the car, at the house event,' Lydia said. 'Your people know me, don't they? But, from where I was, you seemed to do it all with real warmth and polish.'

'It's encouraging that the house can resume its normal, proper role,' Sally said. 'So it was natural for me to show pleasure.' She liked doing a slice of high-command spiel now and then. The words seemed to boom around beautifully inside the Focus, but worth a bigger audience.

'We heard Regnal's been busy trying to find a bond between you and Frank. Some real digging. Has he said anything? But would he? Not till he's finished. Anal retentiveness of the face, if you ask me.'

'They deserved a public mark of our admiration – those people taking the house. Some families would find it too unsettling,' Sally replied.

'Of course, Frank believes you held back your radio call on the day to give him and others longer to get clear. And it worked – for him.'

142

'Frank wasn't there.'

'I can understand his gratitude, but I hate it,' Lydia replied. 'You'd expect that, wouldn't you? The fucking magnum, the flowers.' She had the briefcase at her feet and glanced down. 'I want to buy you off, you know.'

And so the business suit? 'I minced the flowers,' Sally said. 'You needn't fret about them. They went down the disposal with aplomb, as if they'd cultivated themselves with that in mind. "Behold the lilies of the field – but be quick beholding."'

'And behind the magnum and the flowers, behind all the woozy, gooey, backstreet, park-hut historical stuff, there's real, solid thankfulness. How do I fight that, for God's sake?'

'Do you have to?'

'To hold him.'

'He's confused,' Sally replied. 'The trial would be a huge stress, especially for someone who so absolutely knew himself innocent. Like Frank. Not even near the scene. Like Frank. Any gratitude, any thankfulness should go to you, Lydia, for the way you presented the bonk-and-bonk-again alibi. Although it was true, you could still have been shaken by cross-examination, but, no, you stayed superbly with that open-legs tale, and the jury could not believe you lied and lied. Only that you got laid and laid. A performance, a true performance. In the witness box, I mean. Can't speak of the other.'

'That woman will die.'

'Which?'

'In the hospital. Do you know what happens if she does?'

'Avril Kale, the injured lady dealer?'

'Months of coma. Now she could be near the end.'

'Really?' Sally asked. 'I hadn't heard that.'

'She's got very heavy family and friends in London.'

'The Kales, yes, famous. South of the river – they run it. A dynasty.'

'If she goes, they come looking for who did it. I'm

surprised they're not around on the vengeance trek already
– Avril so damaged.'

'They can't do much, though, can they? The lad who
clobbered her is inside. They'll keep him segregated for
safety.'

'I want Frank to get away from here. I want us – him,
me, us together – to get away from here. Now.'

'Frank?'

'People like that – the Kales – they're not fussy about
where they hit. They just want to retaliate, do the bit for
family honour. If they can't get the actual one, they'll look
around. They can't get the other two Lexus people either,
can they? So, who else was in the raid? That's how they'll
think. And then there's the cash . . . They know someone's
sitting on the fat part of that. They'll regard that money as
their money. It's time for Frank to get clear. Disappear. I
thought Portugal or Italy. Not Spain. Spain is getting tricky.
Less a haven for people like Frank than it was. He could
still help the other three's families, wherever we are. Bank
transfers. That's important to him.'

'Frank?' Sally replied. 'Why Frank? The Kales read the
papers, watch the news. They'll know Frank wasn't there,
won't they? They'll know the jury decided he was on an
epic afternoon belt with you at the time.'

'Does it hurt you, Sally, offend you?'

'What?'

'That I fuck Frank, live with him. You still have yearn-
ings? The past really is alive? Oh, Lord! I'm sorry.
Honestly.' She put out a hand and touched Sally's arm.
That was all right. Sally did not stiffen or flinch.

'Are you scared the Kales won't believe the alibi – won't
accept the not guilty?' Sally said. She gave this astonishment, as if such scepticism would be strange.

'What do you mean, "minced" the flowers?'

'Which part of Portugal? The Algarve's more and more
built up and flashy-vulgar. Try further up. Oporto's lovely.

Café quarter alongside the river. Or the old capital, Guimaraes. Castle. Fine floral square.'

'Will you get intelligence on the Kales, if they come looking? Does the Yard monitor a family like that, report their moves?'

'This is months after the incident and injuries. Would they have waited?'

'Death is different from injuries, even bad injuries. You know that. Death is vendetta level. Death requires an answer from them, or they look slipshod, uncaring.'

'What does Frank say?'

'He won't go. Not yet. I tell him it's stupid to wait around. He doesn't listen.'

'I understand that. He won't go because he's sure the Kales have nothing against him,' Sally replied. 'OK, although we know there were four in the raid and one is still missing, we also know it can't conceivably be Frank, don't we, because the jury acquitted him, and, in any case, you can still swear he was home fucking you, fine weather or not? You'd probably acclimatize fast to the sun in Portugal or Italy.'

Ease up, ease up, ease up. Think kindness. This woman held your arm. Big shoulders don't mean she can't suffer.

Lydia said: 'It does trouble you.'

'What?'

'Me and Frank. But why? You hadn't seen him for years.'

'I should be getting back to work. They know what time things ended in Schooner Way.'

'He won't go because of you.' She was almost shouting now. 'This bloody mad gratitude thing, and the bloody past – childhood. Fumbling in some park shed. The grandfather bit. I tell him you're a different person now, a cop, in a steady partnership – with the occasional supplemental sortie to Pal Joey's, so the story says. Love life, sex life, all fixed. But he won't go until he's made some sort of repayment. Honour?'

145

Sally pointed over the sea wall. 'When they were kids, the two grandfathers and their gang used to come here and boil crabs on the mudflats. We heard a lot about that from them. This was before the barrage and the lagoon, of course. The mudflats are mostly covered now.'

'He won't go until he's settled what he calls "the obligations of gratitude", pompous, noble prat. He says he "can't run from such obligations", the mawkish, sincere jerk. Maybe if I told him you destroyed his flowers it might work a change. But I don't think so. He'd think you'd only do something half-demented like that because you're interested, raw.'

Lydia turned and stared out of the side window, perhaps hiding some tears, perhaps hiding some despondency. Sally felt elated. Lydia switched back and became brisk. She picked up the briefcase and opened it. Sally saw packets of twenties. 'He offered money the other night, did he?' Lydia asked. 'Of course he did. That's why he wanted you in the kitchen. And you turned it down, did you? Of course you did. But see it from my side now, will you? Will you? Please. And if you think anything of Frank, see it from his.'

'You should have a chain and wrist clasp, carrying that amount of currency.'

'I want to put this damn idiotic, baby-talk link between you on to a cash basis. That will kill off all the dopey overtones. I don't like them. Yes, a kind of jealousy. It's that, no denying. You might deny, I don't. But take the money, and it all becomes a commercial deal, and nothing else. So much gratitude equals so much boodle. QED. You go off with the briefcase and we can consider things tied up and finished. Even Frank might agree to that then. We'll have turned all the rubbish memories and creepy bonding into an account book entry. Perhaps it would be a let-down for Frank. So, let it be a let-down. Too bloody bad. He doesn't know I'm doing this, doesn't know I've taken a lump of the funds. But I could talk him into accepting the new cash-for-services situation. Then we'd vamoose. Then he'd be secure. If the old-time affections genuinely mean anything still, you wouldn't want him hurt or slaughtered, would you?'

Would she? It was some tangle. Sally worried that Frank would get Brian Edward Aulus. Lydia worried the Kales would get Frank. Did Sally worry about that, too? 'My great-great-grandfather used to run tugboats out of the docks,' she said, pointing over the sea wall again.

'Another factor – as long as we're here, your grass is in big peril,' Lydia replied. Perhaps she was trained in selling. It was like someone listing the specials in a new Jaguar to a likely customer. 'Once we're gone, he's OK, isn't he? You've got a loyalty there, a responsibility, yes? Someone called Aulus? Did Frank mention him in your kitchen session? Yes, I expect so. He's been researching Brian Edward Aulus of Wordsworth Avenue. Partner, Ann, two kids, Ambrose, Serena. House a semi on three floors – basement. Codename Godzilla.'

'Oh, brilliant for an alias!' Sally laughed a while, nothing mad, nothing obviously meant to hide shock. 'Names. In some ways they're completely meaningless – just labels. And yet they can also suggest all sorts. Godzilla? This is mysterious, supernatural power, isn't it?'

'Like that. He was your mysterious, supernatural power, wasn't he – gets you to Schooner Way by absolute astounding accident at the exact moment?'

'Names. Yes, they can be so influential. Reminds me of another of my grandfather's tales. When a small child, he caught diphtheria and nearly died. His father, my great-grandfather, asked two religious friends to pray for him. My great-grandmother was pregnant at the time. Well, my grandfather recovered in the sana, as the isolation sanatorium was called. No codenames like Godzilla for the patients, but they used to publish their personal number in the *Echo* every evening – Position Unchanged meant nearly dead,

147

Progressing Satisfactorily was more or less OK. As thanks
to the two friends, his father called the new child by their
first names, Charles and Henry. My grandfather said, even
in later life, every time he met his younger brother, the
commemorative Charlesness and Henryness of him gave
my grandfather a fever, made his throat sore and, talking
of anal retentive, loosened his bowels – recollection of the
sana's enemas.'

'The money,' Lydia replied. 'I'll leave it. All right?
Closure. I won't have to meet you any more, nor listen to
your fucking evasive drool about your fucking family
bygones. And neither will Frank. I'll have freed him. Do I
want to hear about some ancient Charles and Henry at
prayer? You can have the briefcase as well.'

'No, better not leave it. I'd feel guilty,' Sally replied.

'It's a one-off, a goodbye, a golden handshake, not a
bribe. Your glorious cop purity isn't destroyed.'

'I don't mean guilty like that. But this has to be your
personal savings, hasn't it? Where else would it come from?
Although there's a big bag of swag around, yes, this can't
be part of it, because Frank wasn't there, was he, but tucked
up at home with you? I can't fleece you like that, Lydia.
This money must have been earned at work and carefully
piled up. It would be heartless to take it. Have you been a
working girl?'

Lydia opened the passenger door and swung her fine legs
out. 'Take the briefcase, would you, please?' Sally said. It
had been at Lydia's feet. Sally leaned across, zipped the
briefcase shut and left it on the floor. Lydia bent and gripped
the handle.

'Yes, I'm going to tell him you despised and abused his
lilies,' she said. 'I want him to loathe you.'

Sally leaned across to the passenger side again. She gently
took hold of Lydia's arm above the elbow for a second, as
Lydia had taken hold of hers. 'I wish we didn't have to cat-
fight, but we do,' Sally said. Lydia gave a small shrug and

smiled, but said nothing. Then she walked to her car, the briefcase swinging.

It had been a weird impulse, to touch her like that, Sally thought – a friendly, womanly impulse this time. Yet, just before, when Sally stretched down to close up the brief-case and seal off the twenties, it had been a get-lost-Lydia-don't-fucking-well-insult-me message. Oh, Lydia had her pains, her fears, her galloping insecurity, and was entitled to a farewell flash of sympathy, wasn't she? And there'd been moments in their talk when she seemed to see and understand Sally's dilemma. These deserved recognition, didn't they? Lydia had spoken of the loyalty and responsibility Sally felt towards Aulus. This was right, of course. She felt loyalty and responsibility towards Frank also, but a different kind – more wobbly, more senti-mental, illogical, farcically past-based. Lydia appeared to sense this see-saw in Sally, and, for showing that much sensitivity, deserved a couple of seconds' warmth, surely. Surely.

Lydia drove down to the yacht club gates and turned at the dead end of the esplanade. When she came back, she gave Sally the full ignoral, just stared forward. Caught like this, her profile was terrific – composed, ladylike, not too beakily aquiline, not really at all. The car should have been bigger for the snootiness and snottiness to rate as major, but if someone had that kind of profile, you knew when you'd been snubbed. Rejecting a gift could always cause rattiness. Didn't Cain turn evil when bent smoke showed God disliked his sacrifice?

The glow on Lydia's dark hair seemed better than shampoo and might have been nature. Although her car amounted to nothing much, she still looked moneyed, and would have looked moneyed even if Sally didn't know about the rich, jam-packed briefcase Lydia had to put up with for company. There was a sort of glow of plenty to her. Sally had noticed that before, but now it shone stronger, although glimpsed only like this, briefly, through two car windows, one of them moving. It seemed an affluence of her own, perhaps inherited, or squirrelled away over time, different from the bribe cash she'd brought and stayed stuck with. She had grandeur. For instance, Sally could imagine her putting something hefty but unmetal into a busker's collection cap, and then hanging about, graciously listening to the music for a while, never mind it was a piss-artist's all-thumbs din.

Sally tried Godzilla again on the mobile. It had appalled her, of course, to hear Lydia fit the codename to his real one, and appalled her more that the tie-up came from smart, evil inquiries by Frank. Oh, yes, Sally had produced a nicely controlled little laugh –*so* amused and surprised, don't-you-fucking-know, by the Godzilla tag? But what about her padded-out, half-baked, drifting sanatorium saga that followed? Drool, as Lydia called it. Sally had needed a spell to rebuild her calm, and to stop any more questions about Aulus/Godzilla. Keep talking, ancient gibberish or not. Lydia probably saw the tactic.

Again Sally reached Ann's recorded, gushing set piece at the Wordsworth Avenue number. Now, though, this should be a true comfort, shouldn't it? Godzilla and the family really had done a bunk, had they, and done a bunk soon enough? They'd find obscurity somewhere for a time, security somewhere for a time, Brian Edward, Ann Temperance Mayhew, Ambrose and Serena. Goodbye, Frank. Godzilla picked up hints, saw dangers early. Well, yes, he would – very basic skills of a good grass. They kept ahead or they were dead, professionally, maybe literally. *Often* literally. Sally had seen something in the papers lately about the spate of potential gangland executions the Metropolitan Police reckoned to have thwarted. And how many had they missed thwarting? A lot of the victims – saved or otherwise – were sure to be informants. Ann Temperance Mayhew Donovan and Godzilla would go on piling up the days they'd survived together – survived *and* survived together, dammit.

So, stop worrying about Frank getting to Godzilla for vengeance? Instead, worry about a Kale vengeance party getting to Frank if Avril died from head wounds. *When* Avril died. Yes, Lydia was probably right and, for avengers, a death really brought things to a crux, whereas someone's injuries were only regrettable, par for the villainy course. Perhaps the Kale clan were already assembling at the hospital, specially called because her condition had reached touch-and-go. Sally would need to find out soon.

God, but how crazy to be sitting in on two lives like this, Godzilla's and Frank's, and to be trapped by the detail of protecting both, including one from the other. Fears for Godzilla were routine, because a detective had duties to her/his informant. Fears for Frank? Mystical, folk-lore stuff? Was this the past badgering her, the school days heritage? She felt a kind of daft rivalry with Lydia in looking after him. Lydia had been ready to lash out weighty cash to keep Frank unhurt – OK, keep herself unhurt as well, but mainly it was *his* safety that obsessed her. Love? Certainly. Sally had sensed this and found it infuriated her. And, if now she *had* fancied taking the money, the fact that it came via Lydia would have made her refuse – that is, the fact it came via Lydia and was meant to preserve him, and her relationship with him. Sally felt ashamed of the bitchiness. How could those silly bits of history still mean so much – mean anything at all? Mad possessiveness. Who wanted to possess a crooked killer like Frank? Wasn't that juvenile past gone, and gone completely? Surely it couldn't hold her. A park hut.

For the love of Pete, Pete save me from this bloody-minded idiocy! Occasionally when she caught herself in some stupid excess, she'd want to cry out to him like that. Sally needed his management mind to tell her what really counted now, a grown-up analysis. *Give me a business plan,*

Pete. Once she got it, she'd rubbish it, of course, as she'd rubbished the lilies. All right, they had been more or less together for more or less five months, but that didn't mean he and his damn intellectual rigour could run her, did it? Although intellectual rigour was fine, it cut out so much.

She had paperwork from other cases to deal with, and spent a couple of hours at her desk. In a way it was a pleasure to revisit topics with no emotional tug for her, no personal fret – just cases, just work, answerable, as a matter of fact, to intellectual rigour, or as much of it as she could assemble. And in another way it was total drudgery, it was dodging out of what mattered. She could not concentrate on these papers properly, anyway. When assembling witness statements for a mugging trial, her mind was half the time with Avril Kale in hospital. Or, not so much with Avril Kale herself, but with her visitors now. Sally needed to see the people who might come hunting Frank, inventory them at the bedside, list them and wonder whether she and he had an answer to them. One day she must definitely get herself trained with guns. Frank would be capable already, judging by Schooner Way, from where, of course, he and his Colt .45 happened to be so very absent on Lexus day, and so *provably* absent.

If Avril Kale really was about to go under, relatives and mates would turn up in gangs. There'd be some urgent Mercedes and Volvo M4 travel from London and elsewhere once the university hospital said 'Critical'. Villain networks put on large public displays of sympathy and solidarity when one of their own went – and not just at the funeral, with those comically grand wreaths extorted from terrorized florists. This public grief always expanded for a death caused by violence, modelled on Remembrance Day at the Cenotaph. Avril Kale was older daughter of S. E. Kale himself. The initials did not indicate names but the fact that he and his firm and family and friends controlled most major crime and criminals in South East London, from the

Old Kent Road to Bromley. Reversed, Sally saw it as the way Rhodesia, now Zambia and Zimbabwe, came to be called after Cecil Rhodes.

Avril had lived for years with Neville Nelmes Scott, but Avril kept the Kale surname and so did their children. Naturally. It would have been a huge help for her in most situations, but no use against someone gone cash-frantic and blood-frantic, possibly ignorant in any case of metropolitan thug dynasties, and swinging an all-purpose sledgehammer. Although Neville died from three bullets in the chest and abdomen at Schooner Way, he was not a Kale and would rate much lower than Avril for retaliation, if at all. Today, during Bullfinch's PR ploy, Sally had been invited into the house by the proud new occupiers to see what they had made of the place, and had observed an old, decrepit-looking whippet asleep in a dog basket in the living-room spot where Neville Nelmes Scott was found. Momentarily, she'd thought this offensive, but recognized it immediately as another of her stupidities. Faded whippets were surely entitled to comfort and sleep as their time ran out. It was a *living* room. The people here intended no insult to Neville Nelmes Scott through the whippet. They were seeking normality for the house now, escape from its history, and Sally understood. She wanted to escape history herself, but did damn badly at it.

Blood tracks had suggested a crawl across the room before Neville's finale. Perhaps he'd been trying to get to Avril, or perhaps only crawling because crawling, even crawling, was life, and he needed to prove he still had some. That is, prove to himself. Nobody else but Avril would have been interested, and she was most likely out of it by then. Sally in fact *wanted* to think he crawled just to crawl. It would be intolerably sad to imagine he'd made all that haemorrhaging effort to reach Avril, hoping to put handkerchief skull swabs on such acres of damage. To attempt to patch her up might have seemed vital to him, because he'd worry how S. E. and his advisers would take it when they heard Neville had failed to save Avril from a bumping, and had been dim enough to get shot three times. He couldn't have been sure at this point that the shots were fatal.

Sally worked on the other cases through her lunch hour and then drove to the hospital. There was a nominal police watch on Avril despite her condition because in theory she would stand trial for trafficking. The officer could get to the canteen or concourse now and then, but not leave Avril unattended for long. Sally had done a few sentry turns in and around the four-bed ward herself, and another was scheduled. She knew the layout. Talking of hopeless effort, she didn't really see what she could do here now, yet she had to go. It wouldn't be possible to enter the ward, in case the guard were around and word reached Bullfinch. How would she explain her anxieties about Frank to him? On the other hand, perhaps he'd understand them too bloody well.

She parked and sat for a while watching the main entrance. S. E. Kale should be recognizable from dossier pictures. The Met sent nice portraits of all their London connections once Avril and Neville Nelmes Scott had been identified after Schooner Way. She thought she could recall S. E.'s appearance all right. It would be simple to identify an uncle of Avril, S.E.'s younger brother, Theo, one-armed following that famous five-hour gun, chain and machete street fight around their patch in 1998 – a limb of Satan, as the other arm came to be known. S. E.'s first names were Velazquez Prosper, after the painter and a French writer, according to the printouts. He and Theodoric Horatio had come from an aspiring Dulwich family, the father a Kensington hairdresser, but they must have decided to aspire in a special style.

Dossier photographs showed S. E. as fairly robust and suave, although born in June 1930. Four of the half-dozen pictures of him she'd seen had him smiling – genuine, reassuring smiles, not defiant or threatening. Although he'd done at least one long term, his skin seemed all right, untouched by that permanent Edam-cheese look a good spell of cell life could leave. He was tall, thin, long-faced, and with what could be his own teeth in good shape. Parents who picked names for their boys with such judgement would probably also stress dentist visits. From S. E.'s expression, many might think him genial, and if someone asked why people called him South East, he would probably say he was famed for loyalty to the Elephant and Peckham districts, despite some admittedly troublesome elements. He had all his hair, or a really expert, curly, mousy-to-dark wig, and a strong neck. Sally noticed necks.

She went into the hospital and up to the second floor. She walked along the wide corridor and when she came to Avril's ward on the right, kept going but did a quick glance inside. All the beds were occupied. There was no one near Avril's. Sally turned and walked back. This time, she entered the ward and crossed to Avril. She was as she had always been during Sally's duty spells – very still, very white, not obviously breathing, her head bandaged down to below her ears, tubes in from two drip feeds. Sally did not see the oxygen Regnal had mentioned. She bent and spoke to one of the covered ears: 'Holding on, Avril, love, or not? Yes, yes, hold on.' But she did not know whether she said it out of sympathy for Avril or worries over Frank. Two of the other patients also seemed unconscious. Sally smiled at the fourth and said: 'Yet once she was so active, pulling a trolley case, for instance.'

She left and went down to her Focus and sat watching again. After about an hour, two cars, apparently travelling in convoy, arrived and found spaces. Seven people climbed out, one of them S. E., another Theo. There were two more men and three women. Sally had been wrong about the vehicles. Theo's was a Jaguar and S. E.'s what looked to her like a vintage Bentley, silver, a bit boxy, beautifully preserved. It might be the car S. E. kept for certain occasions. Such sensitivity could probably be expected from someone with a long face and almost credible smile like his.

So, perhaps Bullfinch was right and Avril hadn't long to go. Sally realized she should have brought a camera. Instead, she made short notes as the seven moved towards the hospital entrance. They were head-on to her, luckily. Also luckily, one of the women walked very slowly and the others took their pace from her. Sally had her notebook on her lap. She slumped in the driving seat as far as she could, so as not to be noticed, and pulled the sun visor down. She had to keep her eyes on the targets as much as she could before they disappeared, and wrote without looking at the page, in capitals to improve legibility, she hoped. S. E. and Theo she need not describe. They were as they should be, though S. E. put on a dark fedora hat over his curls as soon as he left the Bentley. Somehow, it made him look like a woman transvestizing as a lounge lizard in a thirties French film. Both he and Theo wore what Sally thought to be excellent dark suits, the cuff of Theo's empty left sleeve enclosed in his jacket pocket. Wouldn't he bother with a false arm, for some reason?

MAN 30–35. FROM BENTLEY. DRIVER. MINDER? 170LBS. 5 FEET NINE. JEANS. DARK CREW CUT. PODGY WIDE-AWAKE FACE. COUNTY-FAMILY-STYLE JACKET – YELLOW-BEIGE WITH RED, ORANGE INSETS. VENTS. WALKS BEHIND S. E. AND PRESUMABLY WIFE. GUARD POSITION.

WOMAN, LATE SIXTIES. FROM BENTLEY. BOTTLE-BLONDE. WIDE, BROAD-NOSED FACE, UNMADE-UP, ONCE BEAUTIFUL? WORN. WEEPING? ALONGSIDE S. E. WIFE/PARTNER? FIVE FEET FOUR. GOING BURLY. BLUE SMART RAINCOAT UNDONE OVER BLUE BLOUSE,

DARK SKIRT. LONG RAINCOAT – THAT'S LONG ON HER. BLUE AND WHITE TRAINING SHOES.

WOMAN, FROM JAG. FAT – 180LBS. SLOW MOVING. FIVE FEET SIX. FORTIES – LATE. THEO'S? BILLOWING, LOOSE LIGHTWEIGHT PINK DRESS TO FEET. HEAVY-FRAMED SPECTACLES ON SMALL-FEATURED, INTELLIGENT FACE. HEELLESS BLACK SHOES OR SLIPPERS. BROWN, BUNNED HAIR.

WOMAN, FROM BENTLEY. THIRTIES. SLIM, FIVE FEET SEVEN. DARK, EXPENSIVE SILK SUIT. TANNED. SHORT DARK HAIR. OLIVE-SKINNED. MEDITERRANEAN? HEAVY-FEATURED. BROAD SNUB NOSE. BORED-LOOKING BUT ATTRACTIVE. S. E.'S OTHER? MAISON À TROIS?

They entered the hospital. The remainder of her notes Sally had to do from memory. She could look down at the page now and write in normal script.

Man, from Jag. Fifties. Heavily built – 185lbs, five feet six. Hair reddish, but scanty. Dark suit, black shoes. Goes ahead. Theo's driver/guard, checking for possible trouble? Rough-house square face, possible cheekbone depression.

Sally sat on a while, but then returned to headquarters. She had a canteen meal and afterwards checked her notes against the material sent by the Met after Schooner Way. The women received mentions only in reference to S. E. and Theo, which would mean they were not regarded as lawbreakers, actual or likely. The dossier actually had S. E. properly as Velazquez Prosper, and named his wife, Penelope Rose Marta, and Theoderic Horatio's, Rhiannon Lynne. Sally could find nothing on the other woman with the S. E. group, nor anything about the home set-up.

157

The younger man, from the Bentley, was Leonard Paul Nottage of Grove Park, near Bellingham, described as formerly a taxi driver, building-site worker, sales representative and barman. He had minor theft and violence convictions. The dossier photographs showed him in similar vivid, manor-house jackets. Leonard Paul had decided on his style and stayed with it. Either that, or he'd burgled an upmarket tailor's and couldn't find a fence to unload such squirish stuff on. Familiarly, he was known as 'Gear'. The dossier did not explain why. It could be the jackets, it could have a drugs sense. He had belonged to two gun clubs and, the dossier said, 'might carry'. He was in a long-term gay relationship with a senior social worker. This opened another possibility about the jackets, and Sally wondered whether it was the partner who liked Gear in such gear. Because of the grubbiness of so many of the homes they visited, some social workers did come to envy and imitate upper-crust modes. Leonard Paul Nottage's present position was 'aid, chauffeur, possible enforcer in the Kale organization'.

The second man would probably be Hugh Garston Innes Philigan. There was a picture, but not a good one, and dated. The age given – fifty-four – seemed about right, though, and the height and weight. No convictions were listed, which might explain the absence of good head-and-shoulders photographs. The notes said he was a self-taught accountant and book keeper to the Kales, and in his youth a promising amateur welterweight boxer. That might account for the dented cheek. The fact that he'd gone ahead of the rest to suss out things suggested he might have other roles besides money management. No firearms information was included. Just the same, she found herself thinking of Philigan as possibly the most dangerous. She could discover no reason for the idea, except that Nottage's gorgeous jackets seemed to settle him in her mind as someone tamed and would-be genteel. Another of her absurdities?

Late in the afternoon, Bullfinch called a further meeting.

It was for all those sent on the routine watch of Avril. Ray
Regnal also sat in. Raging Bullfinch still looked poised and
formidable in his uniform. Sally wanted to admire him.
Never had she spotted the least bit of dandruff on his collar.
Regnal said: 'As you all probably know, according to the
hospital, Avril Kale is not likely to survive for many more
days. A party of her relatives and others have arrived in the
city, and will stay until . . . until she dies or improves. They
have booked in to the Comprador Hotel, all on the second
floor, in four rooms, three doubles and a single. There are
seven people. I have a list here. Each of you will receive
a copy and I want you to familiarize yourself with it. You
should be able to recognize any of them when they visit
the hospital.'

Bullfinch was standing near his desk. He nodded several
times. 'Essential,' he said. He seemed strong and calm.
Sally was surprised and happy for him. She would have
expected Raging to fall into rage, jitters and self-pity at this
invasion of his realm by big-city – bigger-city – hellhounds
and their companions. 'They should not be harassed in their
ministrations to Avril Kale, nor in their grief, should it come
to that,' he said. 'Of course, they are dubious people – at
least dubious. Some a lot worse, including Avril Kale herself.
But Avril Kale is also a severely hurt, probably dying,
woman and, confronted by that tragedy, we must show tact
and understanding. That is only human, and I hope I always
opt for humanity in our treatment of folk, even when these
folk are undesirables.'

Regnal said: 'We don't want complaints to the media that
we behaved in an unfeeling way. This was a spotlighted
case. Such publicity is damaging.'

'A consideration, certainly,' Raging said. 'But, even
without that, I'm convinced – a gut thing, if you will – an
emotional thing – or, I come back to that word – a human
thing – I am sure we should – must – see this as a family
tragedy. All right, some may say, "And what a fucking

159

family!" but I still feel we should not seek to make things worse by crude intrusiveness. When these visitors are present at her bedside, our guard should withdraw – not appear to be turning this sad occasion into a sly opportunity for surveillance or vindictive reprisals. Surely, we are bigger than that!'

'Surely, indeed, sir,' Regnal said.

'This party must be free to move as they wish between their hotel and the hospital out at the Heath. You will know that in some travel guides a hospital is signified by the capital letter H, maybe especially one in the Heath district! Likewise, road signs indicate a nearby hotel by that same capital letter H. But H for our purposes now signifies, perhaps, humanity and humaneness.' Although Bullfinch might feel pleased with the neatness of this thought, he kept his face matter-of-fact and totally unvain. Sally considered he should have had a flip chart for maximum impact. There'd be an H-for-hotel page to be turned back, revealing an H for hospital behind it, and this one finally displaced by the culminating Humanity and Humaneness message. Pete knew about flip charts. He'd told Sally several times that they had proven a success in getting stuff right into people's heads and – this was the point – making it stick.

'None of the Kale group has current charges against them and they may therefore be treated – indeed *must* – another must – *must* be treated as ordinary folk fulfilling the obligations of a distressed family and of distressed friends,' Bullfinch said. 'Now, one is not naïve, and I obviously recognize they are notorious. It is, therefore, elementary policing for us to know where they are staying, but this is primarily so they are not intruded upon there, rather than the opposite.'

'Folk.' Bullfinch seemed fond of the word. To Sally it usually suggested people who'd qualify as at least salt of the earth and possibly pillars, cornerstones, buttresses, stanchions, posts, props, girders, stalwarts, backbones, spines, lifeblood of their communities. She found the term strange when applied to S. E. and Theo, especially, and perhaps to Nottage and Philigan as well. '*Ordinary* folk' was even more difficult for her. Ordinary folk had ordinary jobs and ordinary home lives. They did not put their daughter into top-of-the-range drugs dealing, or collect a 'might carry firearms' classification, or get an arm cut off with a machete in a trade spat.

At the start of this meeting, it had surprised Sally to see and hear Raging so non-raging and settled. Now, it surprised her that, in this briefing, neither he nor Regnal mentioned the possibility that some of these ordinary folk would decide to go looking for Frank Latimer if Avril died. They must see it. They knew the rigid, tit-for-tat crook logic after a killing. 'Custom and practice' could have been entered as cause on many villain death certificates.

'Image. The police-service image,' Bullfinch said. 'Now, I hope I never mistake image for substance . . .'

'That would be the day, sir,' Regnal replied.

'But image does have its importance. We must not appear crude and harsh in our handling of an undoubted personal catastrophe, however much that slippery slag in the hospital with half her head off brought it on herself.'

'This fact will make our kindly treatment of the lice recently arrived here to offer soiled goodbyes all the more praiseworthy in the public gaze,' Regnal said. 'And that *is* important in these days of consultation, efficiency league tables, complaints procedures and all the rest of that worthy shit. They will see that you – you and the force, generally, sir – have a heart.'

'Ah, another H, Ray! Good! Completely unrehearsed, I should tell you all. Simply lucky, happy evidence that we're on a consistent theme. There are times when one must be proactive in this respect – the H for heart respect,' Bullfinch replied.

Naturally, it struck her then that he and Regnal might

161

like these *folk* to go after Frank Latimer. Was this how to
tidy up the Schooner Way leftovers? It should get Frank
unofficially and finally dealt with for being present there –
though officially missing, of course – on the day of the
Lexus. And it should get Frank unofficially finally dealt
with for nabbing – but officially not – a couple of hundred
thousand in gains. Bullfinch and Regnal did not want these
folk to feel oppressively and restrictively watched in the H
for hospital or their H for hotel, and perhaps she had spotted
why. They wouldn't like the Kales scared off doing Frank.
If these ordinary folk felt they were under observation, they
might decide that reprisals against Frank would bring subsequent trouble. By this they would mean trouble for themselves, the ordinary folk, as well as the trouble they'd bring
to Frank. They'd fear they could get police and trial trouble
once Frank had had *his* trouble, for instance from the sports-
jacket lad who 'might carry'. Or Frank's trouble could even
come from S. E. himself. Although S. E. provided very
good-natured dossier smiles, this would not be the total
personality. Think – Stalin could do a sweet smile. True,
S. E. was old, but he looked trim and had both arms. The
fact that Bullfinch and Regnal might like to see Frank obliterated by grieving villains did not mean Bullfinch and
Regnal would neglect to get after whoever obliterated him
once it had been satisfactorily done. This was law in action.
If only policing could have started with an H.

'Are there questions?' Regnal said.

Well, Sally would have liked to ask about Frank's situation, supposing Avril did go now. Not on. She guessed
they might be waiting for this giveaway. It would help
confirm whatever Regnal had unearthed about her background and childhood – confirm that she knew Frank,
possibly favoured him at the trial, possibly shared some
of the lovely hijacked spoil as *quid pro quo*. If the Kales
failed to get Frank, Bullfinch and Regnal would still get
Sally. In policing, small victories were sometimes the only

possibility. When you lacked speed to nail the tearaway Porsche, do an invalid buggy instead. Of course, Sally hadn't favoured Frank in court, just favoured dull old limited truth. Of course, Sally had none of the money. However, Bullfinch and Regnal were not required to believe either of these claims. Disbelief came easily to them. It came easily to police of all ranks, but the higher the easier. For God's sake, you didn't get a beautiful smooth uniform like Bullfinch's by thinking well of colleagues.

Regnal passed around profile sheets and photographs. They covered six of the Kale party. Still nothing on the younger, Med-skinned woman.

Bullfinch said: 'I'd like to pinpoint one phrase in this material. It is, of course, "might carry". You'll see that entry in the Leonard Paul Nottage notes. Now, perhaps you'll ask why I'm allowing someone who could be tooled up to come on to our ground unchallenged.' Briefly then, Bullfinch seemed about to go into one of those furies, as if his judgement and motives had been challenged – as if he was to be attacked again by those whose sole reason for existence was to fuck up him and his schemes. Sally thought it probably pleased Bullfinch that Nottage might carry.

'*"Might* carry,"' he said. His voice was high-pitched for emphasis, but nowhere near a scream. '*"Might."*' And then, almost immediately, he resumed a virtually normal, sensible tone, no excess spit on his teeth or lips. Sally reckoned he deserved praise for control. Perhaps he'd signed up for a course in anger management. She longed for him to hang on to such poise. 'I don't think I'm the kind of officer who believes we should act on mights and maybes,' he said.

'No way, sir,' Regnal replied.

'Obviously such a dossier warning is relevant and potentially useful. Although I don't think I'm the kind of officer who believes we should act on mights and maybes, I think I *am* the kind of officer who believes in caution when caution is due. If we have a "might carry" on our ground, we need to know where he/she is at any time. I do not *act* on mights and maybes, and I don't want any of you to, but I do bear mights and maybes in mind. That, I think, is as far as one needs to go, at this juncture. At this juncture. As far as one *should* and *can* go. We know the hospital ward and we know their accommodation. Yes, this is another reason I wished for details on the hotel and rooms. Given this information, we can remain comfortable. We are ready. Leonard Paul Nottage might, indeed, carry when he is at home in South East London, that famed tip and creeping jungle. But, when sick-visiting on distant ground, he could well feel this is not necessary or even appropriate. Some of these seeming thugs have surprisingly precise, even decorous, behaviour codes, as have several animal species which at first sight seem driven only by savagery.'

'Surprisingly precise,' Regnal said.

'I'm thinking of the wildebeest and, certainly, the cougar.'

'Certainly,' Regnal replied. 'Oh, yes, the cougar. *And* the wildebeest.'

'The word "thug" itself comes, of course, from an admittedly barbaric, yet at the same time religion-based and ordered, form of assassination in old India called "thuggee",' Bullfinch said. 'Always the victims had to be strangled, you see.'

'System,' Regnal replied.

They were looking to Leonard Paul Nottage – in his county-family jackets for hunting flair – were they? This would be the nearest they could get to the cougar or wildebeest or the Indian thugs who used to do thuggee. And to exercise hunting flair, he'd need more than the gentleman-farmer jacket, wouldn't he? He'd need a weapon. But Sally did not ask. Were such questions necessary or even appropriate?

'You're talking about a kind of rough justice, aren't you, Sally?' Pete said, when she described things to him at home in the evening. This was the point about Pete – business and communications seminars had taught him how to look at apparently complicated situations and immediately stick clear, simplifying labels on them, or short, bold terms suitable for a flip chart. She'd heard him refer to this procedure as 'cutting through the bullshit'. Sally definitely did not despise it. After all, hadn't she invited him over tonight to hear his thoughts? She'd given him more or less the whole scene. Often she admired his mind. He looked great – lean and relaxed in jeans and a short-sleeved blue shirt – but could also come up with ideas. She did not bring up the cougar or wildebeest or thuggee, feeling Pete would regard them as beside the point.

'They'll leave a route clear for one or more of the Kale set to do Frank Latimer,' she said. 'They're enraged he wasn't convicted – justifiably, maybe – and they're *very* enraged he finished holding so much of the money.'

'And therefore rough justice.'

'Bullfinch and Regnal are not supposed to go in for rough justice, just just justice,' she replied.

'But they think justice failed, don't they?' Pete said. 'The same way the Home Secretary thinks justice and the judiciary fail him on asylum law. People like that believe justice has to be helped out, given a kind of *natural* justice boost – for its own good.'

'Do you consider it all right?'

'What?'

'To send Nottage after Frank Latimer? Or it could be someone called Hugh Garston Innes Philigan, a boxer-accountant who's with them.

'Bullfinch and Regnal are not actually *sending* him – them.'

'Well, not making it difficult for him, them,' Sally replied. 'Do you consider it all right?'

'All right in which sense?' Pete said.

'In any sense.'

'Clearly, not in a strictly legal sense.'

'What do you think about that?' Sally asked.

'It's important to be realistic. By realistic I mean—'

'Yes, I know realistic.'

'They, you, are powerless – have been made powerless by the court.'

'Who?'

'Who what?'

'Who are powerless – have been made powerless?'

'The police,' he said. 'The Prosecution Service. Latimer, in a sense, is laughing at them, and at you.'

'Not me.'

He grew snarly for a moment. Occasionally, Pete's strong, thoughtful face could take on what Sally thought of as a touch of the Sealyham, square-jawed, yes, but doggy square-jawed, a jaw made for Winalot biscuits. 'Oh, you don't like to hear that, do you?' he said. 'The damn childhood link. He'd *never* laugh at you, would he? Not at *you*. At your chiefs, yes, but never, never at *you*.'

'He thinks I'm an ally.'

'Very well, very well.' He put some weariness into that. 'You're an ally.'

'No, I'm not,' Sally replied. 'He *thinks* I am.'

'He's laughing at police as police – that's all of you.'

'Possibly.'

'Your bosses know this.'

'Possibly.'

'Your bosses probably think *you're* laughing at them, too, if they believe Latimer is an ally.'

'I've told you, he's not.'

'*I* might know this. They don't.'

'You *do* know it, Pete, do you?' she asked.

'That's not material.'

'Do you?'

'What's material is their powerlessness,' Pete replied. 'They can do nothing via the usual channels – prosecution, the courts. Latimer's been cleared. Irreversible. He gleams with righteousness. The three sent to jail are a foil to his glory.'

'So, Bullfinch and Regnal are right, are they, to pass the job of destroying Frank to Mr Might Carry or Mr Bookkeeper – welterweight? But Mr Bookkeeper, welterweight, has no firearms form.'

'Right? I'm not applying judgemental criteria. That doesn't appear to be my function. I'm trying to present matters as your superiors see them. The actual picture. What I meant by realistic. They seek other forms of power.'

'Subcontract to the Kale firm?'

'Perhaps Latimer must also become realistic, Sally. He should recognize that the legal protection he thinks he has since acquittal might not work.'

'He should accept the role of target – is that what you're saying?'

'He made targets of others, didn't he?'

'So? He's a villain. The Kale team are villains. We're the police. They don't have to worry about what's right. We do.'

'The police are powerless.'

'I know Latimer did not hammer Avril Kale,' Sally replied.

'He was there, wasn't he? He probably shot one or more of them at the house. The Kales won't care about niceties. They'd suspect the court was wrong. They'd probably *know* the court was wrong. Latimer is the enemy, and the only enemy they can reach.'

'And we're supposed to let them reach him?'

'He could disappear,' Pete replied.

'He could. He won't – not until he's squared with me.'

'For?'

'For nothing. He can't see that, though. Refuses to see that. It's like pride.'

'This won't last,' Pete said. 'Sentimental bunk based on a myth about childhood.'

David Craig

The curtness, the certainty, of his answer angered her. It made Frank and the tie with Sally seem trivial. And, simultaneously, the curtness, the certainty, of his answer pleased her. It made Frank's chances of survival sound good. If Lydia went back and told him another offer had been turned down, perhaps he'd see it was useless and give up. After all, the buzz would soon let him know the Kales and their attendants had arrived. He might decide now it was wisest, safest, to go.

True, Pete's views would probably come touched by big bias. He'd prefer Frank out of the way – and that private, childhood connection to Sally too. Cutting through the bullshit, he would cut to favour himself. But at least Pete's recommendation suggested Frank should get lost, not wait around for slaughter. His solution was a decent, even kindly, solution, a practical, large-minded solution. Humane and human, in Bullfinch's terms. Sally hoped Frank would choose it. She did not want him hurt. But she did not want him messing up her life, either, nor messing up, possibly wiping out, Godzilla's. For the moment, Godzilla might be safely out of reach, but his business was here and he would have to come back eventually, and he would be at mortal risk if Frank hung on.

More and more she felt she had been right to ask Pete over, to brief him and profit from his sharp dissection of things. Obviously, he brought his own interpretations and his own prejudices and jealousies to these problems. But she had wanted this personal approach, was grateful for it, was comforted by it. In bed later, but only a little later, she decided this was definitely not merely reward sex – neither for him nor her. If so, would she have moistened up so fully, for heaven's sake? It was the love-making of a great relationship, a loving relationship. They could pleasure each other like this because – because they had something good going, something that could last five months plus, and which made possible helpful, intelligent, constructive talk

168

between them, like tonight's discussion, and the warm, intermittently filthy talk now. The bedside phone rang and she certainly did not reach out from under Pete to answer. That would have been damned unfeeling. Priorities had to rule. To bring something as unfleshly as the receiver in with them couldn't be helpful when fleshliness was all that counted, for now. She felt ashamed that she had even heard the bell, given how things were just then. She should have been deaf with ecstasy. Instead, she had to *pretend* she missed it. Wholeheartedness was crucial. The bell stopped.

Just after one thirty a.m., while Pete dozed, she switched on a lamp and keyed 1471 to trace the call, expecting, as almost ever, 'number withheld'. But the mechanical voice recited digits she'd been trying all day – Godzilla's. She dialled at once. There was no reply, not even Ann on tape. Oh, God, why the hell hadn't she answered? Was lovemaking sacred? Was just another bout of love-making after nearly five full months of a relationship sacred? Oh, God, why hadn't she put her phone on to automatic answer and record? It was rotten security for him to ring here, just as it had been rotten security for her to ring Godzilla earlier. Unless things were critically bad, he wouldn't have done that. Had he needed instant aid? Sally left the bed.

'What?' Pete muttered.

'I have to go out, love.'

'What?'

'Have to go out.'

He half sat up and looked at his watch. 'Go out where? Pal Joey's?'

'Sleep, Pete. It suits you.' This time she did not drive into Wordsworth Avenue. Cars were conspicuous and noisy at two a.m. She parked outside what had been the snob school and walked a couple of hundred yards to Godzilla's place. What would the snob school have made of someone called Godzilla living so near, in an avenue named after an exceptionally worthy poet associated with fine lakes and

169

mountain views? Was this one of those signs of social decline people moaned about? But, of course, Godzilla might not have been born when the snob school was the snob school, even if Wordsworth had been.

She'd put on a dark coat, black bobble hat, and wore trainers for silence. She took a tyre lever with her from the car. Although Sally had never hit anyone with anything, she had gone through baton training as a recruit. The lever was shorter than the new baton, but she thought she could adapt. She kept it up the right sleeve of her coat, the thin end resting on her folded palm. In her left hand she carried a torch, not switched on yet. She felt more or less all right – a bit preposterous, perhaps, and certainly scared, but still able to put one foot in front of the other, and her brain was reasonably functional.

An upstairs light showed in Godzilla's house. It was faint and probably not a room light but filtering through from the landing. She walked past slowly. She saw no damage to windows or the front door. The avenue was well lit and she thought she'd have spotted breakages and signs of entry. But why should there be any? What did she expect here? She went over the sequence. There'd been a phone call to her – not taken. She found it came from Godzilla's number and rang back, assuming the family must at last have returned to the house. No reply, not even from the eternal answer machine. So? Perhaps when they couldn't reach Sally they'd all gone to bed and ignored or slept through the ringing. Possibly the phone was downstairs, not audible in the bedrooms. The light on the landing might be routinely left on to reassure the children.

If they didn't hear the phone would they hear the door-bell? She'd give it a try. What else? She went back to the house, climbed the few steps to the front door and pressed the button for a good ten seconds. She could hear the ringing inside and nothing else – no movement or voice in response. After about a minute she tried the bell again, for more like twenty seconds now. The same. She glanced about. The street remained quiet. No twitching curtains.

She'd had one useless trip here and could not repeat that. It would be pathetic to turn up with a tyre lever in her sleeve and dressed like a burglar, then go home because nobody answered the doorbell. The house had a basement reached by a longer flight of steps. She descended quickly. There were a pair of casement windows and she squinted in. It was darker down here. She switched on the flashlight and moved the beam through what seemed a study in a very mixed style. It had a big, old-fashioned roll-top desk in what could be oak, alongside a veneer, home-office workstation table carrying a computer and printer. An ergonomic-looking operator's chair stood near the workstation. Elsewhere in the room were a couple of shiny, basketwork easy chairs, and a Victorian-Edwardian sofa covered in what might be red velvet. The walls had been painted dark green and framed photographs of children hung from a picture rail above the roll-top desk, presumably Ambrose and Serena. The room was tidy and, as far as she could tell, undisturbed. She saw an up-to-the-minute lightweight telephone on a Pembroke table. Might that be the only extension and its bell too far from the upper floors? She felt preoccupied by telephone bells tonight.

Sally found she feared the normality of the basement. Why? She could not have explained that, so perhaps her brain wasn't working very well after all. She looked at this room and wondered about the rest of the house. She looked at this room and its calmness and neatness struck her as like a deception, a con. By this, Sally didn't mean that someone had set it up to lull her. No, but she knew *she* wanted to lull *herself*. She'd like to believe that, if this room was all right, the rest of the place must be, too, her worries foolish, and, by the way, her break-in plans deeply improper for a police officer. Then, she could return to her

171

car, shed the tyre lever, drive home and climb back into bed with Pete, supposing he were still there. And, supposing he *were,* and supposing he woke up, she'd apologize for being snotty when she left, even though it had been a disgusting insult to suggest she would actually quit one man, even Pete, to go and look for another at Pal Joey's in the middle of the night – the middle of the *same* night, for God's sake. Did he imagine she'd bring someone back while he was still there? Did he think she'd never heard of decency?

Despite her earlier resolve, the temptation to retreat again from the avenue did start to take hold of her now, and, in order to kill this before it grew ungovernable, she let the tyre lever slide down until her fingers were around the broad end. The smoothness, the efficiency, of this movement heartened her. While the lever was up her sleeve, she'd had to cup her hand so it nested there and did not slip to the ground. Now, she could adjust that position, half uncrook her fingers and allow the metal to run slowly and nicely controlled through the relaxed grip until it was fully out, then take a good hold on the wide, body-warmed base. The base was octagonal or something like that, shaped for closing a hand around with real tightness. She felt right on top of the practicalities. This was what mattered now. To hell with the quibbles about danger or propriety.

She switched off the flashlight and set it on the ground under the window so she could get two hands to the lever for pressure, one hand at the base, the other halfway down. She jammed the flattened-out tip behind one of the window frames and gave a sustained tug with both hands. The timber started to squeak and to give. It was beautiful. She loved to put a bit of structure under stress now and then, *only* now and then, and get it groaning. The structure could be wood, a relationship, a hierarchy. She pulled harder and the frame around the catch broke up. Thank the Lord, no double-glazing. The window opened. She paused. If the house was alarmed, she might have to do a runner now up the steps, down the avenue, around to the ex-snob school and away. But she'd seen no warning box on the house façade. Business folk like Brian Edward Aulus, in the kind of business that business folk like Brian Edward Aulus went in for, tended not to alarm their properties in case police responded one day and took the chance to nose all through the interior and came across papers or cash or commodity related to the business that business folk like Brian Edward Aulus went in for. The house remained hushed.

She pushed the lever back up her sleeve, a weapon now, not a tool. Who was here? She took the flashlight and climbed in. Deeply dodgy conduct for a police officer, as she'd decided earlier? Well, God, yes. But better than chickening out? Better than dousing her instincts? Maybe. Some carry-on if Ambrose or Serena crossed the lit landing on their way for a pee and saw Sally coming upstairs, all in black. The lump of iron in her hand would have made it worse, but not much. *Just tell me you and the family are all right, Brian Edward Aulus, and I'll vamoose at once, never expose you again to the risks of grassing, never infringe again upon your Godzilladom, and pay a carpenter from my own cash to come around and fix the window tomorrow.*

She stood near the red sofa and tried to telepathize this offer to wherever he might be in the house – in fact, tried to get some telepathy going through the whole place, feeling out, sniffing out, intuiting out, who might be here and where. Some breaking-and-entering regulars she'd dealt with reckoned they could twiddle their antennae in a property and deduce at once whether it was unoccupied, and, if it wasn't, exactly where the residents might be. Sally waited for such a bit of magic. No reliable communication came, though. No communication at all came. Maybe she lacked that kind of sensitivity. She found, instead, she was listening for the sound of a lavatory tank refilling or an occasional snore. No. In the original Godzilla films, the monster was only awoken from its millennial slumbers by H-bomb tests. This Godzilla could be another epic sleeper – if he was here. She switched on the flashlight. At two forty a.m. it shouldn't get noticed from the street or by neighbours and, in any case, this was a basement room, the windows looking out on to a small paved area and a wall. But she kept the beam down, part-screened by her leg.

A wide, uncarpeted flight of eight stairs led up to the ground floor and she made for that now. The stairs were varnished wooden planks on a metal frame. They looked liable to creak and she took them very carefully, like a child, one foot gently first, then the other alongside it on to the same stair, and in that one-two style to the top. She would have liked to put some of her weight on to the metal banister rail and off the stairs, but because of the torch and tyre lever, she lacked a free hand. All the training said don't hang about on stairs. You could be hit from above and/or below. Just the same, she kept to this slow climb, maybe not wanting to get to the next floor all that much, nor the one above that, in case of what she might find. At least she was passably quiet. Did it matter, though? Increasingly, the skimpy antennae she did have told her there was nobody else in the house. Or nobody else in the house who could hear things. Nobody else in the house alive. That notion had been around from the start, but now it really ripped at her equilibrium, for a second hit her muscle power, and her hand under the tyre lever slackened. The lever slid, but fast this time, fast and away from her. Sally was on the seventh stair from the basement and the lever struck the wood near her left foot, rolled to the sixth and then the fifth, and dropped through the space between the fifth and fourth to the basement floor. And, oh, God, she was the one, wasn't she, who'd felt so proud of her flair for practicalities? She stood still, waiting and listening for any response to the noise. In any case, she knew fright had taken her strength and coordination for now, and would have stopped her moving any further upstairs even if she tried.

Her mind did keep moving, though. She'd never seen Ann or Serena or Ambrose, yet what devastated her was an imagined picture of all four of them, children and parents, strewn across one bedroom, dead from gunshots, a sight as bad as that room in Schooner Way, although no sledge-hammer featured in her vision here. It was the children who gave this present tableau its special horror. They lay face up, their features graphic in her head. The girl had fair, cropped hair, plump, fresh cheeks, a deep forehead, deli-cate chin. Ambrose, a baby still, was fair, too. His features had not properly formed yet. The forehead looked similar to Serena's, but he possessed a stronger, boyish chin, and had no podginess in the cheeks.

All this turned out utter bollocks and panicked make-believe. She had no gift for clairvoyance. Godzilla must have driven Ann and the children to some safe spot, or to an airport or ferry port en route to some safe spot, and returned alone to keep his business alive. He sat alone at the kitchen table on the ground floor in the rear of the house. He had been shot in the head, perhaps two or three times. The destruction was bad and made the number of wounds indeterminate. He sat bent over in a straight-backed, white-painted, wood-slatted dining chair, his face resting on the table, his tongue protruding and nailed to it. There were two new large-headed nails which shone very silver against the redness under Sally's torch beam.

Near him she saw a wall phone, so the basement set was not the only one. Had he seen something, heard something, and tried to call her? Another question, of course, was whether the nailing had been done before or after the rest of it. Perhaps forensics could determine that. She was not sure she wanted to know, but the word would get around. Possibly Ann needn't discover any of the details. Could they be kept from her?

When the tyre lever had bumped itself down three stairs and then to the floor without causing any answer elsewhere in the house, Sally had decided she needn't try for subtlety and silence any longer. Once the daft moments of second-sighting the children were over and her body felt undodgy again, she'd moved quickly on to the ground floor. She found a small sitting room and then the kitchen. Briefly, now, she put the beam on Godzilla and tried his hanging wrist for a pulse. Oh, God, God, she caught herself hoping there wouldn't be one. It was a foul thought about someone who'd whispered good information and brought her a green antique vase, even if stolen. But how would she get his tongue free if she needed to? No pulse.

She went upstairs then with her dreads and visions all appallingly busy, but Ann and the children were not there. Would it make things worse or more bearable for Ann that they'd had the seven, almost eight, years together? Was the past like money in the bank? Often, Sally wished she knew something about longer relationships. She returned to the basement, picked up the tyre lever and left through the window. Outside the school, she sat for a few seconds getting her morale and composure back into something like shape. Apparently, her grandfather's parents had insisted he went to the snob school. They aspired socially. They were large-C Conservative. Most people in their working-class street had been. There was an upper-Grangetown and a lower-Grangetown. Bargoed Street was upper, or regarded itself as such, which meant the same. To vote Labour would have been regarded as demeaning. The air-raid trot home from Grange Council Elementary School had covered several small but vital social gradations on its way from lower to upper.

She drove back to the flat. Pete was still there. She

undressed and climbed into bed. He turned and put an arm around her. 'I'm sorry I was rude,' she said.

'Oh, my fault. Probably. Duties? Anything much? Or can't you talk?'

'*I* can talk,' she said. 'Not everyone can.'

'What? What's that about?'

'But I'd rather sleep,' she replied. 'Or try to.'

Eight

In the morning Sally still felt shattered by sadness and shock. But she had slept, and could sleep some more. Although she was listed for sentry duties with Avril at the hospital, these did not start until two p.m. Pete stayed in bed a couple of hours extra with her. Saturday. No office. His croissants and papers trip could come later. The leisureliness of things helped soothe Sally, and she moved in and out of unconsciousness, woken now and then from about eight o'clock by hunger and habit. In a stupid half-doze moment, she wondered how the snob school would have reacted to news that someone called Godzilla not only owned a property in Wordsworth Avenue, but was dead there with his tongue abused. Could a monstrous event like that have happened in the snob school's day, or Wordsworth's? Yes, things must be in non-stop, non-stoppable decline, as so many thinkers out there beefed on about. Could police on their own cope with this? Some police had probably not even heard of Wordsworth.

Pete lay close. A couple of times when she part-surfaced, he had a hard-on, but he did not try to proceed – most probably just accidental contact. The restraint was fine. Cock urgencies could stay shelved. Instead, she sensed true considerateness, a sign of good domestic practice and understanding. Their relationship did not depend entirely on the blood-up frenzies of fucking, hearty as fucking could be. They had stability. She needed to establish this after finding Godzilla. That was bound to shake anyone's belief in the

178

settled, continuing way of things. A seven-year – almost eight-year – partnership had been so abruptly and terribly destroyed.

She put an arm around Pete as he had put an arm around her when she returned from Godzilla's just before three thirty a.m. She made sure her arm rested only lightly and stayed high on him – aligned along his right shoulder. It was not a sexual contact but a self-consoling search for the solidity of Pete and his living warmth after Godzilla. Pete's shoulders were good – unbony, but also unblubbery. He went to the gym a few times a week. He looked after himself.

Her other arm and hand, down in the bed, she kept absolutely clear of him for now. In no way did she disapprove of the erection, or even twitchily distance herself from it. Mornings, horniness happened – like the sun coming up. If you slept with a man, you expected to bump into an inadvertent stiffy now and then. But it was irrelevant to the comfort she looked for this morning to sweeten her sleep. She wanted reassurance that their five months really counted and gave them something mature and steady, with as good a chance of lasting as any of the link-ups among people she knew. She would not ask for more than this. She would not even have demanded that much except for seeing Godzilla in such an awful pose. Although Pete could occasionally take her close to seizure through boredom, at least a standard management career should never get him victimized like that.

She went to sleep again on that *Just be grateful, bitch* thought, and dreamed that, in fact, his tongue *had* been nailed down, but to a big, oval executive-suite table in what could be rosewood, and with nails whose heads looked made of brightest gold, not just bright base metal, and with a radiant convexity. He seemed alive and sat at the table head, beautifully and formally dressed in a chalk-stripe three-piece, probably chairman, his tie obscured by the tongue

179

but almost certainly muted in design. Other directors occupied places around the table with water carafes and leather-covered folders. None of these people was fixed to the furniture as Pete was, and they threw suggestions and arguments to him in respectful but confident tones, only one bothering to get low to the table and level with his face when he spoke. The business seemed to be private twilight homes.

Pete left the bed very gently and quietly when going for the croissants and paper, but she did partly wake again and was glad to get out of that meeting. 'Beware boardroom coups, Pete,' she muttered.

'What?'

'Oh, nothing. It's nothing.'

The phone rang while he was out and woke her properly. She had put it on automatic answer, but listened in. 'This is Ann Donovan. Ann Temperance Mayhew Donovan, Brian Aulus's partner?' No need for the modesty of a question, because Sally recognized her voice at once, even though still blurred by sleep. Hadn't she heard Ann a lot lately? Sally considered cutting in and taking the call direct, but then decided against. What would she say, for God's sake? The discovery at Wordsworth Avenue was not to be spoken of, not spoken of to anyone, and certainly not to Ann Donovan by telephone. 'I'm sorry to ring. I know it's not really allowed, but Brian did say . . . Look, the children and I are in France. Concarneau. Fortress town? It was his idea. He thought it best to get across the water for a while. But he's told me several times that if there were ever difficulties and he couldn't be reached, I should speak to you. Well, look, there *are* difficulties. I can't get an answer when I phone the house. I've been trying for twenty-four hours. But he said he'd be standing by for a call, to know we'd arrived all right and were into accommodation. He hasn't rung me on the mobile, either. This is totally unlike him. He'll be desperate for contact. He worries about the

180

children and me. Well, obviously – that's why we're here
safe, and he's there, maybe not so safe. Miss Bithron –
Sally, may I? Sally, I wondered if you could go to
Wordsworth Avenue and . . . well, and see what's what,
and why. OK, I realize that's not allowed either, perhaps
even more so, the informant protocol . . . keep away from
each other's domicile . . . oh, definitely, I know about that.
He doesn't tell me much, but he mentions the safeguards.
To calm me. Well . . . all right, there's a protocol, but I
have a dread, you see, Yes, I have a dread. Perhaps you
think I'm – you're probably more used to handling crises
than I am. But, if you could – it would be such a . . . well
. . . relief. Or, I hope it would be. So, please? I don't know
who else to ask. He wouldn't try anything on with you –
like alone in the house. I'm almost sure of that. You've met
him already in all sorts of private places through work,
haven't you, and there haven't been any attempts, have
there? So, please?'

She gave a landline and a mobile phone number. Sally
did replay that bit of the tape and wrote them down. They
could become important. They were already important. She
had a big urge to call her back at once and say, 'Stay there
– stay abroad in your fortress.' It would have invited Ann
Temperance Mayhew Donovan to do the opposite, though,
wouldn't it? She'd ask why Sally thought she should keep
away. If Sally told her, Ann would insist on coming home
at once, to be with him in death. People were like that.
Death drew them. This was a tributes age. That could be
another symptom of decline – obsession with decease. The
more terrible the death the more compulsive the tributes.
Remember Diana. A wreath pile as big as the Ritz. Flowers
in cling film.

And, if Sally *didn't* tell her . . . Ann had her 'dreads',
and they'd increase at Sally's silence. Ann might return to
find out why she shouldn't return. This was a seven-year
– almost eight-year – partnership, plus children. She could

not just forget all that, not when she sounded so bloody chuffed about it on their answerphone. Sally was pissed off, also, by the suggestion that Godzilla would never make a pass at her, even if the circumstances suited. Damn smug cow.

Sally replayed the end of the recording once more, and double-checked the digits. 'Stay there – stay abroad in your fortress. Your dreads are intelligent, but can't live up to the vile facts. Watch the kids always and do a change of address every couple of months at most.' She spoke this, but to herself only. His reading of things had turned out right, hadn't it? Ann and the children were safe. No question the dangers had been real. Ask Godzilla, but expect no reply, for two reasons – one nails, the other death. Christ, she hoped she had this sequence reversed.

Pete said he could tell in the shop that the croissants today were perfect, and so he'd bought them two each. Weekend treat. She liked the notion. Pete sometimes did nice touches like this. He was not against impulses. Perhaps he sensed she needed something out of the usual. Breakfast always seemed to Sally a symbolic meal, a face-the-day-together meal, and twice as much of it helped convince her about the permanence of things. When, afterwards, Pete undressed and climbed back into bed, that helped convince her too, a little. If you yearned to be convinced and had half convinced yourself, anyway, then sex did help a bit further along that route. In her experience, sex could definitely signify something worthwhile occasionally. She didn't have to worry about how she touched Pete now. Eventually, she said: 'Oh, look, I've left bits of croissant around him. That's the thing with croissants when they're good – *so* sticky. Leave it. Oh, leave it! I wouldn't mind another half-hour's snooze. I've got a grim afternoon ahead.'

'Shall I guess where you went last night?' he replied.

'You did.'

'No, not Pal Joey's. I don't know *why* I said that.'

182

'But you did.'

'I can see why you'd fly off the handle.'

'No, I don't think I flew off the handle. I had to leave. For elsewhere.'

'Let me guess again.'

'No, Pete,' she replied.

'Why?'

'Because you'd never get anywhere near, darling.' Just as Ann Temperance Mayhew Donovan's dreads would never get anywhere near the actual, and Sally couldn't give her help, except the dud help of silence.

Pete said: 'You see, I think—'

'No,' she said. Rattiness took half a hold. '*No*. No point.'

At the hospital, she sat with Avril Kale for half an hour in the afternoon, and then her mother and father arrived. Sally followed the Bullfinch instructions and prepared to leave. There had been no movement from Avril and, of course, no word. The bed curtains were closed around her permanently. That was new. The doctors must really think she might go any time. When the visitors came, Mrs Kale drew back one of the curtains a little and pushed her vivid, dark-roots head through, only her head at first, like in a pillory. She looked tense. Because of the curtains, she might think Avril already dead.

Sally stood and the movement seemed to give Penelope Kale a signal. She obviously decided the police would not watch if Avril's life was over. Mrs Kale said: 'Any . . . any sort of signs of anything, dear?' and came closer to the bed. The two men followed.

S. E. said: 'The doctors will tell us, Penny. No need to ask *her*. She doesn't care.'

'Velazquez, love, don't be so . . . well . . . fucking negative,' she replied. 'This is a girl who's been alone with our daughter and might have observed a development, might even have heard her speak. These are things to be acknowledged.'

'I wish I could tell you something good, Mrs Kale,' Sally said. 'But Avril's as ever, I'm afraid.'

'They hover, that's all,' S. E. said. 'No shame. Vultures.'

'Oh, sweeten up, Vel, dear,' Mrs Kale said.

'Why does *she* have to be here?' S. E. said.

'Because your daughter's a bumper-edition crook,' Sally replied.

'Because our daughter's a bumper-edition crook, Velazquez,' Mrs Kale said.

Sally said: 'And if she comes round . . .'

'But she won't come round,' Mrs Kale said.

'No, I'm sorry,' Sally said.

'You don't give a shit,' S. E. replied. 'You're paid not to give a shit. Police – if they give a shit about people their pension's stopped.'

'Which people?' Sally said.

'People,' S. E. said.

'What are *you* paid for?' Sally said.

'Forgive Vel's sick mouth,' Mrs Kale said, 'but he's in such despair over Avril.'

'Of course,' Sally said.

'Such special despair,' Mrs Kale said.

'As I would be for any of my family,' S. E. said.

'Such special despair,' Mrs Kale said.

S. E. turned to Sally: 'I don't know how you're mixed up in this.'

'In what?' Mrs Kale asked.

'All of it,' S. E. said. 'How she's mixed up in the deaths. I know she's mixed up in it all, but I don't know *how* she is. I'll find out, though. We had a more or less son-in-law killed at that docks house. This Neville Nelmes Scott . . . well, Christ, him – but still a son-in-law, give or take a wedding.' He waved a hand towards Avril. 'And the injuries.'

'Perhaps it doesn't matter now,' Mrs Kale said.

'It matters,' S. E. said. 'Am I supposed to let people scheme when my daughter's like this?'

184

'Which people?' Sally said.

'She was set up,' S. E. said. 'A Kale, but she and her man are set up. Penelope, that's what I don't know yet – I don't know where this bit of law and order figures in setting them up.'

'She's here as a guard, that's all,' Mrs Kale said.

'Do you understand why something like this happens?' S. E. replied. He waved towards Avril again.

'She went into tricky places, this time with a trolley case of cash,' Sally said, 'Cash in that quantity can always bring trouble, whether it's on wheels or not.'

'Right. Tricky places,' S. E. said. 'What *are* tricky places?'

'Drug-deal spots. A commodity shop. No rules there. Money rules.'

'Tricky places are places off our home patch,' S. E. said. 'There are no tricky places for Kales on our ground. Arrangements have been put in place over many years.'

'She's not allowed out of Peckham?' Sally replied. She was on the far side of the bed from the Kales. They talked across Avril. Her stillness stayed total. So did the whiteness of her face, the bedlinen, the bandage. Mrs Kale sat down in an armchair.

'There are places she'd have been safe because of respect – respect for that name, Kale,' S. E. replied. 'This respect is big. It's big in quality, it's over a big area. It's been earned. You say Peckham. That's your ignorant little, crude little, joke. But think about Croydon, think about Lewisham, think about right out to Eltham, Sidcup, Chislehurst. These are all zones where the Kale writ reaches.'

'Do they name streets after you, like Queen Victoria or Mandela?' Sally replied. 'Velazquez View?'

'Would anyone say there wasn't enough scope for her there? No. Never. There was enough scope for *her* because she's been brought up to know what scope means, and what limits mean. "Know your limits." I instilled this.'

David Craig

'"Know your limits." You, you instilled that, did you, Vel?' Mrs Kale said.

'But then Avril gets herself tied up with this Scott – Neville Nelmes Scott, wiped out now – and, of course, he's not part of the area, he hasn't got the instinct, he's outside the thinking, outside the methodology. All right, big word. But that's what it is, methodology – not something to be learned in a fortnight, or even a year. This is something absorbed over a long, long period, like, say, ancient Assyrian by a scholar or soil moisture by an oak. But Neville can't be content with what's been built and made secure over decades – yes decades – can he?' Theo came through the curtains and stood at the head of the bed looking down at Avril. S. E. said: 'He's got to show her he, Mr Neville Nelmes Scott, has his own plans, his own brilliance. Neville thinks he has to prove to her and the rest of us the individual himness of him. It's an old tale. He's from Preston or Grimsby, somewhere like that. What could someone of his sort know about anything? Or possibly Exeter. Tradition? He had no feel for it.

'And he's not content with what she brings him – the grand, worked-for Kale reputation. No, he has to expand, he has to go into new regions for what he most probably tells her are higher-grade supplies, cheaper supplies. This is Mr Neville Nelmes Scott the fucking business genius.'

'Nev was an independent thinker,' Theo said. 'As far as that could go, given defects.'

'So, he takes her into a strange diocese, where he and Avril aren't familiar with the people, where the Kale name might still be known, yes, admittedly owing to the inevitable spread of fame, but not known the way it's known in its own domain, like a currency. How could it be? Wales. Wales! There are people called "ap Something" here. There's a nurse called "ap Something". I've seen it on a noticeboard. And "Jones-Williams-Jones". That's another name. Names. I'm not making this up. But Neville

186

persuades her they can do things in Wales. This is a fucking different *country*. Road signs in mumbo-jumbo-speak. Its own flag and love spoons. He thinks he's not just Neville Nelmes Scott, he thinks he's *Captain* Scott and must explore unknown lands. Well, I should have said, "*You* explore, Neville Nelmes Scott, but don't take my eldest with you."'

'Captain Scott's ship, the *Terra Nova*, sailed from Cardiff on the South Pole expedition,' Sally replied.

'They're in a house in a street called Schooner Way! Schooner Way!' S. E. replied. 'It's wrong for them – schooners, barques, sloops. We're people who live with the Underground, shopping malls, whore cards in payphone booths. And that district they were in. What's it called?'

'The Bay,' Sally said. 'Cardiff Bay, now. Used to be Tiger Bay.'

'Bays. There you are, then. Maritime. So, of course, they're lost, lost, and Neville gets his in the house and my Avril . . .' He sent his hand to float out towards the bed again and cried a bit, letting the tears run on to his cheeks, no handkerchiefing or embarrassment. 'I should have stopped them, kept them on our territory. Why have I looked after a territory like that year on year if I don't make sure my own daughter stays there?'

Theo said: 'Different generations – they'll always want to experiment, Vel. You can't fence them in. This is not something to blame yourself for.'

'He'll make himself ill,' Mrs Kale said. 'He's not happy till then. He has to prove something.'

A consultant came through the curtains. 'Here's Mr Jones-Williams-Jones now, as a matter of fact,' S. E. said. 'We've just been speaking of you, Mr Jones-Williams-Jones.' S. E. did wipe his face then. 'And this here is the fuzz, in case you weren't aware, Mr Jones-Williams-Jones.' He nodded at Sally. 'She was in the trial. Press pictures – and TV. I'd say she knows about these injuries to my girl, but her chiefs

187

still let her come here and sit by herself with Avril. Is this decent?'

'That's a police matter,' Jones-Williams-Jones said.

Mrs Kale said: 'It's best someone's with Avril when we're not.'

'Someone, yes. But this one?' S. E. said. 'Crowing.'

'I never went on the crowing course,' Sally said.

'I don't want this one here,' S. E. said.

'This one's as much use as any,' Sally said, 'and that means no use at all, unfortunately.'

'We should talk about Avril's condition now,' Jones-Williams-Jones said gently. Too gently, maybe.

Sally left and went down to the concourse restaurant. She bought tea and a newspaper to see if Godzilla had been found. A milkman or postman might notice the busted window. She wanted him found, because it was appalling to think of the body there. And she *didn't* want him found, because Regnal and his boys and girls were sharp and might discover something in the house, or from the neighbours, something that pointed to DC Sally Bithron. They didn't come better at pointing than Regnal.

She tried to run through her brain all she had done at Wordsworth Avenue in the night, and also tried to re-see a picture of the whole street as she approached and left. Had there been movement at a neighbouring window, which she'd been too excited to notice, but which might be in her subconscious? This she more or less recognized as crap, though. She believed in the subconscious, but not much. If anyone had been watching, she would have noted it in her *un*subconscious – in her very conscious consciousness – and, had it happened on her approach, she would have abandoned the scheme to get in and retreated to her car. She'd been gloved, of course, and had carried only two loose items, the flashlight and tyre lever. No question she brought both away. She wondered whether full-time burglars fretted like this after a job. But perhaps they worked to such a set ritual they knew they'd left no giveaways. Some still got caught, though.

Theo Kale appeared at the edge of the concourse and looked about. When he saw Sally, he raised his hand slightly in signal, then chose himself hot chocolate and a Danish pastry and joined her. They gave him a tray. He carried it really fine, very level, no spillage, wrist power. 'That scene by the bed – distressing, unnecessary,' he said. 'But Vel and Av were always close. Are still close, as far as Vel's concerned. I don't say there was ever anything . . . anything *specific* there, but very close – now, you mustn't misunderstand . . . that disregard for Neville Nelmes Scott probably does *not* come from jealousy – but just close, the way a father and daughter can be . . . often wholly above board. It's only that Nev kicked against the regular pattern of things, which, in the ultimate, as we've seen, is foolish. And all that mad grey hair.'

'I found S. E. quite moving.'

'You're kind.'

'A supreme fucking hoodlum, almost one hundred per cent venom, but still quite moving once in a while,' Sally replied.

'Many do refer to him as S. E., although his true names are Velazquez Prosper. And this is the point, isn't it? I'm glad you raised the matter by speaking of him as S. E.'

'Am I going to call him Velazquez Prosper, for God's sake?'

'That had to be earned – the S. E.,' he said. 'A reward for much steady achievement in often hostile circumstances, not something simply plucked from a bush. And then to see it spurned by Nev. Grievous. In view of the consequences. And yet, of course, the consequences did not come unaided.' He bit into his Danish.

'Which of course is that?'

'Down here, off our patch, we don't hear everything – not like in SE,' Theo replied. 'Naturally, we've brought a researcher, a very gifted researcher, but we have no established network. What reaches us via such channels as we *do* have is the matter of this number-one detective – Regnal? The one at the trial, and not too happy there – DS Raymond Regnal, out looking for, let's say, an involvement . . . call it an involvement . . . Excuse me, I must personalize. It seems indelicate to be discussing this topic while eating a pastry.' He covered his mouth with his hand so as not to give offence by showing half-chewed-up stuff. 'But an involvement, yes – namely, you on the one side, a piece of villainy on the other.'

'Is that right?'

'We're bound to be interested in such involvement. You'll understand that, I'm sure. I mean, in view of Avril's state. She is a dear niece. Formerly so charming, vivacious, witty. She had a wonderful way with amusing anecdotes and supported many charities, including Poppy Day. Ask your brother, Mark.'

'What? You know Mark?'

'That flat you have – mainly thanks to him, I gather,' Theo replied. 'A good arrangement.'

'How do you know Mark?'

'Avril – very much a woman with her own agenda, yet not pretentious.'

'A pusher. Top-scale, but still a pusher.'

'I certainly don't go all the way with Vel in regarding Neville Nelmes Scott's death light-heartedly – and I hear there's a whippet's basket on the spot where he happened to pass on, which can at least give Vel a smile at this very harsh time. But the head-job on a fine, talented woman like Avril – this has to be a quite different consideration. And, of course, she's blood, Kale blood. Clearly, that will not mean as much to you as it does to us, but for family members like Vel and myself, the Kale bloodline is . . . I don't say sacrosanct – that would be arrogant, lurid – but the bloodline is of value . . . yes, of value, and to be defended. I'm

190

entirely with Velazquez in regarding her wounds as a serious challenge. I think I can reasonably speak of wounds as an insider.' He put down the remains of the Danish pastry on the plate and touched his empty sleeve. 'It would have been neglectful and flippant after the severance of my arm, for instance, if the loss had not been noted and responded to. When I say noted – well, obviously it would be noted by one's self and all who knew one, but noted in the sense of highlighted in the firm for recompense. Now, I'm naturally aware you are a police officer, and I will not embarrass you by saying too much about that response, the recompense. But it took place. And, similarly, we are bound to regard the savagery against Avril with real soul darkness.'

'Someone's inside eternally for it, and probably getting stabbed and beaten up weekly by clinked pals of S. E., or suborned warders.'

'I wonder if you've thought enough about how Aulus knew events were due in Schooner Way,' Theo replied. He had a smallish, neat face which stayed controlled really well. He launched Aulus's name, but without showing any special satisfaction at flinging a surprise. A tidy, fair, minia-ture moustache helped give him the look of someone who in another career might have liked to win people by harm-lessness or mild jokes. Sally could visualize him as, say, an announcer on the radio music channel, Classic FM, full of quaint, utterly undammed verbiage, his voice gross with amity. She remembered that his and S. E.'s father was a considerable hairdresser in the smart end of London, and Theo might have inherited some instincts from him. His own hair, as well as the moustache, had obviously been thought about a lot as to style, and she felt this was a lad who would never come out with a rubber-banded pigtail in middle-age, the kind of thing some might do to make up for an arm off. His chewing, as he finished the pastry, remained moderate.

'And yet you seem to have adjusted remarkably well, if

David Craig

I may say, to the loss of a limb, Theodoric,' Sally said. 'Was it your gun hand? Did you have to retrain?'

'This Aulus is Brian Edward Aulus,' Theo explained. 'Poet's corner address, according to our last soundings. I feel, and Velazquez does, too, that it's reasonable to ask not just *what* a grass supplies but *how* he or she acquires his/her information. The route.'

'I hadn't realized . . . well, in your term, the *closeness* of S. E. and Avril,' Sally replied. 'But yes, perhaps a hint or two from Mrs Kale in the ward, now I reflect.'

'Oh, yes, a closeness. There's another daughter, and a closeness there, also, a *family* closeness – let's refer to it as that – and natural, but not the same sort of . . . well, closeness as with Av. Not the same, as it were, *degree*.'

'And yet Mrs Kale seems genuinely upset about Avril.'

'Yes, she does seem like that, doesn't she? And, of course, Avril is still her daughter, her first-born, regardless. Penny fought it. This dye one week, a different one the next. Higher heels. She's a trouper, Penny is. I wouldn't try anything there ever. I regard a sister-in-law as a sister-in-law.'

'What interested us, of course, was how often Avril and Neville had already been to the Bay for supplies,' Sally replied. 'We were bound to wonder whether a long-time, inward bulk movement existed that we didn't know about. I'm not Drugs, but I can appreciate the concern. People here like to think of the Bay as fresh, untainted, a fine emblem of a sweet future, not as a site for bucketsful of substance.'

'Aulus tells you, yes, but who tells Aulus?' Theo said. 'Perhaps Aulus notified the Lexus group as well. Anything to get rid of potential trade rivals like Av and Nev. They buy here, so maybe they'd sell here, too. He'd want to look after his interests. There are dependants, aren't there?'

'We're talking, are we, of importers established in a very bijou marina property and attracting dross like Avril and

192

Neville Nelmes Scott? Oh, this would be regarded as wholly against the spirit of the development,' Sally said. 'These are premises for a certain kind of living – an elegant, waterside, twenty-first-century kind, not for illegal trade depots. After all, the Welsh Assembly building is just down the road. This is very much a cachet area.'

'Look, I know a detective can't ask a grass to reveal sources. Or, rather, a detective *can* ask, but is not going to get an answer. A grass who tells where his information comes from is liable not to get any more. And worse than that. In the case of Schooner Way – you were down there alone, despite the possibility of numbers. The possibility and, as it turned out, the actuality. Eight people, if we include the Lexus driver. But you try to handle all that solo. Is this because you lacked total faith in what Aulus told you, and did not feel it justified a major police presence until things actually started happening? Oh, I know you said you were only there through luck, but . . . Let's be grown-ups, shall we? I'm really curious, you see, about whether Aulus indicated a source for his knowledge. You'll spot why this is so, I expect. Oh, more than curious. This is vital.'

'Aulus? The dealer? Does he come into this, then?'

'It's unpleasant to think that within the Kale organization there might be a voice who would murmur to an outsider like Aulus matters concerning a daughter very dear to Velazquez, plus, as it happened, concerning Nev Scott. Now, I'm aware, naturally, that you might not normally pass on to someone like myself the name of a source known to your grass, even if the grass provided it. But this case – is it different, do you think? Knowing your brother, for instance.'

'But how?'

'Possibly this does make it a privileged situation.'

'On a business basis? You know Mark through business?'

'And, then, in addition, I had an idea you might want to compensate for allowing an incident to take place, in which deaths and an appalling injury – probably also unto death – yes, compensate for allowing such an incident to proceed, although you'd been briefed ahead of time. This would look poor for you, if published – in a general sense and especially with your high-ups. I don't say, not in the least, that you foresaw as a certainty such brutal damage to humankind would be caused. Probably you genuinely hoped not. You risked it, though. Perhaps you suffer awful guilt at that. A massacre you were an accessory to – it's tough to have that in your memory. To me, you look the sensitive kind, the unforgiving kind – unforgiving towards yourself, I mean. I felt it a duty to offer you the chance to escape some of that guilt by letting me know where your tipster, Brian Edward Aulus, otherwise, amusingly, Godzilla, got his information. This voice from within the Kale organization could also have murmured to one or other of the Lexus group personally, rather than letting Aulus do that. This could be a voice that was determined to get Avril and, as it happened, Nev, one way or the other – either through you and a posse, tipped off by Aulus, or by that quartet of bandits, one with a hammer. It would be aimed at hurting Avril, yes, and, as it happened, Nev, but the real target was Velazquez, wouldn't you say? This must be someone very aware of the appalling pain he would suffer – someone who might actually delight in it.'

'Penelope? Are you saying Penelope Kale?' Sally said. 'She told the Lexus boys they could get rich at the Schooner Way meeting – as long as they wiped out all resistance? You think her grief now over Avril is an act?'

'Two receptacles of information, probably. One the Lexus barbarians. The other Aulus.'

'Aulus? I don't see how he's concerned. He's a trafficker of sorts himself, isn't he?' Sally replied. 'Does he grass, then? I have to doubt that.'

'You say someone is in jail for Avril, but I expect you see now this is not the whole matter – quite apart from the lost money factor,' Theo said. 'Two hundred K plus. We need to trace things back, for the sake of the continuing integrity of the Kale conglomerate. That's uppermost in my thinking. I feel myself as a kind of guardian of the Kale reputation. Oh, you'll probably reply, we should ask Aulus himself, or, of course, the Lexus lad, Latimer, whom Regnal seems to think you have a special . . . well, *closeness* with. That's according to our research. And it's entirely possible we *will* ask them, but I wondered, seeing you relaxed here, and in view of knowing Mark, I wondered whether in the course of a civilized little chat we might get to things more easily, given that you most probably – and commendably – wish to make up for your terrible error in permitting such foul violence. Indeed, actually promoting it. I don't believe it's unfair to say that. Call this opportunism in me, if you will. But perhaps call it, rather, a kindness in me – a longing to help you diminish, possibly eliminate, self-condemnation for the state of that dear girl upstairs, not to mention the slaughter of poor Nev and others.'

'God, though, you think Mrs Kale . . .' Sally replied. 'No, surely.'

'You'll obviously want to ask how do we know about you and Brian Edward Aulus. I am in a position to say that—'

'Here's S. E. and Mrs Kale now, as it happens.' They were coming towards them. Sally thought the concourse brilliant – circular, high-ceilinged, airy and spacious, and around the edge shops, a bank, an information desk and the coffee stall where Sally and Theo sat. A good number of people rambled about. Watching S. E. and Penelope's approach, Sally thought they blended in well and looked less rough and villainous than some other visitors. Hospitals had all sorts. They bought teas and then came to the table.

'How is she?' Sally asked.

'Has Theo been giving you the standard bollocks about me leaking to Aulus and/or the Lexus team on account of

Av and Velazquez?' Mrs Kale asked. 'He gets off on fantasy. It's almost harmless.'

'How is she?' Sally asked.

'Leonard and Charmaine are with her now,' Mrs Kale said.

'Charmaine?' Sally asked.

'Charmaine does a lot of research for us,' Theo said.

'Charmaine's the Spanish or Italian-looking lady?'

'Research, yes,' Mrs Kale said. 'A lot.'

'Charmaine says she thinks Aulus shipped his family to Brittany or somewhere like that, but might have come back himself, Theo,' S. E. said. 'I won't ask our cop friend here if she's heard the same. We'd get lies and more lies.'

'Velazquez, don't be so fucking rude,' Mrs Kale said.

'Aulus? Does he come into all this?' Sally replied.

'Vel's scared of chaos when Avril dies,' Mrs Kale said.

'Don't, Penny,' S. E. said.

'Don't what?' she said.

'Don't just say it like that – "when she dies" . . . "*when*".' S. E. began to cry again and let the tears fall once more down that long, unfriendly face.

Mrs Kale leaned across the little table and said in a normal voice into that long, unfriendly face, 'When she dies, when she dies, *when* she fucking dies.' She was crying herself now. Her own square, plump face had become more unfriendly than S. E.'s – perhaps into the hate region. 'Why don't you ask your researcher, Charmaine, to work out date and time. She's got a particular interest, hasn't she? Hasn't she?'

'Before you arrived just now, Penelope, Velazquez, I was speaking about my arm and tried to put it into the context of the, as it were, annals of the family, though I hope not in a pushy fashion,' Theo said.

Across the concourse, Sally saw what might be Coldfinger – Roger Basil Chancel – her other grass, her official and officially paid grass, her alive grass. Last time,

196

he'd stalked her via the car basement. Now, the concourse. He stood in what appeared to be a religious bookshop, perhaps run by the Society for the Propagation of the Gospel, and had an open volume up in front of him, giving it some real study, or not. Perhaps there was a market for devotional writing in hospitals. The book masked most of his face, though she could just about make out his eyes. Brown? Could she make out the colour? Did she remember Coldfinger's correctly? These eyes might be doing a good sample read before purchase, or they might be watching her, trying to send a message to her. *Yes, it's me. Yes, I'm here.* The bulkiness of the body and big spread of the face were about right for Coldfinger. She would have liked to see him move. Although Coldfinger carried weight, he was agile. She had a flashback to the way he'd dodged among vehicles under the flats. In a while, he lowered the book briefly while turning over a page. He didn't look down at what he was doing, but now, definitely, across the big crowded space towards Sally. Although visitors shifting about interrupted her line of vision, she could be sure – yes, Coldfinger.

His eyes fixed on hers briefly. Brown? He stared. That was all. That was enough. Then he seemed to decide she'd had time to identify him and guess why he was there, and he lifted the book up as cover again. Perhaps he liked spiritual writing. Or perhaps he had studied a different kind of book at home, a manual on elementary self-conceal-ment methods. But he believed himself a bit of a chameleon, anyway, didn't he? He'd hope to blend in with the loaded shelves and get mistaken for a hospital padre. Possibly he thought she'd have trouble spotting him because of his flair for disguise, and so the big, commu-nicative stare.

'And her sense of guilt – her reasonable sense of guilt,' Theo said. 'Yes, we spoke of that.'

'They don't get guilt,' S. E. said. 'Not people like her. The

197

skin's too thick. They don't have any morality, not in the usual meaning of that word, the meaning *I'd* attach to it.'

'I certainly did not want to make her feel we would hold her to personal account for Avril's destruction – and, of course, dear Nev's,' Theo replied. 'Even though she was complicit in those cruel events at Schooner Way – and some would say more than complicit.'

'Chalk and cheese,' S. E. said, with aching sadness.

'Who, Vel?' Mrs Kale asked.

'Her brother and herself,' S. E. said. 'Mark, a gentleman. Her? She disgusts me. Doesn't she disgust *you*? His chin glinted wet with tears. 'The same background, yet such amazingly different development.'

'I don't understand how you know Mark. He's never mentioned any of you,' Sally said.

'When I referred to my arm, all she could think to ask was about shooting,' Theo said. 'I didn't resent this, but let's say it seemed off-key, shall we?'

'Excuse me now, will you?' Sally said, standing. 'I have to report in and the managers don't like cellphones used on hospital premises. They jinx scalpels. I'll go into the grounds for a second.'

She walked to the exit and waited outside. After a couple of minutes, Coldfinger joined her. He carried a paperback book called *A Bundle of Papyrus*. 'Novel about the life of St Paul,' he said. 'I thought I'd better buy something. Like for credibility. Authentic details are vital.'

'You'll enjoy it.'

'I heard you had a duty here today.'

'Heard where?' she replied.

'Let's walk a bit. The Kales – they're sharp.'

They strolled further into the grounds. 'Do you tail me sometimes?' she asked.

'I have to keep up to date.'

'What are you driving these days – and nights?' Sally said.

198

'I thought that was one of the questions officers never asked an informant.'

'A Citroën? I noticed a Citroën in the early hours lately – Newport Road area. Nothing else on the road.'

'Now there are others asking around about Frank Latimer,' Coldfinger replied. 'Not police, and not about *you* and him this time, just about him. Trying to find where he and the girl are living. Lydia? I thought this was sure to be of interest. You have a sort of link to Latimer?'

'Who's asking around?'

'This is quite a piece – twenty-five, twenty-six. Very tidy arse – I'm told.'

'She looks Spanish? Or maybe Italian?' Sally asked.

'In that kind of ballpark.'

'Alone?'

'A lad in a jacket – say, thirty-three, thirty-four.'

'In a jacket?'

'A class jacket. Like russets, reds, yellows.'

'Asking with her?'

'With her, anyway. She seems to be the research element. He the heavy? They're Kale people?'

'What about an older guy who looks like an accountant who used to box?'

'What would that look like?'

'It's all a bit sensitive at the moment, Rog. But I'm noting everything, for payment later.'

'Kale people, tracking him?'

'It was a real lesson – the way you merged in the bookshop, unnoticed behind the novel,' Sally said.

'I read the end of it. As a Roman citizen, Paul gets the axe, you know. Not the sort of book for Avril Kale, suppose she was in a reading state.'

Nine

Bullfinch said: 'We wondered, Sally, whether you'd recognize him. That's why we sent for you at once. This death has quite considerably changed our thinking – suggested new likelihoods. When I say recognize, possibly that is not quite the word. It might be better, fairer, if I phrased it differently, such as, *Do you think he could possibly have been number Four in the Lexus?*'

'A sort of general answer,' Regnal said.

'Or do you consider this an impossible question, Sally?' Bullfinch said. 'Is it preposterous even? What we're after is, I suppose, the most general estimate – indeed guesstimate. General, as Ray says. That's the furthest we could reasonably invite you to go in identification. After all, don't we know, from the trial, about your scrupulousness on such matters?' Venom bubbled momentarily, then ebbed. Bullfinch crouched for a few seconds to try a closer look at the body, but continued talking upwards to her over his left shoulder. 'It would be ironic in the extreme – in fact it would be absurd – oh, yes, absurd – if we expected you to say this could definitely be number Four when the only reason we have to ask you if this could conceivably be number Four is that, out of a fine and, yes, famed respect for total truthfulness, you felt unable to confirm in court Frank Latimer as number Four!'

Despite the awkwardness of speaking from down with the body, there was a supreme, rhythmic crappiness to this statement, probably not achievable by someone who was a slave to daft fury. Perhaps Bullfinch had progressed. Ray Regnal, standing next to Sally, chuckled for a while about Bullfinch's patterned wordage, and when Bullfinch straightened again he, himself, chuckled also, with some wryness. Sally didn't think she'd ever heard him do wryness before. Skill in something as delicate as wryness also might suggest he was learning how to control his little wrath fevers better. It all chimed with that quelling of temper just now about her part in the trial. A turn to wryness might indicate modesty – a recognition that he ought to change. Wry Bullfinch would be so different from Raging.

He said: 'Let me tell you how our thinking shapes up, Sally, may I? To go right back, we know from you there were four in the raid. Your invaluable, first-hand witness report. This means that, although we captured three, we are still bound to search for the one man who has evaded us. A duty. Now, I know, of course, that number Four in the Lexus was hooded. So what it comes down to is, would the physique of this present dead man on the floor here now fit your recollections of Lexus Four – the weight, height and form, possibly shape and size of head? Obviously, all these are on record for us to check, but Mr Regnal thought that, should you actually see the body here now, it might mean more than such mere statistics. If you'll excuse the term in these circumstances, the body might animate – "animate" as a paradox in the admirable sense of what someone said, "truth standing on its head to attract attention" – animate memories rather better than notes and data could ever do. I agreed.

'We've left him as when discovered, of course, because the Scenes of Crime people and our photographers have to do their stuff. But Mr Regnal considers this might not be how the body was immediately after death and for some time afterwards. He doesn't think it lay on the floor then, against the chair like this. His view is that the victim could have been seated in this kitchen chair, leaning forward over

201

the table and slightly to the right, with his tongue double-nailed to it. The body has been here some time and Mr Regnal believes that there would be a decline in the consistency and strength of the tongue – as there would be of any tongue of any corpse – yes, a material decline during that period and eventually the weight of Aulus, dragging slightly, yet constantly, reckonably, right, caused the tongue around the nails to tear, thus freeing the body, which then slid to its present position. Neither Mr Regnal nor myself is a forensics expert, but I think he could be correct. You'll see there are two nails embedded in the table, with some furls of flesh about them, which might be tongue flesh, though we need confirmation of that, clearly.'

Regnal said: 'The lab will certainly be able to give a definite finding as to tongue or not.'

'And the residual tongue within the body's mouth might be damaged,' Bullfinch said. 'Obviously would be, if our previous speculation is accurate. However, that is not the kind of invasive inspection we, as non-experts and simple plods, feel entitled to go messing about with – forcing jaws and so on.'

Regnal said: 'Obviously, we've all known Aulus for a long time, but these circumstances perhaps suddenly put him into the frame as a possible Four. To recap what is really rather historical now, we had thought Frank Latimer was Four but the court said no. This left us with an obligation to continue the search and correct our error. That requirement is uppermost in our heads when we come upon something like this. We ask ourselves, is this that final, elusive element in the Schooner Way story?'

'But, Sally, you'll want to know – and reasonably want to know – why do we connect the corpse of Brian Edward Aulus with the Schooner Way raid? Or rather, why do we ask whether you as witness can connect his body shape with the Schooner Way raid? Or not even ask whether you can connect it, but whether you would have to eliminate it outright as a feasible number Four because of blatantly wrong build? Well, this is how Ray Regnal and I see it – very tentatively see it.'

'A theory,' Regnal said. 'Admittedly. Yet perhaps not to be dismissed out of hand as only theory, since we found to our astonishment that we had both hit upon this explanation independently of each other almost immediately upon seeing the body and the table traces. Perhaps – perhaps – this conjointness does lend weight.'

'Aulus was, as we all know, a middling-to-major dealer,' Bullfinch said. 'Our Drugs people have a case in preparation against him. That's his scene. Was. This being so, he might have picked up trade gossip concerned with new people operating in Schooner Way – gossip about a lot of commodity on the premises from time to time and a lot of money, trolley case, carrier bags, what you will. Perhaps we should have seen him as a possible much earlier. We can wonder now, seeing him in this state, did he recruit rough talent – three rough talents, including a sledge-hammer man and a driver – did he recruit these wild bravos to help him do a snatch – and to squash an incursion by competition?'

'"Squash" has to be the right term, sir, tragically.'

'That poor, brutalized moll in the hospital,' Bullfinch replied. 'Avril Kale. Avril. I have no objection to French names. The parents, such as they are, wanted to give her a continental flavour. How could they have known she'd end up brain-banged in a South Wales drugs nest? I don't mean they had a life as an art scholar at the Louvre in mind for her, but not a culmination with her head under metal in what was once docklands.'

'The story goes she was close to S. E.,' Regnal said. 'I mean, close.'

Bullfinch said: 'And then it's not simply the details of the raid per se that led Ray and me into this identical idea, or we might have shortlisted Aulus as a probable before.

203

But now –' he nodded with sadness towards the shot, tumbled Godzilla remains – 'but now it's the degree of violence and abuse, isn't it – that is, if we've got it spot-on re the tongue? This is not a "normal" killing – suppose there is such a thing. Almost certainly it has gang implications, wouldn't you agree? This savagery seems to us of a piece with Schooner Way – from the same kind of ruthless culture. A hammer. Nails. And, yes, bullets. How would it be if relatives and mates of those convicted three think number Four skipped out of it by some chicanery with most of the loot? Perhaps he hasn't shared it around as might have been expected, and promised. Possibly they thought the money was here. Possibly it is, was. We haven't had a real look through yet.'

'The tongue has to say something to us,' Regnal added.

Bullfinch cupped a hand to his right ear, as if trying to catch faint sounds. 'Not this tongue,' Bullfinch said. 'Especially not now.'

Regnal had another chuckle and himself held up a hand, a mea culpa hand, for the poor use of language. 'To rephrase: the tongue treatment on Aulus must contain a message. Perhaps he's suspected of grassing, i.e., using his tongue to fink, though I don't recall Aulus on our register.'

'He can afford this very pleasant house in a fine district commemorating great literary figures – Wordsworth Avenue, Cowper Place, Southey Street,' Bullfinch said. 'All top-notchers. These were writers who could not have been more keen on Nature. Many an outdoor scene in their work – hills, lakes. This neighbourhood has resonance. The house furnishings – at least passable.' He tapped the kitchen table twice with his knuckles. 'Solid pine, not veneer, so nails can get real purchase. And the chairs – like Charles Rennie Mackintosh design. If you're going to lie dead alongside a chair, this is a beautiful chair to lie dead alongside. Plainly, nothing can truly dignify a death of this sort, but the chair does add some marginal cachet. Aulus's family are not here at present and, according to neighbours, have been away a while, so has he another property somewhere? Abroad? Tuscany? France? No doubt he drives a decent vehicle.'

'An Audi, we understand,' Regnal said.

'How does he afford it all?' Bullfinch said. 'We ask that, and others may have asked it, too, and come up with an answer that made them bitter and jealous. Murderous.'

'In a way, I'm glad he's fallen like this,' Regnal said. 'It would have been a hell of a sight otherwise for the kids who found him. That's nightmare material. They'll be offered counselling, but nobody can counsel away the memory of a familiar member of this community tongue-nailed to furniture.'

'Which kids?' Sally said.

'Kids from up the street looking for a missing kitten. They come down the basement steps and see a window has been forced.'

'Forced?' Sally said.

'A crude, grossly obvious job,' Regnal replied. 'These kids know the Auluses as neighbours and so they worry. They open the window properly and shout.' Regnal made his voice treble and called out, 'Mr Aulus, Mr Aulus.' He said: 'No good. While one of them is shouting, the other goes back up to the ground floor and does a good squint in at the window there but sees only normality. A conscientious child. It's a semi-detached house, and she nips to the rear and looks in at the kitchen window this time. She can make out Brian Edward Aulus's feet and the lower part of his legs. She returns to the front and descends to the basement and her pal. They both climb in through the damaged window then, go up the stairs and find how bad things are. They belt home and we get the nine-nine-nine.'

'I felt I must come personally,' Bullfinch said. 'It seemed to me almost certain there would be overtones.'

'One is grateful, sir,' Regnal replied. 'This is something that needs the widest kind of interpretation.'

'It's what one is paid for, Ray.'

'If I may say, sir, some are paid for it, but are not able to provide it,' Regnal said.

Sally had to speculate hard about what these two babbling fuckers were playing at. There were times when she felt the sympathy she gave Bullfinch was not earned, in no way reciprocated. Of course, he and Regnal knew Aulus could never have been number Four as described originally by her for the trial. Too short, too frail, skinny-necked. Number Four was six feet and well built, Frank Latimer's height and form, naturally. Aulus might be five foot six. Regnal would not need to be reminded from notes about Four's dimensions. Detectives lived by such knowledge and it stayed in their heads. Bullfinch himself would probably recall the figures, too.

And what else did the pair of malevolent sods know and remember? Had Regnal discovered in those trawls described by Coldfinger that Aulus was her grass, and did they deduce he had probably whispered something that put her into Schooner Way with such brilliant luck? Not everyone had believed fully in that brilliant luck, anyway, or even believed in it a bit. Bullfinch and Regnal would have had big, very sensible doubts. And did they also suspect that Aulus, as a talented informant, gave her actual names of the expected raiding group? They might imagine these names included Frank Latimer's. They might believe she had suppressed it. They'd think she refused to cooperate, by improving her evidence to convict him, because he was something from her childhood. Had they brought her down here for a view of Aulus in horrible situ in order to impose sudden punishment trauma, and to let her gather they had her marked – perhaps, in her shock, shake from her admissions of treason? Look at him, Sally dear, and look at the flesh-festooned nails in the fine pine table. You caused this. The show might accomplish nothing much in the way of crime-solving. Frank could not be tried again. No, their object was to stick true suffering and confusion on her as a nice thank you, Sally, for your fucking betrayal. At the higher levels, this was known as policing. Bullfinch occupied a very high level and wanted to go higher – believed himself entitled to go higher. He would bear a grudge against anyone who seemed to mess up those plans for himself, such as Sally. Possibly he had taught himself lately how to apply such detestations in a more calculated, less fluttery and farcical, way than before. They'd probably be wondering about perjury charges, but, even suppose they couldn't stand those up, there was this chance to give Sally some good, possibly mind-wrecking pain. She hoped they would not start traces on her recent phone calls in and out.

'No,' she said. 'He couldn't be number Four.'

'Is this a sort of instant, instinctive, verdict?' Regnal replied. 'Do you think you should get down to floor level and aim for a more considered, informed opinion?'

'No, he just couldn't be,' Sally said.

'In what sense couldn't be?' Regnal said.

'Couldn't,' Sally said.

'Obviously, when you say "couldn't be" with such firmness, it isn't, is it, because you – like the rest of us – feel, despite the court, that Four might have been Frank Latimer after all, and feel also that he and his big floozy, Lydia Mastille, are sitting on something above two hundred hijacked K?' Regnal replied. 'Oh, when I refer to " the rest of us", I exclude, naturally, that damned deranged jury.'

'This is to put matters very strongly, Ray,' Bullfinch said.

'But possibly justified, sir,' Regnal said.

'Is Sally "damned deranged" also, if she doesn't feel, as you feel, that Four was Frank Latimer?'

'I don't mean to suggest that, sir,' Regnal replied.

'I would trust not,' Bullfinch said.

Such sweet reasonableness, the liar. Bullfinch would have liked to suggest it himself, but was performing his new, temperate part. 'Physically nowhere near right,' Sally said.

David Craig

'We did fear that,' Bullfinch said.

'I don't understand why you ask me if this dead man could have been number Four if Mr Regnal is sure Four was Latimer,' Sally said.

'A fair point,' Bullfinch replied at once. 'But Mr Regnal is not sure. How could he be sure when the court has said the opposite? We are all police officers and, I trust, accept that what the court decides is truth. Mr Regnal does accept that truth, I know, in the matter of Latimer and all other matters, but, just the same, he feels there can be a gap between what we might call a "not proven" verdict on someone like, say, Frank Latimer, and an actual guarantee of innocence. We somehow failed to prove that Latimer was there. I certainly don't say you were responsible for that failure, because of your evidence. I hope I'd never allege that.'

'Thank you for that clarification, sir,' Regnal said. 'Oh, thank you. This is the kind of flair in the interpretation of things I spoke of earlier – that wide interpretation of things – and yet, also, a very precise interpretation of things – the distinction between sureness and feeling, the distinction between not proven and innocent. This clarifies my own understanding and, I'm sure, DC Bithron's as well.'

'We think possibly two separate break-ins at different times,' Bullfinch said. 'There's the rough, absurdly amateur job on the basement window which Mr Regnal referred to, but also possible signs that a rear window has been much more capably worked on and then reclosed. Which came first we can't say, not at this stage. Our look at the place has been very hasty.'

Regnal said: 'The job on the basement window must have created a big din and alerted anyone inside. So, Aulus might have been dead, killed by the first intruder or intruders.'

'Naturally, the first suspect in a domestic murder has to be the spouse or partner,' Bullfinch said. 'Especially when that spouse or partner is missing. But Mr Regnal and I both

208

think this is probably a wrong assumption here. There are the break-ins. Also, the tongue aspect. This would suggest something more than a marital or lovers' squabble. The family have to be traced, though, as a matter of urgency. Assuming that the partner didn't do him, I imagine I personally shall have to tell her of the vile end to her man.' Again for a second he seemed about to revert to a God-how-I-pity-me spasm. It was that heartfelt word, 'personally'. But then once more he recovered and became noble. 'Very well, very well. This, also, is what one is paid for.'

'Had he been a possible Four, we could have reduced the suspects list,' Regnal said. 'It would be reasonable to assume someone, or more than one person, connected to the three who were jailed. Now, the field is open.'

'But you'll get there, Ray,' Bullfinch replied.

'Oh, of course, of course, sir. We owe you that. We owe the public that.'

On Sunday morning the phone rang early. Control told her Avril Kale had died and that Sally's scheduled hospital duty from ten a.m. was cancelled. Pete slept through the call. She lay awake for a while and then decided it would be good if she went herself for the croissants and papers today. She liked the notion of waiting on Pete, for a change. It seemed to give a welcome, additional domestic solidity to things. She still looked for that, perhaps even more now. It wasn't just the awful rerun of those horrors at Wordsworth Avenue. But yesterday when she returned from there and now again this morning she found herself full of uneasiness about occupying this flat. She no longer liked the notion of living here. It disturbed her that Theo and S. E. knew her brother. These splendid, central Cardiff residences cost up towards the half million. How did Mark pay for such a place, as well as owning a big house in Chiswick? She realized she was floating the same doubts about Mark as Bullfinch had about Godzilla. Mark ran genuine and successful baby-clothes

209

businesses, no question, and until now this had been enough explanation of his money. Was that all he did, though? Sally paid him rent for the flat, but something only very nominal. Suddenly, she did not want to be obliged to Mark. As a result, the domestic set-up which had obviously part depended on the flat now seemed damn shaky. This brought the urge to do her housewifely trip to the shop, as a substitute sign of her and Pete's settled togetherness.

But, oh, God, was she really into that kind of creepy need? Pathetic. Croissant therapy? She would have to buy two each again, wouldn't she, to prove there'd been no retreat from the dim cosiness of yesterday? Yes, pathetic. She must not let this kind of thinking move in and get permanent, compulsive. Sometime later this week, a trip to Pal Joey's, and so an endorsement of the *Not Just Friends* book. If she gave up living in the flat, one important loss would be the club as a haven and life-enhancer she could walk to and from. The simplicity of that was such a help. Taxis might not be so convenient. They would make things seem calculated – not like, 'I live near. We can stroll there if you feel like a bit of air after the bar.' And, obviously, her new accommodation couldn't be anything like as impressive.

She bought four croissants and then tried to decide which paper would be Pete's most likely free choice. She picked the *People*, convinced this couldn't possibly be correct, however free the choice. Interesting to watch Pete at moments when he thought he'd encountered a bewildering taste or culture gap between him and her. Politeness would always make him try to hide his irritation but he never managed that altogether. His eyes sharpened. His breathing became slow as he forced himself to stay civil. She thought it vital to let him know they were not the same, and in some ways not even similar. She hated to feel crowded by someone else's personality. That's why Pal Joey's was important. In those encounters, personality couldn't get much of a look-in. No time. They were about something else.

And then on the way back to the flat with the domesti-
cating croissants and the deliberately alienating newspaper,
she had one of those fits of regret that would come now
and then, and Sally wondered whether occasionally – often
– she was damned harsh to Pete. She began to worry about
him, in that daft off-on way of hers. Especially, she worried
about this change in breakfast duties. She'd come out, he'd
stayed in bed. On the day that Avril Kale's death was
announced, was it wise to reverse the early-morning roles?
S. E. Kale and Theo obviously thought she earned most of
the blame for what had happened to Avril. He believed
Sally had known what was likely at Schooner Way, but,
for her own murky reasons, had let it happen. Suppose that
talented research lady had discovered the normal weekend
shopping arrangements. Suppose she knew the layout of the
apartment block and of the flat itself. Suppose S. E. sent
Leonard Paul Nottage around in one of his splendid jackets,
and with a pistol in one of the pockets of one of his splendid
jackets, to settle up with her for Avril. Or the pug accountant,
with no known firearms skills, but since when did the Met
know everything, or anything much? What if, as he sometimes did, Pete had sunk low in the bed and was covered
from the top of his head to his feet under the duvet. Someone
like Leonard Paul Nottage, or Hugh Garston Innes Philigan,
might not hang about making sure he'd got the right target,
because the research had specified Sally was always the
one in the bed at this stage in the a.m. rituals. Was it even
possible that her brother, Mark, had mentioned to his friends,
S. E. and Theo, these funny little rituals? Now and then
Mark had been in the other bedroom while she and Pete
slept together. After all, this was an established relationship – nearly five months – and not something to hide.
Obviously, Mark would not have spoken about the croissant trips to them for any dark reason, just as chit-chat. But
chit-chat could be used, couldn't it?

She hurried now – grew really scared for Pete. But at the

door of the flat she actually paused for a moment, frightened of what she'd find. Then, she went in. There was a small hallway and, standing in it, for a moment she caught herself sniffing for the tang of cordite. Pete called out, but he was not in the bedroom. His voice came from the lounge: 'Visitors, Sally,' he said.

'Lydia and Frank?' she said.

'Of course,' Frank replied.

Of course.

As she joined them, Frank said: 'We're leaving, really leaving.'

Thank God. 'Oh?' They all remained standing.

'Don't ask where we're going,' Frank said.

'No,' she replied.

'It could be best you don't know,' Lydia said.

'This is mystifying,' Pete said.

'Abroad?' Sally asked.

'Which paper is that, Sally?' Pete said. 'Which, for heaven's sake?'

'It could be best you don't know where we're going,' Frank said.

'So, what's changed?' Sally said.

'Avril Kale dead, for one thing,' Lydia replied. 'The word's out. So I badger him.'

'Why should Avril Kale's death trouble you?' Sally said. 'I don't get it.'

'Of course you get it,' Lydia said.

'Plus, we've come to recognize that you'll never accept any recompense,' Frank said. 'Lydia has convinced me.'

'Recompense?' Pete said. 'For what?'

'So, we clear all the debts and obligations with a very, very token gift,' Frank replied. 'No question of illicit gains. Something nominal, only nominal.'

'What debts and obligations?' Pete said. 'I'll put the croissants in the oven, shall I? Were they out of other papers?'

'Here we are then, Sal,' Frank said. He handed her a

small package in gift wrap. She opened it slowly and with a good helping of dread.

'What's that?' Pete said.

'The monster, Godzilla,' Sally said.

'I remember him. Films – a series starting in the 1950s but around till the 90s?' Pete replied.

'From an antique toys collection in Jacob's Market,' Lydia said.

'Thanks,' Sally replied.

'Very individual,' Pete said. 'I mean, as a present.'

'No damage to him at all, despite age,' Frank said.

'Goodbye, then,' Sally said.

'Absolutely no damage to him,' Frank said. 'Some Godzillas are lucky. Some.'

'Goodbye,' Sally replied.

'Aren't you rather ungracious, Sally?' Pete said. 'Wouldn't they like a coffee? Perhaps a croissant, as you've so brilliantly bought four. If they're going to be travelling.' He sounded thrilled they might disappear for good. Naturally. Some breakfast for each should mean they'd be nourished enough to complete their journey to wherever – and let it be distant. She'd half expect him to offer them a guide to house purchase in Monrovia with the coffee and croissants.

'No. Goodbye, Frank,' Sally said. It was as good as over now, her and him, such as it had been. He'd looked in to taunt her about Aulus. That would have taken some forgiving and she did not feel like trying.

'If toys can seem realistic, this one does,' Pete said. 'You'd think he could talk.'

'I wanted one who looked like that,' Frank replied. 'Godzillas talk a lot.'

'That right?' Pete said. 'I don't recall it from the films.

When they had gone, Sally set out the breakfast. In his forgiving way, Pete read the *People* with true interest. Someone rang the doorbell. Pete stood.

213

'No,' Sally said. 'Me.'

'Why?'

'Me.'

'Are you sure it's all right?'

'No.' She went to the security peephole and saw Lydia weeping outside. Sally opened the door. 'They've shot him,' she said. 'In the street. Frank's dead, I know it. They're calling an ambulance, but he's dead, I know it.'

'Who?' Sally said. She took her arm again and brought her back to the lounge and made her sit down.

'From a car,' Lydia said.

'What car? A Bentley?'

'Bentley. No, no. Smaller.'

'Who?' Sally said. 'Someone in an all-colours sports coat? Or an accountant-looking guy who might have once been in the ring?'

'What?' Lydia asked.

'I don't get it, either,' Pete said. 'Boxing ring?'

'Didn't you hear it?' Lydia said.

'Double-glazing,' Pete replied.

'How would they know where to find him?' Lydia said.

'Research,' Sally said. 'They'd located where you live and followed him. Was there a woman in the car?'

'Who researches?' Lydia said. 'Who?'

'You don't think I told them he was here, do you . . . do you?' Sally said.

'Who?' Lydia replied. 'You? How could you have? It happened immediately. You wouldn't do that, would you? Would you? Not to Frank. But, my God, would you?'

Sally drove her to Accident and Emergency at the University Hospital. It was becoming a focus. Lydia had it right, though, and Frank was dead on arrival. Regnal turned up soon after, and then Bullfinch. They both said how terrible it was. 'Especially terrible,' Bullfinch added, 'when Frank Latimer had escaped a trial conviction and must have felt so happy. Then to be unaccountably blasted. Why? Why?'

'Indeed, why?' Regnal replied. He wanted a witness state-
ment from Lydia and she agreed to go to headquarters with
them. Afterwards, she would return to her parents in the
North. Bullfinch took Sally aside. 'Ann Temperance
Mayhew Donovan has been traced to Concarneau, France.
The local police will inform her what's happened.'

'Oh, hell,' Sally said.

'I didn't tell them more than that Aulus was dead,'
Bullfinch said. 'Perhaps she need not know the rest of it,
ever. I feel for her.' But he said it without theatricals – did
not sound as though, because he felt for her, he felt it all
worse than she ever could. He was definitely growing up.

But Sally could not leave things like that. In the evening,
after Pete had gone home to polish some report or his shoes
for work next day, she telephoned Ann Temperance Mayhew
Donovan, hoping to get her before the police arrived. Ann
said: 'It's something bad, is it? You've been a long time.
You didn't want to tell me?'

'Yes, bad.'

'Really bad?'

'Bad,' Sally said. 'A kind of trade shoot-out, I gather.
They happen.'

'What kind?'

'He was killed. Regrettably.'

'Yes, I got that.'

'Instantly – if it's a comfort.'

'How do you know?'

Sally said: 'We think the one who did it was killed
himself not long afterwards. Well, we're sure.'

'Is that good?'

'What will you do?' Sally replied, but the phone had been
put down at the other end.

She thought of ringing Mark in London to say she would
have to quit the flat because of his Kale connections. But
then she realized that, if it were not Sunday and the club
shut, she would have liked to get round to Pal Joey's tonight.

215

It had turned into a strained day and she needed relief. She decided the club's nearness was, after all, fairly crucial. To move from here would be to give it up, most probably, and perhaps that was not necessary. She put off telephoning Mark. One painful call a night seemed enough. It could be argued that for Mark to know S. E. and Theo was not itself an offence, though close. They might have a social side. When she became too old for Pal Joey's, she could think about moving out of the flat on principle. Of course, her address would certainly be known to the Kale research department, but she doubted whether this was a risk. The payback for Avril's destruction had most likely been made now, despite Theo's chilly chat to her, on the concourse, about blame. She felt reasonably safe – safe, but weak with a double sadness. Although the link with Frank had fractured, she could still regret what he had chosen to become, especially when he finally seemed so dim at it. Oh, Frank, why did you have to go the way you went, and then have to go, die, the way you went? God, you're a disappointment – bopped by strangers in a home-patch street.

She put Godzilla on the mantlepiece and didn't really mind it there. That lovely green antique vase he gave her wouldn't have fitted in well with the monster, though.